SYDNEY GOMMER

Off Balance

Off Balance

SYDNEY GOMMER

Acknowledgments

To everyone who shaped this story, from family, friends, teachers, partners, classmates, choreographers, roommates, and the brief strangers in passing, whether you're still here or not, whether your impact felt gentle or sharp. Your kindnesses and your hard edges both taught me how to keep going. Thank you for the lessons disguised as love, and the lessons disguised as loss.

To the places that held me, studios, porches, long drives, late-night kitchens, thank you for being soft landings when words ran out.

To the girl I was: you did your best with what you knew. Thank you for getting me this far.

To the person I am now: keep choosing peace, keep choosing yourself.

And to anyone who finds themselves somewhere in these pages, may you feel a little less alone.

I

Part One

First Semester

Chapter 1

I watched the heavy beige door as it shut, the latch clicking when it closed. The sound seemed to echo in the room, bouncing off the bare white walls before fading into silence. This was the moment I had been picturing for the past year, maybe even my whole life, and yet now that it was here, I wanted nothing more than to go back.

My orientation leader's cheerful voice replayed in my mind, "Welcome to your new home." The words had sounded bright and promising when she said them, but they felt almost cruel now. This place was anything but home. The room was large, but not in a way that made me feel comfortable. It felt empty and hollow, like a space that belonged to someone else. The faint chemical smell of paint lingered in the air and mixed with the musty scent of the old carpet.

I rubbed my eyes, heavy with exhaustion. I had managed exactly two hours of sleep the night before because of my usual procrastination. Even though my new "home" was only two hours from my actual one, we still needed to leave at six in the morning. Emphasis on leave, not wake up or start packing, but leave. That meant I had been awake all night, frantically cramming things into bins and hoping I did not forget anything important. Now it was four in the afternoon, and I was exhausted and starving. Apparently, rest was for the weak in college, because freshman welcome was set to begin in thirty minutes.

The beige door creaked open again, pulling me from my thoughts. I realized I had not moved since watching it close behind my parents an hour earlier. My roommate, Natalie, slipped past me without saying anything and went straight to her bed. We had not chosen each other; we had both chosen the corner dorm on the first floor. There had been no matching comforters or roommate photo shoots, just two strangers who happened to land in the same room.

The only text she had sent me all summer was to let me know she had bought a shower curtain. When I arrived earlier that day, she had mumbled something about going to the library and left before I could even ask which side of the room she wanted. Now she barely glanced in my direction.

It hit me all at once. The person I would be living five feet away from for the entire year already disliked me. What a great start.

I tried to convince myself that silence was better than fighting, but in that moment, the quiet felt suffocating. It pressed against me like heavy air. Even an awkward conversation would have been better than the weight of nothing.

Natalie looked a little like me, which somehow made the differences feel sharper. We both had long brown hair and brown eyes, but she looked polished while I looked plain. Her dark hair shimmered with blonde highlights, and her skin glowed with a sun-kissed tan. My hair was flat, a single dull shade, and my skin was pale. Ballet had kept me out of the sun all summer, locked in a studio while other girls lay on beaches.

From eight in the morning until five in the evening every day,

I had danced in a hot, windowless studio. It might sound like torture to some people, but for me it was passion. Ballet was not just what I do; it's who I am. It's the reason I chose this large out-of-state college. I had been dancing since kindergarten, thirteen years now, and I dreamed of one day owning my own studio. Right now, though, that dream felt far away.

My phone buzzed in my pocket, pulling me back to the present.

"4:30 p.m. Freshman Welcome."

I looked up and saw Natalie in a short red dress, her hair styled in two neat Dutch braids. She looked like she belonged here, perfectly prepared, while I still felt like an intruder. She grabbed her phone, brushed past me again, and opened the door. I caught a glimpse of the rest of our dorm group gathering in the hallway. Their laughter echoed down the corridor as she disappeared to join them.

I hurried to grab my key and ran after them.

Raylon University was massive. By massive, I mean seven thousand freshmen massive. Every single one of us seemed to be headed to the courtyard at once, a flood of red and white shirts filling every sidewalk.

The hallway thundered with noise. The marching band played somewhere outside, but even their booming drums could hardly compete with the shouts of a thousand girls in Grace Hall. Grace was an all-female dorm, something people often called unlucky, but to me, it was a relief. After my messy breakup with my high school boyfriend, the last thing I wanted was to share a dorm with college boys. I was not ready for them. I could not even handle my own roommate.

By the time I reached the courtyard, the August sun was beating down, relentless. Heat radiated from the concrete and mixed with the press of thousands of anxious, excited bodies. The air buzzed with energy, a cocktail of nerves and adrenaline that made my skin prickle.

"You have got this, Brianna," I whispered to myself. Except the music was so loud that I must have said it louder than I realized. Heads turned. A few girls giggled.

Before I could sink into the ground, a soft voice spoke behind me. "Yeah, you do. And don't worry, I am nervous too."

I spun around and found myself looking into hazel eyes. The girl smiled warmly. "I am Adeline, but you can call me Addy. This is my roommate, Clarissa. You should stick with us tonight. There are too many people to be wandering around alone."

Addy's hair was dirty blonde, tied in a messy bun, while Clarissa's faded blue hair fell over her shoulder. Both of them looked effortless in a way I envied.

"Okay, thank you," I said quickly, grateful for their kindness. "I definitely need that. My roommate already ditched me."

Before I could say more, they each grabbed one of my hands and pulled me into the crowd.

The courtyard was alive. Booths lined the paths, stacked high with shirts and free food. The smell of popcorn and fried dough drifted through the air. Music pulsed from speakers. Students danced in circles, others posed for pictures under the lights, and some just lounged in the grass watching everything happen. It felt like a carnival had taken over campus.

After wandering for an hour, we ended up at the dining hall.

Clarissa spotted a group of people she knew from high school and rushed off before I could blink. Addy headed toward one of the chain restaurants, where the line already snaked out the door. I gave in and picked the "generic Chinese food" option, balancing a carton of fried rice as I searched for a table.

I sat near a window, opening my food, but when I glanced up, I saw Clarissa tugging Addy into her high school group. Together they ran out the door, laughing, forgetting I even existed.

So much for sticking together.

I put my headphones in and tried to eat, but even music felt overwhelming. Silence was better.

That was when I noticed him. A tall guy with shaggy brown hair and piercing blue eyes left his laughing group and walked straight toward me.

"Why are you sitting alone?" he asked casually. "Want me to join you?"

I glanced at his friends, still watching, laughing like this was a joke.

"I'm good, thanks," I said, staring down at my carton. "I'm waiting for someone."

"Here, take my Snapchat. I will talk to you later."

Before I could respond, he swiped my phone off the table. My phone, unlocked and in his hands.

"Hey-" I reached for it, but he yanked it out of reach, grinning as my fork clattered to the ground. He swiped quickly, then tossed it back to me like it meant nothing.

"Have a great semester," he called as he walked away. His friends clapped him on the back like he had accomplished something.

I sat frozen for a moment, then quietly finished my food.

By the time I left, the sun had set. Lights were strung through the trees in the courtyard, glowing like stars, but the air was thick with noise. Music blared. Students shouted. My head pounded with it.

I pushed through the crowd and slipped back into Grace Hall.

The sudden quiet felt like a blanket.

Natalie was not back yet. Relief washed through me as I changed into pajamas and crawled into bed.

The room was small with high ceilings. Our beds were lofted, and a single wide window separated the two sides. My wall was covered with pictures of home, taped against the stark white paint. My family. My pets. Little reminders of who I was.

How had this day gone so backwards?

I reached for the book I had started last week. Its cover was colorful and lighthearted. A story that was not stressful. Exactly what I needed.

At some point, I drifted off, the book falling onto my chest.

The door slammed open, jolting me awake. Light poured in. Natalie stumbled in, laughing with her friends, and disappeared into the bathroom.

I turned toward the clock: three in the morning.

At least one of us was enjoying college.

I smoothed the crumpled pages of my book, set it aside, and pulled my blanket over my head. Three more days until classes begin. Maybe tomorrow would be better.

But even as I lay there, listening to Natalie's shower run, my mind refused to settle. Thoughts chased each other endlessly. I tried to focus on one thing. Tomorrow could be a reset, a chance to start again.

It was another hour before sleep finally found me.

Chapter 2

I slowly opened my eyes and let them adjust to the morning light. For a few seconds, I lay perfectly still, not wanting to face the day, clinging to the blur of sleep. Then the memory of yesterday hit me.

Oh no.

It had not been a nightmare at all. Everything that had happened was real. The weight of it rushed back through me so suddenly that it felt like getting hit by a bus. Not just any bus, but one loaded with my own emotions, driven by anxiety, and stopping for no one.

I grabbed my phone and slid beneath my covers, cocooning myself against reality. A text from my mom blinked across the screen, a picture of each of our dogs just like she promised. My throat tightened, and I quickly wiped away a tear. No, I told myself firmly. I was not going to let this define me. Today would not be a repeat of yesterday. I would get up. I would stay busy. I had a list of things to do, and if I kept moving, maybe I would not have the chance to drown in sadness.

I sat up and slid out of bed, but my bare feet hit the floor with such a thud that my knees buckled under me. I fell to the carpet with a groan. Pushing myself back up, I made a mental note to actually use the ladder next time instead of leaping down like

I was indestructible. I gathered my bathroom essentials and slipped quietly into the bathroom, trying not to disturb Natalie with the noise I had already made.

The shower was brisk, more functional than relaxing. The hot water beat against my shoulders, washing away some of the tension but not all of it. I dried off quickly and dressed for the day, pulling on short denim overalls over a black t-shirt. I scraped my hair into a tight ponytail and tugged on my white Converse, their rubber soles squeaking faintly on the linoleum floor. Phone. Key. Bag. Ready. I stepped through the heavy front door of the dorm and out into the morning.

The campus was still quiet. The sky was pale and soft, the kind of early light that made everything feel like it was holding its breath. Most people were still asleep since classes had not started yet. The silence calmed me for a moment.

First stop: textbooks.

The bookstore line proved me wrong about the quiet. Apparently, every other freshman had the same idea. The shop was packed with students and their parents, shuffling through aisles of overpriced sweatshirts and key chains. I joined the line and waited. The minutes dragged. By the time I finally stepped outside with a bag that felt like it weighed as much as a small child, an exact hour had passed. I trudged back to my dorm, arms burning from the load.

Once I dropped the books off, I decided to map out my classes. Most of them were in the dance and band building. That made sense, since ballet was my major, but of course, it had to be the furthest building from the main quad. A solid fifteen-minute walk, minimum.

I put in my headphones and headed that way, my favorite playlist filling my ears. As I walked, I thought back to the time

I had visited with my parents. I remembered peeking through the tall glass windows of the studios. The memory still gave me goosebumps. The space had been gorgeous, flooded with natural light, mirrors stretching from wall to wall, bars lined up like an invitation. I could hardly believe I was a dancer here now. The thought filled me with both pride and nerves.

After wandering the building for a while, I turned back toward the dining hall. I had not realized before that the entire walk back was uphill. By the time I reached the top, sweat was dripping down my back, my shirt sticking to me.

Inside, the dining hall was chaos. Students packed every line, trays clattering, voices rising above each other. Even the most basic "campus exclusive" food counters had waits of nearly an hour. My stomach growled, but not enough to keep me standing in line that long. With a frustrated sigh, I turned around and walked back out.

The sun was higher now, burning down on my black shirt as I continued toward the farthest lot on campus. My car was parked twenty minutes away, the closest I could get without paying five hundred dollars a month. The walk was miserable. It crossed busy intersections, wove through a neighborhood, and, of course, was uphill yet again. This school seemed obsessed with hills. Maybe the freshman fifteen was not even possible here.

When I finally saw my car, a navy blue KIA Soul, I grinned. People teased me about the shape, but I did not care. It was mine, and I loved it. I collapsed into the driver's seat and immediately blasted the air conditioning. Cool air rushed over me as I leaned back, closing my eyes for a moment.

I pulled out my phone. No notifications.

"Just get out of the car and go eat. You are hungry," I told myself. But my thumb had already pressed my mom's contact. The phone rang, and after a minute her voice filled the car, warm and cheerful.

"Hey, Bri! How are you doing? Having fun?"

"Um, yeah. It is alright," I mumbled. I had promised myself I would not cry, but her voice cracked something open inside me.

"Have you met anyone yet? And wait, why are you calling me? You should be out exploring!" she teased, but I could hear the hope in her voice.

"A couple of people, but I just…" My voice cracked. "Miss you." The tears came hot and fast. I broke into sobs, choking on them. Movies and books always made this part look exciting, magical. For me, it was the opposite. Why was it so hard for me? What was wrong with me?

"Oh, Bri, it is okay, baby. It is hard now, but you will get used to it. You can come home on weekends and-"

"I can't do it," I cut her off. "It is too much. I am terrified and alone. I just want to come home."

Silence. Then, softly, "Just stick it out. Go get something good to eat and find a place you like to sit. When classes start, things will feel better. Remember why you are there. If by the end of the year you still hate it, you can come home. But give it time."

I could hear her holding back her instinct to tell me to quit, to drive here and scoop me up. She believed in me. She wanted me to try.

"Okay," I muttered, my throat tight. "I will go eat. Love you."

"I love you, baby. You have got this."

The call ended. I sat there in the hum of the air conditioning, breathing sharp and uneven, then finally turned off the car and pushed myself back onto the sidewalk. My mom believed in me more than I believed in myself. That had to mean something.

An hour later, I was sitting under a giant tree in the courtyard, a gluten-free sandwich and potato salad on the grass beside me, my book open in my lap. Food helped. Shade helped. The campus courtyard was beautiful when it was not overflowing with people.

I was taking the last bite of potato salad when I felt it. Eyes on me. Again.

I looked up, and of course, it was him. The boy from the night before: Snapchat Boy.

He waved as though we were old friends and walked straight toward me, his confidence unsettling. He plopped down on the grass beside me without hesitation.

"I am sorry about last night," he said quickly. I glanced around him, scanning for his friends. "I am alone, if that is what you are checking for. They were jerks. Honestly, I just hated seeing a girl like you sitting alone. You are beautiful. I know there are terrible people out there, and yeah, I was terrible last night, but I would love to make it right. Let me take you out."

His eyes were steady, almost pleading.

"I do not even know your name," I said, unwrapping a half-melted piece of chocolate.

"Oh, sorry. I am Jack. And you are?"

"Brianna."

"Perfect. Now we know each other. Look, I will leave you to your book, but please meet me here tomorrow night. We can go out, and you can even tell me all about your book." He smiled, winked, and leaned back as if already waiting for my answer.

I sighed. "Fine."

"Great! Tomorrow at six, Brianna," he said, jogging off toward the library.

I watched him go, my stomach twisting. A date. With the rude boy from last night. Wonderful.

I popped the chocolate into my mouth and bent back to my book.

Hours slipped by. I read until the sun shifted in the sky, and I turned the last page. My life might be unpredictable and messy, but at least stories had neat endings, tied up with bows, happily-ever-afters guaranteed.

When I finally looked up, the courtyard had transformed into something almost magical. Not packed like the night before, but alive. Students were sprawled across the grass, some with guitars, some laughing over food, some reading, some skateboarding across the walkways. It was noisy, but in a softer way. Chaotic, but peaceful. For the first time since I arrived, I felt like maybe I belonged here. Like maybe I was a puzzle piece finally fitting into the picture.

On my walk back to the dorm, I kept my head up instead of staring at the ground. I noticed the bright flowers by the paths, the smell of cut grass, and the murmur of excited conversations. Maybe Mom was right. Maybe this was an opportunity.

I had made it here. Kindergarten-me had never imagined ballet as a career. It had been a hobby, something fun, something light. Now here I was, in a college with an incredible program. Terrified, yes, but finally a little excited again.

I practically skipped the last stretch to my dorm. The moment I opened the door, though, optimism faltered. Addy and Clarissa were in the kitchen, laughing over a tray of cookies. The smell of warm sugar wafted into the hall. They called out to me, their voices cheerful, but my stomach twisted. They had abandoned me the night before, left me to eat alone. Maybe it had not been their responsibility, but it still hurt. I forced a smile and kept walking. Not today.

In my room, Natalie was gone again. Relief. I pulled out my favorite pajamas, oversized sweats from my high school dance program, and a giant shirt from my dad that could have fit me twice over. I tugged my hair down from the ponytail, the elastic snapping against my wrist, and slid under the covers.

The picture of my dog glowed from my laptop's home screen. Instead of crying this time, I smiled. I would see her again soon enough.

I opened my comfort show and performed the theme song, singing into my phone like it was a microphone as the familiar music washed over me.

Halfway through the first episode, the door flew open. Natalie ran in, grabbed her purse, and darted out again with a quick word to her friends.

"She is so weird," one of them laughed in the hall.

"She is not that bad," Natalie replied. "But maybe I will still take you up on that offer." Their voices faded down the corridor.

I sank deeper into my bed. At least I was not the worst roommate on the floor. Small victory.

Dinner did not happen. I was not going to change back out of pajamas to face the dining hall. I dug out a microwavable mac and cheese cup from under my bed, filled it with water, and waited for the hum of the microwave. Outside, the courtyard filled with music again, games, and voices rising into the night.

I stirred the pasta, added the cheese, and curled back into bed. Headphones in, screen glowing, I let myself block out the world.

Five episodes later, my laptop slid to the nightstand. My eyes were heavy, my body sinking into the mattress. Tomorrow would be even crazier, but at least today had offered me a small spark of optimism.

Chapter 3

My Saturday morning started off about the same as my Friday morning. I woke up thinking I had a terrible nightmare, only to find that it was real. The memory lingered for a second, heavy in my chest, before the familiar wave of panic rushed over me. I lay there, eyes on the ceiling, willing my breath to slow down. Then, like the morning before, I forced myself to move on, holding onto the fragile hope that today might be better.

I reminded myself that I had two more days before classes started. Two days to prepare myself, to try and feel a little steadier, to prove that I could make this place mine. That determination was what pulled me out of bed. I walked my class schedule again, tracing the paths I would take starting Monday, trying to commit them to memory, then headed to the dining hall once again. I was beginning to feel like I lived there, like the dining hall had become the center of my existence.

This time, though, I decided to try something new. There was a small restaurant tucked into the corner that I had not braved yet, and they had gluten-free bagels. I ordered one and carried it out carefully, surprised by how warm it still was from being freshly baked. The cashier, who had no reason to do so, had gone to the back to grab one just for me. That small act of kindness stayed with me as I walked back out into the courtyard.

I returned to my new favorite spot under the tree and sank down, unwrapping the chocolate chip bagel. The steam curled up faintly from the dough, and the maple cream cheese container gleamed invitingly beside me. Since I didn't have a knife, I dipped the bagel directly into the cream cheese. The sweetness of the chocolate and the maple together made me close my eyes in contentment. Maybe my orientation leader had been right about it being a "campus exclusive." Maybe it was silly to let a bagel brighten my mood, but sometimes it really was the smallest things that made me happiest.

When I finished, I reached for my bag to pull out my book, only to remember that I had finished it in this very spot yesterday. A sigh escaped me. Mental note: bookstore or library trip soon. I needed something else to distract me, to pull me out of my own head when it started racing. For now, I settled on watching a couple tossing a Frisbee back and forth while their golden retriever leapt in between. They looked like they had everything figured out, their laughter light, easy, unbothered. I wondered if I would ever feel that at this school.

Not even five minutes later, the sky opened up. I gasped as fat raindrops splattered across my skin and bag, and I scrambled to my feet. Within seconds, it was pouring, the kind of heavy rain that makes your hair cling to your forehead. I sprinted toward the nearest building, my Converse slipping slightly against the wet pavement, and shoved myself through the slowly closing door just before thunder cracked overhead. My heart pounded in my ears.

Inside, the air was cool and smelled faintly of paper. I shivered and dug through my bag, pulling out a sweatshirt that was damp but better than the tank top clinging to my skin. I tugged it over my head, grateful for the warmth. My new Raylon sweatshirt was soft, still fuzzy on the inside since it had not been through the dryer yet. It was a deep maroon with the university name stitched proudly across the front, and when I pulled it down, it brushed just past the hem of my jean shorts. Only the bottom edge of the shorts peeked out, which made it feel oversize in a cozy way.

I finally looked around, and my breath caught. I had stumbled into a library, but not just any library. Directly in front of me, a giant spiral staircase wound up three floors, each level lined with shelves that seemed to stretch forever. My eyes traced the endless rows, the leather-bound spines, the soft glow of reading lamps. The rain had accidentally brought me to the exact place I wanted to be.

The silence was almost startling after the storm outside. I could hear the softest sounds, even the clink of a pen falling on the third floor. It made the entire building feel alive, as if every little sound carried a story.

I wandered slowly through the aisles, letting my cold fingertips trail across the worn book spines. The first few rows were filled with thick, dense volumes labeled for history majors, the kind of books I would probably never crack open unless I had to. I moved deeper in, searching for something closer to my own world, but after skimming rows and even trying the computer catalog, I realized there was no real "dance" section. Just a shallow shelf of classic children's books, with nothing substantial for ballet majors.

I laughed softly, shaking my head. Of course. I had written essay after essay about dance, pulling articles from databases and journals, but here, in the heart of this massive library, ballerinas did not seem to exist.

Still, my eyes lingered on a copy of *The Nutcracker* in the children's section. I slid it out carefully and opened it, flipping through the pastel illustrations. My throat tightened. A tear escaped before I wiped it away and put the book back.

The Nutcracker had been an anchor in my life for years, a tradition at my home studio. This time last year, I had been rehearsing for my senior show, cast as Snow Queen and the Sugar Plum Fairy. The biggest roles. The dream roles. Those nights had been magical, each one filled with music and lights and the strange illusion that, for a few hours, I had actually become a fairy or a queen. And now it was gone.

This would be the first time in seven years that I would not be part of the performance, and the emptiness of that realization hit me hard. I tried to remind myself that I would have college-level shows ahead, but the ache remained. What I needed now was an escape, and nothing worked better than an addictive romance novel.

Thankfully, this library delivered. The romance section spanned several rows, overflowing with titles. There were enemies-to-lovers, fantasy romances, and small-town stories. Even books I had seen trending online sat here, waiting, some in multiple copies. My fingers itched to take them all, but I narrowed it down to two, clutching them like treasure as I searched for a place to read.

In the far back corner of the third floor, I found the perfect spot: a wooden bench tucked against a tall window, hidden by surrounding shelves. I curled up there, knees tucked against the glass, head leaning into the cool pane as I opened the first book. The rain outside continued, lightning flashing faintly in the distance, thunder rumbling softly under the building. Safe, warm, hidden, I let myself sink into the story.

Until I wasn't alone anymore.

"Hey!" a voice called out.

My head snapped up, and my stomach dropped. Addy and Clarissa. Of course. In a college this massive, with all the hidden corners I could have chosen, somehow they had found me. It was like they had a tracker on me.

By the time I looked up fully, they were already standing too close, cutting off my escape.

"Why are you avoiding us?" Addy demanded. Her voice carried too loudly for the library. "We saw you multiple times, and you ran from us." Clarissa stood silently at her side, chewing her gum and watching.

I blinked, incredulous. "Excuse me?"

"What do you mean? Excuse me? It was a simple question. You keep running when you see us, and I want to know why. We were nice and let you stick with us the first night, and now this is how you show appreciation?" Addy's tone sharpened with every word.

Clarissa smacked her gum and looked around like she wasn't part of this at all, which only irritated me more.

"First of all, I only walked past you once," I said, sliding a random receipt into my book as a makeshift bookmark before setting it down. I straightened, finally facing her fully.

"I wasn't done yet, so please don't interrupt me," I added firmly, and Addy's mouth snapped shut. "Secondly, you ditched me an hour after you said we could stay together all night because it wasn't safe to be alone. I watched Clarissa drag you into her friend group, and the two of you ran out without a word. I ended up sitting alone at dinner, but don't worry, I had company. A random guy decided to flirt with me, and now

I am somehow going on a date with him when I really don't want to. So thank you for that."

Clarissa's brows shot up in amusement. "Wait, now you have a date? Who was the guy? I wonder if he's in one of the frats. Maybe he can get us into a party."

Addy elbowed her hard in the ribs, glaring, but Clarissa just shrugged. "Fine, yes, I brought Addy with me, but she said you were eating and probably leaving soon anyway. This isn't my fault, so I'm leaving. The first soccer game is in four hours, and I have to get prepped. Addy, I'll see you later. Oh, and stop dragging me into your problems."

Before either of us could reply, Clarissa spun on her heel and walked off.

"Clarissa, wait!" Addy called, but she was already gone. Addy groaned. "Ugh, whatever. Anyway, I don't know why both of you are against me. I turned, and you were gone, so I figured you left. Plus, you seemed bored with us, and Clarissa needed me to go with her since I had the only room key. Look, I'm not over this, but I'm-"

She was cut off by two campus security guards and the librarian, who appeared like shadows from the staircase.

"Ladies, this is a library. Others are trying to study. The third floor is a silent zone. You are both getting removed for yelling and echoing across the entire floor," the librarian snapped, her cardigan swishing as she crossed her arms. "Next time, stay on the first floor. I do not want to deal with you two again." Her bun wobbled with the force of her glare.

The security guards escorted us both out, their eyes lingering until we split in opposite directions. My face burned with embarrassment. Of all places to get kicked out of, it had to be one of my new favorite spots. I hadn't even checked out the book.

By the time I looked at my phone, it was already five. My date.

I froze. An hour left. Between the storm, the book, and the fight, I had nearly forgotten. My entire skin care routine, the one I had carefully planned, would have to be scrapped. I sprinted back to my dorm, my shoes slapping against the sidewalk.

Once inside, I threw myself into getting ready as quickly as I could. I painted my nails the same maroon shade as my sweatshirt, slipped into a short maroon dress with a high neckline and a skirt that swished with every step, and curled my hair into loose waves. For shoes, I stuck with my Converse, practical after the rain, but my makeup was bold enough to make a statement.

By the time I finished, an hour had nearly vanished. I grabbed my silver purse, shimmering faintly in the light, and headed out into the courtyard. My stomach fluttered with nervous energy.

Chapter 4

At six o'clock on the dot, Jack appeared. He came striding through an archway at the side of the courtyard, his steps loose and easy, like he had done this a hundred times. He smiled as soon as his eyes found me and gave a slight wave, his confidence radiating across the space.

He wore a bright red shirt with the school name stretched across it in bold white letters, paired with black athletic shorts. Red paint streaked across his cheeks, smeared unevenly, as though he had applied it in a hurry. He looked casual, completely comfortable, as if he belonged here. The kind of effortless, laid-back look that comes from not overthinking a single thing.

I looked down at myself and felt my stomach twist. Compared to him, I looked overdressed, like I was going somewhere completely different. Did I misjudge what to wear?

"Wow, you look great," Jack said as he reached me. His grin was wide, his tone playful. "I mean, you are definitely dressed up compared to me, but I love it. I am so excited we get to spend time together. Thank you for agreeing to come with me. This is going to be a great night."

His words should have settled my nerves, but they only made me feel more self-conscious. My eyes flicked over his outfit again, then back to mine, and I winced. We looked like we were headed to two separate events. My chest tightened. Maybe this was a mistake. I could say I felt sick, claim a migraine, and head back to my dorm. Hide. But no. I had promised myself I would try. I needed to get out there. Even if it was awkward. Especially because it was awkward.

I brushed my hand through my hair and forced myself to meet his eyes. He was twirling a single red rose between his fingers, the petals trembling slightly as he spun it.

"I got you this," he said, holding it out. "From the cover of the book you were reading and the description I found online, you seemed like the type of girl who would expect flowers." He winked as if he had revealed some clever secret.

At least he was not wrong. I blushed as I took it. "Thank you. And yeah, I guess I am a pretty obvious hopeless romantic." My voice was soft, and I turned slightly, embarrassed by how warm my face felt.

Jack kept his gaze locked on me, unblinking, almost too steady. It was like he was waiting for something more, though I had nothing else to give.

"Hey, I like your shoes," he said, breaking the tension by tapping his white high-top Converse against mine. "We match. And look, I even brought extra paint so we can paint your face too." He pulled a small container of bright red face paint from his pocket, holding it out like it was a gift.

I blinked at the container, unsure. Where exactly were we going that face paint was required? I had spent thirty minutes on my makeup. I was not eager to smear it away.

"Actually, that's okay," I began. But before I could finish, Jack had already dipped two fingers into the paint.

He lunged toward me with a grin. I tried to back away, but

he caught my chin firmly in his hand. My breath caught as he tilted my face upward, and in one motion, he smeared the wet paint from my temple to my cheekbone. The paint was cold, sticky, and it made me shiver. He repeated it on the other side, pulling his hand away with a satisfied smile.

I yanked my face out of his grip, my pulse racing. He tilted his head slightly, as though confused by my reaction, then casually wiped his fingers on a napkin from his pocket.

"Well, we'd better get going if we want to make it on time," he said, already turning and walking ahead.

I stood there for a second, trying to shake off the discomfort. What made him think it was okay to grab my face like that? Shaking my head, I hurried after him.

We made small talk as we walked. We spoke about our majors, about the weather, about dorm life, and even about the so-called "campus exclusive" restaurants. On the surface, it was an easy conversation, but underneath, I felt the silence pressing between each word. Our walk grew louder with every step, crowds of students joining us until the sidewalk became a stream of red shirts and painted faces.

Was the entire campus going on this date with us?

So much for a quiet dinner or a gentle walk.

Up ahead, the soccer arena loomed, lit up against the sky. My stomach sank. This was our date. When Jack had said it would be just the two of us, he had really meant the first soccer game of the season, surrounded by thousands of other students.

I didn't hate soccer, but as a first date? This was not what I imagined.

Jack, on the other hand, looked thrilled. His grin was wide, his eyes lighting up with each step. He seemed at home in the crowd, while I felt smaller with every passing second. I looked at my outfit again and swallowed. At least I had chosen Converse instead of heels. Small victory.

After thirty minutes of walking and another thirty of checking in, we finally made it to our seats in the center of the student section. The stadium around us shook with the energy of hundreds of students chanting, waving banners, and yelling over one another. The smell of nachos and popcorn mixed with sweat and spilled soda.

It reminded me of my first night on campus. The noise. The crowd. The overwhelming pressure. I had known Raylon was famous for its parties, but I had not pictured it like this.

Jack left to get nachos, and I sat stiffly, trying to take it all in. Thirty minutes crawled by as the crowd pressed closer and the noise swelled.

"Oh, so the date was for the game," a familiar voice teased. I turned and saw Clarissa. She leaned against the row in front of me with a smirk.

"That is quite an outfit. I like the face paint. You will have to give me some next time. Too bad Addy would not come. She said it was too many sweaty people in one place, plus she does not like sports. Anyway, I will be up at the top if you need me. I found a group of senior frat boys. If you want to party, come find me."

She laughed and spun back to join the group of boys whistling at her.

I giggled weakly and turned back toward the field. Addy had been right. The sheer number of people packed into this stadium was overwhelming.

Finally, I spotted Jack climbing the steps toward me. Relief flickered until I noticed the group of guys with him.

"Bri! There you are," he shouted, his voice slurred. "I almost lost our seats. Walked around this whole place three times, but my boys found me. All good." His words were loose, his eyes half-closed.

My relief dissolved. He had been gone thirty minutes, and clearly something had happened.

"Dang, dude, when you said she was hot, I did not picture this. Not your type, but I see you," one of the guys yelled.

"Oh, wait, that is the girl from freshman welcome. The one we all laughed at-"

Before he could finish, Jack shoved him hard. The guy toppled onto the bleachers behind him while the others laughed.

The game started, the players in red jerseys charging through the banner as the crowd erupted.

"Hey, Jack," I shouted, leaning toward him. He tilted his head, barely listening. "Are you okay? What happened while you were gone? I just did not expect this for a date, and now you are acting differently. I feel uncomfortable."

"No, babe, everything is fine," he said, throwing his arm around my shoulders.

"Jack, stop!" I shoved him off.

"Bri, just relax. So what if I had a drink? We have nachos, the game is starting, and this is the best night of the year. Ignore my friends. We are perfect together." His hand clamped on my arm, pulling me close as he leaned in for a kiss.

I jerked away, bumping into the guy behind me, and bolted up the stairs. The roar of the crowd blurred into static. Voices called my name, but I did not stop until I reached the concourse. My chest heaved, and tears blurred my vision as I collapsed on a bench.

I pressed my face into my hands, but then felt an arm slip around me. I flinched.

It was Clarissa.

"Hey," she said gently. "I saw what happened. I had a bad feeling when I saw him coming up the stairs. I am sorry he turned out like that. Look, you probably want to leave, but there is space up top if you want to sit with me. The frat guys are chill, and I will make sure they don't bother you. Plus, popcorn and ice cream help everything."

Her words surprised me. She was not who I expected kindness from, but maybe I had misjudged her. I nodded, too tired to argue.

We bought a jumbo box of popcorn and two chocolate ice creams, then slipped back into the stands, far away from Jack. The top row was empty, quiet compared to the chaos below.

Clarissa eventually rejoined the frat group, dancing and shouting, preparing for victory, as she called it. They included me for a while, then gave up, which was fine. I sat back and watched, giggling at their antics.

For the first time that night, I did not feel miserable.

Five minutes before the game ended, someone slid into the seat beside me. My body tensed. Please, not Jack.

"I am sorry to bother you," a soft, deep voice said. "But I have not been able to take my eyes off you all night. I saw you walk in with him, I saw what he did, and then I saw you sitting here alone."

I stared straight ahead, my heart pounding. Clarissa noticed him, grinned, and gave me a thumbs-up before turning back to her group.

Finally, I turned. Hazel eyes met mine, flecked with blue under the stadium lights. His hair was curly, chin-length, brown, streaked with red highlights from the glow. His smile was soft, steady, and my heart skipped.

I blushed and looked down. He chuckled lightly.

"I am sorry if this is weird. If it is too much, just say so. I would love to finish the game with you, maybe walk you home. But I know I am a stranger, and I do not know why I am rambling like this." His face flushed as he stood quickly.

Without thinking, I grabbed his arm.

"Wait. Actually, I would appreciate that. This night has been awful, and it would be nice to end it with someone new. Not in any way except walking home. Sorry, that sounded wrong. I am going to stop talking now." My words tumbled out, my cheeks burning.

He laughed, his eyes never leaving mine.

"I am Oliver. And you are Bri, right? I heard him yell it."

"Brianna," I said softly. "But Bri for short."

He slid his hand down from my arm to my palm, his grip warm and steady. Together, we watched the final minute of the game, our team scoring the winning goal as the stadium exploded in cheers.

We stood and walked out together. I said goodbye to Clarissa, then walked past Jack without fear. Oliver's hand held mine tightly, and for reasons I could not explain, I felt safe.

Chapter 5

"I live in Grace Hall by the way," I said as I watched the rest of the crowd begin to drift away from us in different directions.

"I just want to get away from the crowd. Trust me. I'm taking you somewhere."

I froze in place. My stomach tightened and my mind leapt to the worst conclusion. Is he a murderer? How could I be so careless and follow someone I barely know?

He must have seen the panic in my eyes because he laughed softly. "Oh stop. I'm not going to kill you. I can see exactly what you're thinking, and I promise you that isn't it. Pinky promise you're going to love this surprise."

He held out his hand, pinky extended, almost like a child daring me to trust him. I hesitated only for a second before wrapping my finger around his. He squeezed gently, and something about that small motion grounded me.

So I followed Oliver, still cautious, but less afraid. The campus was quiet on this side, tucked away from the usual noise. The path we walked ran along the back edge of campus, dimly lit by lampposts whose halos of golden light flickered against the deep shadows. The air was cool after the storm, carrying that damp, earthy scent that comes only after rain. My shoes brushed against wet leaves as we walked, the sound muffled under the rhythm of our steps.

If I weren't silently wondering whether this man could be a serial killer, I would have thought it was the most romantic walk I had ever taken. Unlike Jack, who filled silences with nervous chatter, Oliver seemed comfortable with the quiet. He asked me a few small questions, about where I grew up, what kind of books I liked, and then he simply held my hand and smiled. Sometimes he lifted our linked fingers to point out small things: a stone bench tucked into the ivy, a patch of flowers that had somehow survived the storm, the way the lamplight caught on the puddles like scattered mirrors.

In that walk I learned more about him than I expected. Oliver is a third year photography major. He told me how he has photographed dancers before and how much he respects ballet, the strength behind the softness. He spoke like he really saw it, not just the pretty costumes but the bruises and the hours of practice and the weight behind each movement. For once, I felt understood. He admitted he has his own battles with mental health, similar to my anxiety, though he did not go into detail. His voice quieted when he said it, like it was a truth he kept locked away, and I found myself wanting nothing more than for him to trust me enough to tell me someday. In that moment I thought, selfishly, that I wanted to be his safe place, his home, the person he turned to when his mind became too heavy.

After what felt like thirty minutes, we stopped in front of a small brick building with soft light glowing inside. Oliver pulled the door open and the smell hit me instantly.

Coffee.

"Coffee!" I said, nearly bouncing on my toes with excitement.

"I figured it would be busy, but it's always worth it. I love this place. It quiets my mind." He stood still for a moment, closing his eyes as if to breathe the comfort in. I watched the tension ease from his shoulders. Even if he would not say it aloud, I could tell this cafe was his second home, his sanctuary.

He pointed me toward a booth near the back. "Go get comfortable," he said. "Tell me what you want."

When I started to answer, he shook his head. "I've got it."

A few minutes later he returned, carrying two steaming cups. I took mine carefully, letting the warmth sink into my chilled hands. My first sip made me freeze.

"Pumpkin? But- it's too early for pumpkin. Nowhere has this yet!" I stared at him wide-eyed.

A slow grin spread across his face. "I have an in. I'm here so much they know me, and they might have slipped me some early. Plus, I figured…"

I narrowed my eyes at him.

"You're not basic," he rushed out, his words tumbling over each other. "I just-well, you looked like the type of girl who would love fall and warm drinks and-it's not an insult, I swear. I think it's cute. I just hoped you'd enjoy it."

He rubbed his palm against his cheek, embarrassed, and I couldn't help but smile. There was something disarming about how easily I could read him. His face said everything his words did not. I had never met someone who made me feel that way, like communication was effortless even without speaking.

"Look," he said quietly, "I'm sorry. I felt this connection and I jumped in too quickly. Tonight probably seemed sketchy, even creepy, and I should have just left you alone. Now you're here, in my favorite place, but you're still alone and lost and-"

I stopped him, squeezing his hand until he looked at me.

"Oliver, stop. You saved me tonight. I was having the worst evening and you turned it around. Did I doubt myself when

I followed you? Absolutely. But I'm glad I did. If not, I'd be in my dorm right now, alone. College is already harder than I imagined, and it's only been days. I need someone by my side. I don't know you well, but I want to. Like you said, I feel this too. So don't get self-conscious and leave me now. At the very least, you need to walk me home since I still don't know where I am."

We laughed together, quiet but real. When I checked my phone, I realized it was nearly midnight.

"I can walk you home now," Oliver said, still sounding hesitant.

"No," I said, smiling softly. "I mean, yes, later. But right now, I want to stay. Just a little longer."

He returned my smile and squeezed my hand again. "Pinky promise I haven't traumatized you?" he asked, wincing playfully.

"I mean, I can't say that…" I teased before laughing. "No, I'm kidding. This night has been perfect. I feel like you're my person already, and I know that sounds insane, but it's true. I just want more time to sit with you, to know you."

I held up my pinky and wrapped it around his. Pinky promises were becoming our thing, a secret language that felt childlike and safe.

"So," he said, eyes bright, "you are a pumpkin spice kind of person?"

"Yes, I am basic, thank you very much. Just let me enjoy my pumpkin in peace." I giggled.

"Here, try mine," he said, sliding his cup toward me.

I took a sip, letting the warmth coat my tongue, and then looked at him suspiciously. "Pumpkin?"

He tilted his head, smirking. "Our little secret."

Maybe Oliver really was my person.

When I finally made it back to Grace Hall, I lay in bed staring at the ceiling, too awake to sleep. It was almost two in the morning. Oliver had walked me back slowly, keeping close the entire time, then stood outside the door until I texted him that I was safely inside. We kept texting after that, an extra hour of back-and-forth that felt weightless. Usually my social battery drained quickly, but with him it never seemed to run out.

I had one more day before classes began. Part of me was ready-the textbooks, the schedules walked through, the meals planned. I needed structure again, that rhythm that gave me balance. But another part of me dreaded what was to come. Dance is competitive, brutally so, and I knew the first weeks would be a test. We would all size each other up, trying to prove who deserved the spotlight, until eventually, like always, the walls would break down and we would become family. That was the part I longed for, the friendships that only dance could bring.

I looked at Natalie across the room. She had already found a group of friends but seemed less interested in constant outings now. She balanced her time between socializing and quiet evenings scrolling on her phone. Her fashion design major meant she only had half as many classes as me, three for her degree and two for general education. My major was heavier, relentless, but I loved it. Still, I sometimes envied the idea of fading into the background in a lecture hall, nameless among hundreds. Being a ballerina meant constant exposure, constant critique, constant pain. Leotards, buns, soreness that never really left.

But it also meant growth. Strength. Beauty. Purpose.

I rolled over, thinking of ballet, of the past three days, and inevitably, of Oliver. Sweet, gentle, unexpected Oliver. He carried warmth beneath the armor he wore, a mystery I wanted desperately to unravel. He had walls, but I wanted to climb them, to see the view from inside. He had already eased a pain I didn't know I was holding.

It terrified me, how quickly I trusted him. How fast I was falling. Yet something in me whispered that it was safe, that this was exactly where I was supposed to be.

Eventually the weight of the day pulled me under. I set no alarm, letting the darkness swallow me, hoping tomorrow would be just as much of a dream as today had been.

Chapter 6

Sunday was going by faster than I wanted. I woke up late, the sunlight already cutting across my dorm floor in heavy stripes, then dragged myself through a slow morning of showering, breakfast, and checking my courses online. I filled in my planner with neat little boxes and lists, as if organizing everything on paper could calm the nerves twisting in my stomach. Once I finished, I curled up on my bed and let my favorite show play quietly from my laptop. The room was calm, almost too calm, and with every passing minute the weight of waiting for classes to begin pressed down heavier.

I debated texting Oliver, thumb hovering over his name more than once, but every time I thought better of it. What if I sounded too eager? What if he regretted last night already? I forced myself to set the phone down, but it was almost one when a notification lit up the screen anyway.

"I heard about last night. Lunch?"

It was from Addy. My stomach flipped. I wasn't sure why she cared, or how much she already knew, but I agreed anyway.

An hour later I found myself tucked away at a small table in the back of the dining hall, the window behind me spilling pale afternoon light across the table. I leaned against the glass and waited, picking at the corner of a napkin. When Addy finally arrived, she carried a tray so loaded with food it looked like she had raided the entire buffet line.

"I got enough food for both of us," she announced, grinning as she slid into the seat across from me. "Now, tell me everything."

Her eyes were wide, her grin mischievous. I couldn't help laughing before I launched into the whole story-from Jack to Oliver, from nerves to pinky promises-my words tumbling out in a rush. She listened like a child at story time, chin propped in her hand, nodding and gasping at the right moments.

"Clarissa told me some of that," she said when I finally paused for air, "but oh my gosh! Also, he's nonexistent online. I'm sure he has some secret photography Instagram somewhere, but you need to get me pictures of this mystery man!"

"I'll try to find out if he has one, but no more stalking him!" I giggled, snatching up a french fry. "Besides, I haven't heard from him since last night, so maybe it was nothing."

Addy's expression shifted mid-bite, her eyes flicking up over my shoulder and widening. Her jaw dropped a second later.

I barely had time to process before I felt a hand land gently on my shoulder.

Oliver.

Normally this would have been stalker-level terrifying, but my chest swelled with something closer to relief than fear. I spun around and found his hazel eyes waiting for me, warm and steady. He wore a plain shirt and jeans with red Vans, casual but effortlessly attractive. A grin tugged at his lips as he reached out and offered me a cookie.

"I'm gluten free," I mumbled, startled by the gesture.

"Oh, um, then for your friend. I owe you one." His cheeks flushed as Addy eagerly took the cookie, her face glowing with awe.

"This is Addy," I said quickly.

"Oliver," he replied, shaking her hand. She blushed, and he gave a small, crooked smile. "Sorry, but I'm currently trying to get someone's attention, so don't get your hopes up."

Even as he joked with her, I could feel his gaze lingering on me, warm but heavy, like sunlight that refused to move.

"You okay, Addy?" I asked pointedly, blinking hard twice at her in an attempt to signal that maybe she should stop gawking. She caught the hint, clamped her jaw shut, and stuffed another bite of cookie into her mouth while sneaking another glance between us.

"How did you know I was here?" I asked, my voice sharper than I intended.

"Well, you're a freshman who lives in Grace Hall. Where else would you eat lunch?" He shrugged, almost sheepish. "I figured I would try to meet you here. I was going to text, but my phone died after last night, so I left it in my room and decided to wait. Honestly, I had a ton of precourse work to do anyway, so I've been here studying most of the day. Don't think I was just sitting here only for you to show up."

Charmingly terrifying. I glanced at Addy, who looked just as overwhelmed as I felt.

"That's nice, I guess," I muttered, turning back toward the window.

I told myself not to trust so easily, not again, not after how badly I had been hurt before. Yet something about Oliver slipped past every wall I had built, pulling me back into a kind of childlike openness I thought I had lost forever. He made me feel vulnerable, which could be very good or very bad.

"Well, if you don't mind," I said, forcing my attention back on Addy, "me and Addy were catching up before the first day of classes."

"Oh no, it's no worries. Look at the amount of food I bought. Sit down, Oliver. Join us for lunch!" Addy's grin was bright, almost daring me to stop her.

I glared at her, but Oliver simply smiled. "Um, okay," he said, lowering himself into the seat beside me. His arm brushed mine and I stiffened, staring back out the window as if it would anchor me. I grabbed another fry, chewing slowly while Addy launched a rapid-fire round of questions.

For nearly an hour I listened to her chatter with Oliver while I half-watched the students passing outside. Eventually, with plates scraped clean, we stood to leave. I thought it was over, but Oliver surprised us again.

"Ice cream?" he offered.

As if the mountain of food hadn't been enough. Addy squealed her agreement before I could protest, grabbing my hand as if she were afraid I might run.

The ice cream shop they led me to was crowded, a line snaking out the door and curling around the side of the building. The air smelled of sugar and waffle cones, and though I wanted nothing more than to crawl back into bed, I followed them inside. Eventually, with cones in hand, we carried our melting desserts to a quiet table beneath a wide tree.

We ate mostly in silence, the quiet broken only by small giggles when ice cream dripped onto fingers or napkins. For a few minutes it almost felt normal, almost simple. But then Addy spotted a group of girls she knew from high school and skipped off, leaving me alone with Oliver for the first time that day.

"Is this real?" I blurted, unable to hold the question back any longer. "I can't tell if you're deeply in love with me in some sweet, genuine way, or if you're following me around just to trick me, or kill me. I've played video games with photography-obsessed murderers hiding in basements, and I just-"

Oliver reached across the table and took my hand firmly, pulling my eyes to his.

"I pinky promise I am not a murderer," he said softly. "You are far too beautiful to murder. I know I've been a bit much, and I'm sorry. I just… I really feel connected to you. But I get it, I'll slow down. I'll back off. We live on opposite ends of campus, we have different classes. Let's plan for a date next weekend. Until then, I'll let you reach out to me. No more waiting around and stalking. I mean it."

His eyes held mine, sincere but sad.

"Okay," I whispered, glancing down at our hands. He slowly released mine. I tried to squeeze tighter, to keep the moment from ending, but his fingers slipped away. The loss was sharper than I expected. Did I scare him away, like everyone else?

"I'm sorry," I muttered.

"Don't be. It's my fault. I came on too strong. But I'll wait. I want to talk to you more than anything, but I'll wait. I'll be here when you're ready." He smiled faintly, a shadow of his usual grin, and I forced myself to return it.

Addy returned just then, frowning as she glanced between us. "I left you two alone for five minutes and you broke it off already, didn't you?"

"We're just slowing down," Oliver explained gently.

"Way down," I added, tapping my foot against the ground, my nerves sparking through me.

Addy crossed her arms. "I'm not letting you drift apart. You two are too perfect together."

"Look, I really appreciate today, but it's almost five and I need to get ready for class tomorrow," I said, standing. "My first ballet class is at eight in the morning, and I'm exhausted."

Addy looked at Oliver, then back at me, and shrugged. "Don't let go of her," she said to him. "Give her space, but keep fighting for her." She grabbed my hand and tugged gently. "I'll walk her back. She doesn't need any more reason to freak out today."

Oliver reached for my other hand and squeezed. "You have my number. I'll be here. Call me, text me, find me, whatever you want. And next weekend, a real date?"

I grinned despite myself and gave him a small nod. Addy tugged me away, but my chest ached as he stayed behind, watching us go.

"You okay?" Addy asked once we were out of earshot. "I mean, I get it. His affection is intense, but come on. He's perfect for you. You have to give him a chance."

"I'm going to," I admitted. "I just freaked out and doubted myself. But I feel it too. I feel comfortable with him. Connected. I just need to focus this week without his face haunting me every second."

Still, I wanted to turn back, to run into his arms and stay there until the world made sense. Instead, I let Addy lead me back to the dorm.

The rest of the evening dragged. I ate sushi alone for dinner, did a face mask, and let an old movie fill the silence. I decided maybe it would be my thing-watching classics I had never seen, curled under my dorm blankets at night. Natalie returned around ten, hair damp, cheeks flushed from her own night out. We settled into our routines-shower, clothes laid out, alarms set. By ten thirty she was asleep, her soft breathing filling the room.

I lay awake longer, staring at the photos on my wall. The girl in those pictures felt like a stranger compared to the one lying here now. I thought about how much had changed in just two days, how much more could shift in the weeks ahead. It was thrilling and terrifying all at once.

As the darkness settled, Oliver's voice echoed in my head. I could hear his words, see the sincerity in his eyes. I squeezed my eyes shut, trying to think of anything else, but he was everywhere in my mind. After what felt like an hour of chasing him through my thoughts, I finally drifted into sleep, both nervous and excited for what tomorrow might bring.

Chapter 7

I wake up to the sound of my alarm blaring, the same sharp tone I have used for years, and the noise seems to climb under my skin and scratch there until I fumble for my phone and smash the off button. Silence rushes in, a heavy kind of quiet that makes the room feel even colder. I blink up at the underside of the lofted bed frame, then swipe through the notifications that bloomed overnight. A couple of useless emails, a store promotion I will never open, a text from my mom from late last night with a heart and a picture of the dogs sleeping nose to nose on the couch. I stare at the photo until the edges of my worry soften, then I flick through social media for a minute or two, not reading, just letting my eyes slide over bright pictures and short captions until my brain finally believes it is morning.

I roll to my side and climb down the ladder slowly, one foot then the other, careful on the narrow metal rungs. When my bare feet meet the tile my whole body flinches. It is still August, but the air in the dorm is icy, like the building is pretending we skipped ahead to winter. I wrap my arms around myself and shuffle to the bathroom with my toiletries bag clutched to my chest. I put in my contacts, my eyes watering for a second as the lenses settle, then I brush my teeth until my mouth feels minty and awake. I splash cold water on my face and watch the droplets race down my cheeks, and in the mirror I look like me and also like someone new, someone who is supposed to know how to be a college student.

Back at my side of the room I pull on the outfit I planned days ago, because planning ahead is the only thing that makes me feel steady right now. Jean shorts, maroon shirt with the school logo in white across the front, the letters bold and loud against the cotton. My hair goes up into a ponytail, practical and quick, then I slide on my old black Converse that already know the shape of my feet. Ballet is my first class today, but I tell myself the first day is usually introductions and syllabus and rules. I tuck my leotard and tights into my dance bag anyway, just in case, because the idea of showing up unprepared makes my stomach twist.

I do my makeup in the glow of a small lamp, since Natalie is still sleeping on the other side of the room. She gets to start later most days, which means I am usually the one tiptoeing, the one using my phone flashlight to find a hair tie under the bed, the one turning the bathroom floor into a tiny vanity because I am trying to be polite. I do not mind it as much as I thought I would. The bathroom light is actually good, the mirror is big, and the small inconvenience makes the quiet feel softer, like I am moving through a secret morning before the campus wakes up.

I am not waiting in the dining hall line for an hour, not today, so I pull two frozen waffles out of the tiny freezer and pop them into the toaster. The smell is sweet and familiar, and while I wait I lean against my desk, checking the time again, rehearsing the route to the dance building in my head, counting how long it will take if I walk fast, counting again if I do not. The toaster springs the waffles up with a cheerful click, I drown them in a too-small packet of syrup, and I eat at my desk with my knees pulled up, the plate balanced on my thighs. My room is all quiet humming, the air conditioner steady, the laptop charging, the faint whisper of Natalie's breathing. For a second I feel like the whole campus is holding its breath with me.

I zip my bag, check the contents one more time, and step out into the hallway. It smells faintly like laundry detergent and someone's coffee. The elevator is crammed with bodies and backpacks, so I take the stairs, and when I push through the heavy front doors the courtyard opens in front of me like a loud hive. There are students everywhere, walking in every direction, their voices overlapping into one big sound that fills the sky. The heat of late summer sits on my shoulders, even though the air holds a wet edge that promises rain later. I slide my earbuds in, pick a playlist I know by heart, and let the music carry me forward through the buzz of first-day energy.

I break off from the main stream of people as soon as I can. My first class is across campus, and then some, buried behind the main academic buildings, down past a stand of trees, across a stretch of lawn where sprinklers mist the air and make the grass smell green and sweet. My bag thumps a rhythm against my hip as I walk. With every song I count a little less and look a little more. Someone skateboards by with a stack of notebooks tucked under one arm. A girl sits on the edge of a planter and ties her shoe with calm, methodical concentration, like the rest of the world is not moving around her. The bell in the old library tower rings, and the sound rolls over the walkway, warm and round.

The dance building comes into view at the end of the path, a low rectangle of glass and brick that reflects the sky. Inside, the hallway is already packed. Dancers cluster in small knots against the walls, some stretching their hamstrings on door frames, some leaning on foam rollers that look like oversized marshmallows, some whispering to new friends like they have known them all their lives. The air smells like hairspray and lavender lotion and the rubbery clean of marley floors. My heart beats a little faster as I thread through the crowd, and when I reach Studio Three and push open the door, I stop so fast my bag knocks into my leg.

Half the freshman class is already at the barre, leotards black and neat, buns slick and perfect, warm ups folded under their arms. I look down at my maroon logo shirt and denim and feel heat crawl up my neck. The music is not playing yet, and there is that thin, expectant silence that means class is about to start, and I am in the wrong clothes. I turn on my heel and slip back into the hallway, then into the bathroom where the light is a little too bright. I yank open my bag with clumsy hands and dig until I find the tights and leotard I tossed in last night. Relief floods me so hard I laugh. I wriggle into the leotard as fast as I can, peel off the shorts, tuck them away, pull on the tights, tie my skirt into a clean knot at my hip. I twist my ponytail into a bun and spray until the stray hairs decide to behave. When I look in the mirror this time, I look like I belong in a studio again. My pulse settles.

Back in Studio Three I slide my bag against the back wall and take a spot at the barre that runs along the mirror. I fold forward, letting my body hang for a few breaths until my hamstrings wake up. Around me, everyone is stretching like they are already being graded on it. A girl to my left pulls her leg up onto the barre and lays her chest on her thigh like it does not cost her anything. A pair across from me take turns holding each other in balances, their fingertips a little prayer between them. Some girls talk in easy, low voices. Others have the sharp look of people who are already competing, even if no one has said the word competition out loud.

Three teachers step into the room, and the air changes. The ballet teacher who will run this class stands with her hands lightly together, her chin high, and even her stillness is precise. The modern teacher has a quick way of scanning the space, eyes that seem to catch everything. The third teacher, also ballet, smiles like she knows our nerves are loud enough to drown out thought. They introduce themselves, a graceful exchange, then the married pair slip next door to their studios, and my teacher turns and nods to the corner where the pianist is settling onto the bench.

The first notes float out, warm and full, and the room breathes. Live music fills the gaps a speaker cannot reach. It moves like water around ankles, like air under wings. I close my eyes for one heartbeat and let the sound run through me. Then class begins. Pliés first, simple shapes at the barre, knees opening, heels pressing into the floor, spine long. I find the rhythm of the pianist's hands. I feel my breath set itself to a count. We move into tendus, careful and clean, toes sliding out and in, then dégagés that flick like small sparks. Rond de jambes, hips square, circle the leg, do not let the pelvis wander. The teacher's voice is calm and commanding, and when she walks past me and taps two fingers lightly near my ribs, I lift and lengthen without thinking. I push a little harder in the places where I know I am strong. I let my back soften and my arms trace the line of the music. When the combinations turn to pirouettes, I put my focus on placement and not on counting the turns, because I know this is where confidence can crack. Some girls whip doubles and triples like they could do them in their sleep.

Some wobble and recover. I keep moving and try to look like the music is mine and not like it is chasing me.

We finish barre and step to the center. The light from the tall windows washes across the floor in long ribbons. We carve patterns in the open space, adage that asks for patience and balance, petite allegro that snaps and skims, grand allegro that wants flight. I think about my old studio and the way the floor smelled after long rehearsals, like resin and effort, and for a moment I am both in that memory and here in this room, breathing hard and alive.

When the class ends, applause rises for the pianist, and the sound is as much relief as it is gratitude. I mop my face with a towel and let my shoulders drop. The warmth in my muscles hums like low electricity. I stay in the same studio for modern, because my schedule today pretends I live here. Some girls take their hair down and let it breathe. Others lay on their backs and stare at the ceiling while they slowly open their hips with lazy stretches. I eat a granola bar in small bites, read the schedule posted on the cork board even though I already know it, and twist my bun tighter.

The modern teacher claps once and the room goes quiet. He tells us we will start with a circle, a fire pit, his words, a place where we say our names and share how we are doing. We sit cross-legged and I feel the floor under my palms, cool and slightly textured. People speak one after the other. Excited, nervous, overwhelmed, hungry, tired but happy. When it is my turn, my words come out soft, but they come, and all around the circle, heads nod like they have felt the same thing in their own bodies.

Then we move. He plays music I do not know, something with a heartbeat down low, and the warm up is all about dropping weight and catching it again. We roll on the floor and find the way our spines curve into it. We lunge and suspend and fall and recover. He talks about technique by names I have never learned, names I have only seen in passing on blogs and audition lists. He demonstrates combinations slowly, then again a little faster, and then asks us to try. My knees scuff the marley and sting. My shoulders burn. The center work asks me to move through space like I own it, not like I am borrowing it. I do not know if I love modern yet, but I love what happens to my brain when ballet lets go and something raw takes its place. I breathe like I am learning a new way to be.

By the time class ends, my hairline is damp, my calves feel like they have been squeezed by a giant hand, and every inhale pulls cool air that tastes like the room, chalky and clean. I check my phone. I have two hours until dance orientation, which is not enough time to walk all the way back to the dorm and then return. I sit on the bench in the hallway and stretch my hamstrings again. I watch as older dancers walk by and laugh with each other in that easy way that says they have been doing this together for years. I wonder who in this building will become my person. I wonder who I will be in this building by the end of the year.

A girl stops near me and tilts her head. She is familiar from class, dark blond hair in a neat bun, eyes bright.

"You are Sydney, right," she asks.

I almost laugh, because my name is not Sydney, and the moment is so college it feels scripted.

"I am actually Brianna," I say, smiling.

She laughs and shakes her head.

"Sorry, I just met five new people. Let me try again. I am Lea, and this is Zoe and Alexis. We are going to grab lunch up the hill. Do you want to come."

"Yes," I say before my brain can invent a reason to say no. "And I am terrible with names."

"Same," Lea says, pointing. "Lea. Zoe. Alexis."

They repeat them slower, and they stick this time.

We walk out together and follow the path up the slope to a smaller campus restaurant that looks like it used to be a house before the school grew around it. The line is not long, but when I ask for gluten free bread the order slips to the side and I can see the cook go searching. Lea and Alexis pick up sandwiches that look perfect. Zoe gets a salad that glows green in the light. I stand with my receipt in one hand and a small plastic number in the other and pretend I am not worried I am holding them up. They talk while we wait, and I learn that Lea has a roommate who sets five alarms and sleeps through all of them, that Alexis keeps a stash of granola bars under her bed, that Zoe rides her bike everywhere because it keeps her sane. I tell them about the long walk to the dance building and how I almost showed up to ballet in street clothes. We laugh in a way that feels like we have been laughing together for a while.

By the time my sandwich arrives, the others are already finishing theirs, but they stay and talk while I eat. We go through the list of our old studios and teachers like we are comparing maps. We all have the same kind of scar tissue in the same places. We talk about our dreams like we are saying them out loud to make them real. When we head back down the hill my legs feel less shaky, and when we split at the hallway I tell myself the thing I always tell myself when I am trying to be brave. Show up again tomorrow. That is all.

Orientation is a room full of dancers sitting in a giant oval with the three teachers at the front, and a table piled with papers that slide and shuffle as we pass them down the line. Some are forms we need to sign, some are schedules for the semester, some describe trips the department hopes to take if the budget behaves. The information comes fast, and my hand cramps while I write notes in the margins. When we go around the circle to introduce ourselves I hear hometowns and favorite ballets and reasons people fell in love with movement. When it is my turn I say I am a freshman ballet major and that I am excited and terrified, which gets a small wave of laughter that feels like support.

Afterward I walk back toward my dorm with a group of girls, and two of them turn into my building with me. Lea and Alexis live here too, and that tiny coincidence makes the world feel a little less enormous. We ride the elevator and talk about the first day, and when the doors open I wave goodbye and head down my hall. My room is empty when I push the door open, the bed made perfectly on Natalie's side, a neat stack of sketchbooks on her desk. I let my bag fall to the floor and I drop onto my bed and stare at the ceiling until the sound of my pulse slows. Then I drag myself up and head for the showers, the water beating my shoulders in a way that feels like someone is kneading them clean.

The dining hall is packed when I go later, a buzz of conversation that bounces off the high ceiling. I wind up the stairs to the second floor where the pizza station is, because I know they usually have a gluten free option if you ask and then wait, and I do not mind waiting tonight. From up here I can look down over the whole hall, tables full of new friendships and old ones. The line moves slowly. The air smells like melted cheese and tomatoes and the sweet frosting of the dessert bar. I scan the faces without meaning to, eyes searching for one I have only known a short time but already miss. No Oliver. I do not know if that makes me relieved or disappointed, so I decide I am both.

By the time I get my pizza, the tables have shifted again, new groups, different laughter. I carry my plate to a quiet corner and eat one slice at a time while I read the orientation papers again. My phone buzzes against the table, and the small thud makes me jump. I flip it over. "Hope your first day went well. I am still in class and then I am buried in homework, talk later." It is from Oliver, and my heart does that silly little skip I pretend not to notice. I text back that my day was good and that I am glad he survived his too, and then I tuck my phone face down and make myself focus on the food and the papers and the way the evening light slides down the windows.

Sleep comes like I have earned it. The next day comes early and I move through it like I am following steps I already learned. I dress in the dark so Natalie can sleep, and I thread my way back across campus to my eight-in-the-morning English lecture where the professor is kind and the room smells like old books. After that I run back to my dorm to change, then back to ballet, then to pointe, then to improv, which is funny and scary in equal parts. I stop for food on my way back and let my eyes sweep the dining hall again. No Oliver. I go to my room and do homework while the afternoon folds into evening, and the day becomes a blur of small accomplishments that I try to line up like beads on a string.

Wednesday and Thursday follow the same pattern. Classes and walking and work and more walking. My legs complain and then they get quiet and then they complain again. I stretch on the floor next to my bed while I watch a video for homework and the sound of Natalie's keyboard fills the room in tiny bursts. Sometimes I catch my reflection in the window at night and

I look like someone who almost knows what she is doing. Sometimes I look like a kid playing dress up as a college student. Both can be true. I write that on a sticky note and press it into my planner because I need to see it again.

Chapter 8

Friday feels like a deep breath waiting to happen, this is because I only have one class and my parents say I can come home for the long weekend. It is Labor Day weekend, which means no class on Monday, and it is also my Dad's birthday, which means cake and laughter and the smell of charcoal in the backyard. I pack the small suitcase my mom left me with and I also shove half my laundry into a tote bag, because the stories I have already heard about the dorm laundry room are enough to keep me from trying. People move other people's clothes without asking. Socks disappear like magic. I would rather drag mine home and hug the washing machine like it is a person.

The walk to the distant parking lot is not a mystery anymore, but doing it with multiple heavy bags turns it into a test. The sidewalk is cracked and uneven, and the way the road dips into driveways makes the curb do small jumps that my arms do not love. I shift the straps from one shoulder to the other and then back again. A couple of students pass me with nothing but a backpack and a coffee, and I pretend I am not jealous. When I reach the crosswalk at the busy road I feel people glance at me in that way that says they are noticing, and I stare at the light and will it to turn. It does. I cross, and the hill down toward the lot makes my bags pull at me like small, stubborn children.

When I see my car I say thank you out loud to nobody and everybody. I drop everything on the back seat, slide into the driver seat and turn the air conditioning up high. I sit there for a long minute with my eyes closed, letting my pulse slow. Then I put my destination into the map even though I do not need it, and I drive.

The back roads between school and home are a small miracle I do not expect. Two small towns along the way look like postcards, each with one main street and a brick coffee shop that probably knows every regular by name. There is a barbecue place with a faded sign and a line out the door, even in the heat, and there are antique stores with windows full of old lamps and quilts. Between the towns the hills roll like waves, green and wide open, with cows scattered like punctuation in the fields. I roll my windows down and let the air rush in. I turn my music up until I can feel it in my chest, and I sing like nobody in any of those cars can hear me. The road lifts and drops and I lift and drop with it. For twenty minutes I am happy in the simplest way a person can be happy. I decide I will always take the back roads when I can.

When I turn onto the gravel of our driveway, the sound under the tires is so familiar I smile. The house looks the same, but seeing it now makes my chest feel like it is expanding and collapsing at the same time. I park and catch the movement at the fence, then the dogs notice me and the barking starts, a chorus of joy I did not know I needed to hear. I open the front door and run inside without my bags because I cannot make myself do anything else first. My mom is already coming toward me from the kitchen with her arms open, and my dad stands up from the couch with that smile he has had since forever, the one that always looks a little proud and a little amused. I fall into my mom and she squeezes me.

"Brianna is home," she says, like it is the best news of the year.

"Hi," I say, already teary, "I missed this place and I missed you."

My dad wraps his arms around both of us and squeezes.

"We are so proud of you," he says.

It feels like the week slides off my shoulders, lands on the floor, and evaporates.

We let the dogs inside and the living room turns into joyful chaos, paws clicking on the floor, tails thumping, tongues everywhere. I sit on the rug and let them climb all over me. I laugh in that unstoppable way that shakes your ribs. My mom and dad start telling me small stories from their week. A light bulb that would not unscrew without a fight. A neighbor who brought tomatoes from her garden. A song my dad heard on the radio that he swears I have to look up and listen to on the drive back. I tell them about my week too, the long walks, the classes, the teachers, the cold dorm room, the new friends, the way the library tower bell sounds. I realize how fast everything is moving for me and how still everything looks here, and I do not think one is better than the other. I think I need both to be a person right now.

I carry my bags in and haul them up to my room, setting them down just inside the door. The room looks like someone pressed pause on a movie the day I left. The bedspread is the same, the photos are still taped up above the headboard, the stack of books on the desk is undisturbed, a coffee mug sits where I forgot to wash it. I sit on the bed and it dips in that familiar way, and my dogs jump up and frame me like a living blanket, and for a minute I do not think at all. I just breathe.

Cole, my brother, peeks around the door frame like he is not sure if he is allowed to interrupt. He is taller than the last time I saw him. He has my moms eyes and our dad's smile.

"Hey," he says, shy but trying, "I'm glad you're here, even if it is only the weekend. The house is weird without you. If you want to play a game later, let me know."

"Yes," I say, smiling, "maybe after dinner."

He nods and vanishes, and I know he will be back.

My phone buzzes on the bed, and I glance down. It's Oliver. Of all the moments for him to finally text, it's this one, when I am home and calm for the first time in days.

"Sorry I did not text much this week," he writes, "you know how it is. I thought I would let you focus and then catch up this weekend. Dinner?"

I roll my eyes and also smile. I think about the quiet in my dorm and how a small message from him would have been a warm blanket. I think about how timing can be a coin toss. I type:

"No worries. I came home for the weekend. I hope your week was okay."

He replies fast, like his phone was already in his hand.

"Bri, wait. Seriously, I am sorry. I should have texted you. I hid in my dorm and isolated myself. I will try to be more present in the coming weeks. I get it, you are home, I will let you be. I am here if you want to talk. Bye."

I stare at the word bye and I do not like it, so I answer:

"It's okay. Talk next week. Maybe dinner in the dining hall one night."

"It's a plan," he writes, "have fun."

I put the phone face down, press my cheek into the warm fur of the dog closest to me, and decide I will not think about anything but this house for a few hours.

The next two hours slip by in small good things. I help my mom wipe down the counters and chop vegetables for later. I play a fast game with Cole that I lose in a humiliating way because he has learned three new tricks while I was gone. I take the dogs for a slow walk along the edge of the yard and watch them sniff every single thing like it is their job. The air smells like sun on grass and the faint, mineral tang of the hose someone left dripping. When my extended family arrives, it's like the house swells to make room. My aunt brings a salad that tastes like childhood summers. My uncle stands at the grill and tells the same stories he always tells, and we all pretend we have never heard them. My grandparents sit together on the patio and share a chair cushion like they always do. We eat burgers and corn on the cob, and someone drops a slice of tomato, and the dogs win the lottery.

As the sun starts to drop behind the trees, the backyard turns golden, and the shadows get longer, and the talk gets quieter in that content way that happens when everyone is full and happy. We bring out a cake for my dad and sing in a ragged circle, and he laughs and shakes his head at the number of candles. He blows them out in two long breaths, and we clap like we have never seen someone make a wish before. After the last plates are scraped and the last hug is given at the door, the house settles. Mom, Dad and I carry blankets outside and light the fire pit. The first flames catch and whisper, and then the wood pops loudly as the fire grows. I pull my knees up and wrap my arms around them, the heat on my shins makes my shoulders relax. Above us the sky deepens and one star appears, then another, until there are enough to make me tilt my head back and search for patterns I do not know the names of.

I stare into the fire so I do not have to stare at their faces when I say it.

"I am really struggling," I say, my voice quiet but loud in the dark. "It is a lot harder than I thought it would be. I feel lonely, and I have not made real friends yet, the dance classes are different than I expected, and the school is massive, and I really miss home."

The tears begin without my permission. They slide down hot and fast, and I do not wipe them away at first.

"I know," my mom says, touching my hand, "it is hard." She swallows. "I cry at night because the house feels wrong without you in it. It will get better."

My dad looks up at the stars for a long second, like he is choosing words from them.

"I remember moving out," he says. "It is hard, but it is worth it. Soon you will feel like you never want to come back. You will enjoy the freedom, and you will do great. I am proud of you. We are always here for you, but it is time for you to go be you. You've got this."

I lift my head and look at both of them. Their faces glow in the light of the fire, and there are lines I do not remember noticing before. My mom wipes at her own eyes and then reaches across and wipes the corner of mine with the edge of her sleeve in that automatic mother way she has had since I was small.

"You can come home on weekends," she says, "we are not going anywhere. But do not let your anxiety steal this year from you. You are in charge of your life, and you are brave enough to step into it. Go for it."

She squeezes my fingers, firm and certain. I nod and then I fold, head in my hands, shoulders shaking. I never want to cry in front of people, but this feels like what my lungs need to do to work again. I feel both of them shift closer, their hands on my back, a steady weight that tells my body I am safe.

"It'll be okay," my dad says. "You are smart and strong, we love you, and we support you."

"I love you too," I choke out, messy and honest.

They pull me tighter. We sit like that for a while, not talking, breathing in the wood smoke, the cool night and the quiet. The dogs settle at our feet in warm circles. The embers shift and glow like small cities. The backyard smells like home, and the wind slips through the trees and the sound is like water. I think about the week I just had and the week I will have. I think about the long walk to the dance building and the way the pianist's hands let the room change shape. I think about Lea and Alexis and Zoe and the way their names already feel easy in my mouth. I think about Oliver and the way he held my gaze the night we met and the way he wrote bye like he was trying to disappear and then corrected it with a plan. I think about how I am different than the girl in the photos above my bed, and how I am exactly the same, and how both can be true.

At some point the fire leans into coals and the night leans into late, so we carry the blankets inside. I wash my face in the bathroom where the light is too bright, and I put on the softest shirt I own. I crawl into my childhood bed that still smells a little like the detergent my mom uses. The dogs circle three times and land like commas at my knees. My phone lights up once on the nightstand and then sleeps. I breathe in the quiet. I try a small experiment. I imagine Monday morning. I picture myself walking across campus with a coffee, the air a little cooler, my bag a little lighter because I know exactly what I packed. I picture myself pushing the door to the studio and taking a spot at the barre like it is waiting for me and not the other way around. I picture saying hello first, and I picture the word hello turning into other words. I picture feeling lost, and then I picture feeling a little less lost, and then I picture feeling found, not all at once, but slowly, like light coming up through a window shade.

I do not know who I will be at the end of the year. I know that I will be tired sometimes, and that my feet will hurt, and that I will miss home, and that I will love being away once in a while. I know that I will probably cry again, and that I will probably laugh until my stomach hurts with people who are strangers now and will not be strangers later. I know that if I keep showing up, the steps will add up to something, even if I cannot see it yet. I close my eyes and let the dark hold me. I listen to the quiet of the house I grew in. I fall asleep with the feeling that I am standing on a bridge between two places, and that I am allowed to love both.

Chapter 9

The weekend flies by and I am suddenly driving back to campus, the road folding and unfolding in front of me like a ribbon I have already memorized. It is a great weekend, full of walks, movies, Target runs, home cooked meals and quiet moments with the dogs asleep across my feet, but it is gone in a blink. The car feels too big with only me in it again. I let my parents' words loop in my head like a song I do not want to lose. Come home whenever you want, they said, there is always a place for you here. I grip the wheel a little tighter. I am scared that I will take them up on that every single week, that I will flee the second campus feels too loud or too lonely. I want to make friends, I want to learn the shortcuts on the sidewalks and know the best times for the dining hall and pick a favorite table in the library, I want to feel like I belong, but it is not happening the way I imagined. Is it bad if I go home every weekend, or is it the thing that will keep me steady enough to stay? I do not know yet. Day by day, I tell myself, a quiet promise in the space between the songs.

I roll the windows down and let my music blast into the warm afternoon, the wind picks up strands of my hair and whips them around my face. The hills lift the car and then let it fall again, the way a roller coaster would. I sing until my throat feels scratchy, because it works better than thinking too hard. When my phone buzzes in the console I glance down at the screen for a second at a stop sign. Five texts, a name I cannot see clearly while I am moving. I decide not to read it, my stomach is still learning these curves and I do not trust my eyes off the road for long. I unlock my phone without looking, just to make the screen stop flashing, and as I do, the call pops up on the center display.

Oliver.

My heart stutters and then sprints. He has never called me before. We have texted, but not that much, and suddenly he is a name filling the screen, the call request hovering like a dare. I consider letting it ring out, but my thumb betrays me and taps accept before my brain can vote.

"Are you okay," he says, the words tumbling over each other, "why have you not answered my messages, I thought something happened." His voice is tight and out of breath and he does not wait for me to respond before he stacks another question on top of the first one. I have only been on the road an hour and he sounds like it has been a day.

"I'm driving, geez," I say, trying to sound light, "sorry I didn't text back, I just saw your messages, and I don't feel comfortable checking my phone on these roads yet. Are you okay?" My anxiety leaps to build a whole tower of worst case scenarios. I picture crashes, emergencies, and problems far beyond me.

"Oh, okay," he says, and I can hear him exhale, "well next time text me back, please." The please is breathless and a little bossy at the same time.

"Okay, I will," I say, and my eyebrows pull together. He gets stranger the more I talk to him. "So, did you need anything, or were you blowing up my phone to say hi and make sure I am still alive."

"Right," he says, a laugh caught in his throat, "I got distracted. First of all it was five texts so calm down, second of all I wanted to see if you were free for dinner. They are showing throwback movies at the theater on campus and I thought you might want to go."

"I am still an hour away," I say, checking the time, "what time is the movie."

"That's right, you're driving," he says, "I could meet you when you get here and we can walk together, the movie is later tonight, we could get dinner beforehand."

"I park far off campus and I am not dressed for dinner and a movie," I say, laughing, "would you want to meet me at my dorm in three hours, or is that too late." It is just now two. It should be plenty of time, but Oliver does love a mystery plan. I can feel him doing math on the other end.

"Yeah, sure, that works," he says, "I will be at your dorm in exactly three hours. Meet me in the courtyard by our spot."

"Our spot," I echo, amused, "you've already named it?"

"Yeah, sorry," he says, "I mean the tree, the spot we will always meet at. Anyway I will let you focus on driving. See you tonight. Bye."

"Bye," I say, softer than I mean to, and the call clicks off.

The car is quiet for a beat, like it is listening with me. I still cannot figure him out. I am excited though. Ten minutes ago I was facing a Sunday night alone with laundry and a long face and now it is a date night. I turn the music up again and find every love song I can and sing them all like a pep talk. I press the gas a little harder and watch the hills roll by, green and gold in the sunlight.

Back on campus, I park in the far lot and hike the familiar

route in with my weekend bag banging against my knee, then I bolt up the stairs of my dorm two at a time. I have thirty minutes to turn road trip me into date night me. I sit at my small desk and study my face in the mirror, the tired smudges under my eyes, the bits of sun caught in my cheeks from driving with the windows down. We can work with this, I tell my reflection, and I start. I lay out my makeup like tiny tools that will build a version of me that feels a little bolder, a little brighter. Concealer, a sweep of bronzer, mascara that lifts my lashes into something that reads awake, lip gloss that tastes faintly like vanilla. I pull the yellow dress from the back of my closet because summer is almost over and it deserves one more night, and I pair it with wedges that make my calves look like I have done a hundred more relevés than I have. I straighten my hair and clip half of it back with the small white daisy barrette that always makes me smile. Then the silver necklace, a small pendant resting at the notch of my throat, and simple earrings, and my favorite three rings, cool as they slide on and then warm on my skin.

I stand and spin once in front of the mirror, the skirt lifting and then settling against my thighs, the fabric soft and friendly. The dress makes me feel like a sunflower in a room of neutral paint, which is exactly the point. I grab a cardigan because the air always drops after sundown, and I cram my small purse with everything I think I could possibly need. Chapstick, wallet, phone, room key, tissues, a couple of wrapped candies I shove to the bottom with a secret smile for the movie. When I check the time, I groan. I am already two minutes late. Good thing our spot is twenty steps from my door.

When I push open the door, the courtyard air wraps around me, and there he is under the big tree, the navy polo neat against his shoulders, dark jeans, the kind of outfit that looks simple until you really look. He is staring down at his phone like he is trying to solve a code, but when the door creaks shut his eyes jump up to mine, bright and alert. He tucks the phone into his back pocket and smiles, the kind that lands in his eyes too.

"You are two minutes late," he says, grinning like he is allowed to tease me now.

"It takes longer than the time you gave me to look like something other than a college zombie," I say, glancing down at my dress, suddenly unsure if I am overdressed.

The sun is deciding to leave, the air is slipping cooler under my cardigan, and goosebumps rise on my arms even though I am excited.

"I thought you were not going to come," he admits, a nervous hitch in his voice. He lifts his hand and holds his pointer finger in the air above me. "Spin so I can see everything."

He looks like he will stand there all night unless I do it. I glance around to make sure we are alone, then I slip my finger around his and turn once, the skirt blooming and then falling back.

"Worth the two minutes," he says, and the way his voice softens makes heat climb into my cheeks. He laces our fingers and gives a little tug. "We have to hurry if we want dinner before the movie."

"Okay, okay," I say, laughing, and I fall into step beside him as we cut through the courtyard to the busier walkway.

It is Sunday dinner time and the campus is a parade of pairs and packs, some dressed like they rolled out of bed, some dressed like a runway level of effort. We drift with them toward the dining hall and I angle toward the doors automatically. Oliver squeezes my hand and keeps walking.

"Do you seriously think I am taking you to the dining hall," he asks, and his laugh makes an easy shape in the air.

"You walked me right to it," I say, lifting my eyebrows, "where else is there to eat."

He raises his own eyebrows, half secret, half challenge, and tugs me gently forward.

"Oh right," I say, "Mister insider who knows all the places, it better be good."

I match his pace and for a second I look past him at the sky. The sunset is painting everything in warm honey and orange and red, reflections glossing across windows, the tops of the trees edged with fire. I catch myself staring at him and quickly look away.

We walk for fifteen minutes, weaving off campus to a street lined with small shops and restaurants, until we reach a tiny diner tucked beside a pocket park. The park has one huge tree in the center, arms stretched out like it could gather everyone in the city at once, and smaller trees ring the fence. Strings of warm fairy lights run from the big tree to the little ones, a glowing web. I stop because I have to. The lights make the air look like a story. I feel his gaze slide to me and I can tell he is smiling.

"Go stand under the tree," he says, a gentle hand at my back.

I wander out and tip my head up to watch the lights blur a little. The night is soft and the grass smells sweet and the fairy lights make a halo around the leaves. Oliver drops to one knee and my heart stops.

Chapter 10

"What are you doing," I squeak, and it comes out higher than I mean it to.

"Oh please," he says, laughing, "I was going to take your picture."

He pulls a small camera out of the bag that is suddenly on his shoulder, which I swear was not there before, and my cheeks go hot.

"Spin around a couple of times," he says, lifting the camera.

"Oliver," I say, hands on hips, "I am not posing for a full on photo shoot right now."

"Fine," he says, still smiling, "just one spin, and then later we should do a real shoot. I want to work on movement photography, and a dancer is exactly what I need."

"We will see about later," I say, "but you get one spin right now."

The truth is that posing for photos makes me itch. I was self conscious about my smile for years, and even though I eased into it a little in high school when I did promo pictures for that local dance wear company, I still feel safer when I am moving, not when I am trying to be a regular person being looked at. I turn quickly, the skirt blooming again, and then I walk back to him and he takes my hand, squeezes once and leads me into the diner.

Inside, the place is all chrome, red vinyl, a long counter with stools, a row of small booths, a jukebox in the corner that probably still works. Only one waitress is on the floor, and an older couple sits at the far end of the counter sharing a plate of fries. Oliver slides into the corner booth and reaches across the table to help me in, and when we settle he pulls a lighter from his bag and lights the small candle on the table. The flame dances and the light lands gold on his cheekbones and I have the sudden urge to draw what I see, even though I am a dancer not a painter.

"It is nothing too fancy," he says, a little shy, "but I figured it was nicer than waiting an hour for a place everyone goes to."

"It is perfect," I say, and I mean it.

"Also," he adds, leaning in like he is telling me a secret, "I came by earlier to make sure they had gluten free options, and when they said they did not, I went to the store and grabbed a few things to help. So I recommend the burger."

He winks and sits back, proud of himself in that easy way that is warm to stand near.

"That sounds perfect, thank you," I say, and the words come out more quietly than I expect.

The waitress appears with two waters and a smile, and we order cheeseburgers and a basket of fries to share and one milkshake with two straws because sometimes clichés are clichés because they are right.

The food is simple and somehow more than that. The burger is juicy and salty and the bun is soft and does not fall apart, a gluten free miracle. The fries are hot and taste like the fryer has a story. The milkshake is thick, cold and sweet enough to make my tongue happy. We talk, and the talking is easy.

He tells me about his weekend, which was studying and shooting photos for a small event the university hosted. He tells me the job pays almost nothing but buys him practice and the occasional pass into places students do not usually get to go. I tell him about my weekend without mentioning the part where I cried by a fire pit under the stars and my parents held me like I was still ten. I tell him about the back roads and how the hills make it feel like the car is laughing with me.

"I want to see them," he says, "and take pictures when the leaves change."

When we step back outside, the air has dropped more than I expected it to. I pull my cardigan tight and shiver, and Oliver slides his hands up to my shoulders and rubs them fast, that quick friction that sends warmth down my arms. We both blush at how natural it feels. He looks away and then takes my hand like that is the safer choice, and we walk toward campus a little faster than before.

The university theater glows ahead of us, a triangle of light spilling out from the glass doors onto the steps. Inside, a bored student worker sits behind the small ticket stand, tapping on a phone. Oliver pulls his phone out and flashes the confirmation code, and the worker mumbles a theater number without looking up. Oliver turns toward the hallway that leads to the theater and I drift toward the concession stand on instinct. We both stop and look at each other.

"Where are you going," I ask, incredulous, "we have to get popcorn."

"There is no way you are still hungry," he says, taking a step toward the theater, like he can lead me away from destiny.

"Oh, but you would be wrong," I say, delighted and dramatic, "you have underestimated my love for popcorn. Sometimes I come to the theater just for popcorn. I can eat an entire bucket alone. Popcorn is the point of the theater."

I stop talking and slap my palm over my face because I have just announced my ability to shovel food into my mouth on a first date. Perfect. I am about to apologize when I realize he has already walked over and bought the largest tub they have, along with two candy bars and a soda.

"I love it too," he says, grin wide, "I just thought you would think I was a maniac for eating more after dinner."

He lifts the tub and the scent of butter wafts up and wraps around us and my stomach actually growls. I tuck my arm through his and we follow the sticky carpet to the theater.

The room is almost full, the air humming with that pre-movie chatter and the sound of kernels crunching. We find two seats in the back corner, perfect for whispering without bothering anyone, and we scoot past a row of knees and settle in. The lights dim further and the previews blur by. Oliver passes me the candy and I tuck it into the seat cup holder and rest my head on his shoulder like it is the thing I always do, and he breathes in and then out and squeezes my hand.

When the opening credits bloom across the screen I gasp. It is one of my favorite eighties rom coms, a comfort movie I have watched a dozen times. I tilt my face up to his and he is already watching me.

"I love this one," I whisper, like I am sharing state secrets.

"I have only seen it once," he whispers back, grinning, "but I figured."

The projector hums as the light floats dust through the air. We eat popcorn like we have been waiting all day and have eaten nothing else. Halfway through, Oliver stands and refills the tub. We manage to empty it again. The soda chills my tongue, the chocolate melts a little in my fingers, and the whole time my head rests against his shoulder like it belongs there. When the iconic scene plays, the one everyone knows even if they have not seen the film, we both laugh quietly at the same time.

When the movie ends, the lights come up slowly and everyone groans as if to acknowledge they have to leave a warm room for a cold sidewalk. We stepped outside to the chilly, crisp air and the moon and stars shining bright. The campus is mostly quiet except for the distant sound of a skateboard on concrete and the whir of a bicycle passing. The streetlamps paint soft pools on the brick paths. We walk back toward the dorms and the world feels like it has shrunk to the space between our shoulders. I yawn so hard my eyes water. I am not built for late nights yet. Oliver looks completely fine, like he could go photograph a sunrise right now.

We reach the big tree, the one he called our spot, I lean my back against the trunk and slide down until I am a heap on the ground. I tuck my dress under me then let my head fall forward.

"I could sleep right here." I mumble. Oliver laughs.

"Someone does not do well with late nights," he says, amused and affectionate.

"It's been a long day," I say, my words a little mushy, "I drove two hours and then I sprinted through getting ready, and yes I like going to bed early, and yes we have class in the morning, and maybe it is easy for you because you sit in lectures but I have to dance and I need to look like a person while I do it, so no, I don't do well with late nights."

I cross my arms even though I am not mad. I realize I am making the shape of stubbornness but only because of how tired I am tired.

"Do not remind me that tomorrow is Monday," he groans,

then he slides down the trunk too and folds himself next to me on the ground.

I lean my head against his shoulder and he pats my hand, inhaling like he is choosing words.

"Are you doing okay," he asks, "not like right now, but in general, the fitting in, the adjusting, the being here. I know it is early, but when I started it was brutal, and I wanted to check in."

He dips his chin to catch my eyes. I meet his gaze and then look away.

"Yeah, I am good," I mumble, which is the answer I give everyone when I do not have the energy to tell the truth.

"Brianna," he says, gentle and firm at once, "I am not falling for that, I know we just met, but I feel like I understand you a little, and I know when you say fine you mean something else. I was a wreck when I got here. I failed half my classes my first semester, I spent every minute thinking I did not belong. Sometimes I still think it. But it does get better."

He squeezes my hand in steady pulses, like he is lending me a heartbeat.

"It is really hard," I say, and the words break open everything I have been holding.

One tear escapes and then another, I swipe at them fast and sniff. He puts his arms around me and pulls me in. He does not ask a single question after that. He just holds me, and I can feel the pattern of his breathing against my cheek, the rise and fall, the slow even rhythm that says, stay, rest. After a while I lean back against the tree again, wiping my face with the back of my hand, and I keep talking because I finally can.

"I thought it would be like the movies," I say, "and I know that sounds naive, but I did. I thought I would make new friends and it would be fun and shiny and loud in a good way. But I feel more alone than I did at home. I have met a couple of people, and I like them, but it feels like if I stop trying to be an extrovert they will forget I exist. I am anxious and I am an introvert and making friends feels like my worst nightmare. I do not like my roommate. I do not like the dining hall. I am trying to make my parents proud and I am trying to be happy and I do not know what to do. I miss my family and my home studio and my dogs." I took a shaky breath, "I mean, when I think about my dogs my chest caves in because they do not understand why I left. I am trying so hard and I, I just."

The words tangle and I cannot find the next one. He lifts my chin with his finger, gentle as a breath, and he kisses me. At first it is a surprise that tastes like salt and hope, then it softens, a question asked and answered in the same moment. He pulls back before I can lean in again, and I open my eyes and the world is a little less sharp.

"It will be okay," he says, and he sounds like he is promising himself too, "I know it feels like it never will, but it will."

He holds out his pinkie and I wrap mine around it and he squeezes like he is sealing a pact. Then he uses his other hand to wipe the tears that are still escaping and he pulls me in again, and this time I do not stop myself from crying. I let it happen. I make his shirt damp and he does not flinch. When the tears finally thin out, my eyes sting and feel puffy. My body feels like it weighs half of what it did before, which is its own kind of relief.

We sit like that in the quiet for a while, the campus soft around us, the tree steady above us, the night full of cricket music. Oliver reaches into his bag and pulls out his camera, scrolls for a second, then turns the screen toward me.

"Look," he says, "this girl is gorgeous, I hope she will be my new model forever because I cannot get over how easily photogenic she is. What do you think."

The photos are from the park under the lights, the dress caught mid turn, the fabric lifted like a petal, my face tilted up into the glow. It does not look like the girl who was crying two minutes ago. It looks like a character in a film who knows the scene is for her. I look content. I look like I will be okay. I blush and smile in spite of myself.

He tucks the camera away and stands, brushing grass off his jeans, then offers me his hand. When I take it, he pulls me up and we stand there for a beat looking at each other under the huge branches, and I can feel that it is late. Maybe midnight. Maybe later. Time got weird and quiet. He sets his hands at my lower back and kisses my forehead and the simple tenderness of it makes me want to cry again, but in a different way. He spins me once by the fingers like he did earlier, and my skirt lifts and settles, and then he laces our hands and walks me to the dorm door.

"Goodnight, Brianna," he says, "I hope you feel better soon. I am here for you, and it will get better."

He smiles and he watches me walk to the door, and when I turn to wave he is still there. Then he nods and heads back across the courtyard, the lamplight catching on the edge of his shoulder.

"Oh, Oliver," I think as I take the stairs, somehow knowing exactly how to make my night without knowing me all the way yet. Something about how we fit feels like I have been holding a puzzle piece and finally found the space it belongs in. I take a shower that is hotter than I need because I want the steam to erase the last worry lines from my face. Then I climb into my lofted bed and pull the sheets up tight around my waist and stare at the ceiling while the room cools around me.

Sleep does not come right away. I replay the evening like it is a film on the theater screen, me in the yellow dress under the fairy lights, the candle in the diner, the bucket of popcorn that tasted like childhood and comfort, the look in his eyes when I told the truth, the small kiss that felt like a promise. Even though I have a full week of classes waiting, the weight of readings and exercises and rehearsals lining up like dominoes, it feels like time paused and set me down gently and told me to breathe. I let myself wonder about big words I am not supposed to wonder about this early. I mean, it is too soon to say love, of course it is, but he gets me in a way I did not expect. He sees how hard I try. He sees the parts I would rather hide and he does not flinch. He fits next to me in a way that makes my edges feel softer.

I could stay awake all night thinking about the way his voice sounded when he said, it will get better, but sleep matters more than a second replay, so I close my eyes and let them grow heavy. I slow my breath and let the day wash off of me like the shower did. I let the bed hold me. I release the worry I have been holding in my shoulders since I pulled onto the highway. For once I let myself be a person who is carried by good things instead of bracing against bad ones. The last thing I see in my mind is the string of lights between the trees, warm and patient, and the last thing I feel is the weight of his pinkie around mine, a small promise that feels big.

Chapter 11

Weeks pass, then a month, and suddenly it is fall break. September is full of homework and classwork, long dance days and short weekend trips home. I do not go out much, I still do not talk to my roommate, and I only go on one more date with Oliver. The month somehow drags and flies at the same time. This break feels like a breath I have been waiting to take. The first red leaves show up along the sidewalks, the air thins in the mornings, and every cafe smells like cinnamon. It is also Oliver's birthday. We decide to meet on Saturday and take a small trip to celebrate.

Oliver mentions a mountain range he went to as a kid, not far from my hometown. I volunteer to drive. A day trip feels perfect, a slice of fall pinned to the calendar like a leaf in a book.

It is very chilly this morning, early October cold sneaks into my sleeves. I slide out of bed and start getting ready. I curl my hair and tie it with a bow that matches the small green jacket I shrug on. I yank my boots on over my jeans. They are Target fashion boots, not real hiking boots, and I can already hear Oliver teasing me about them, but they are the closest thing I have. I add a little makeup, tuck chapstick and a granola bar into my purse, and head out the door with the kind of jittery excitement that tastes like fresh air.

We agree to meet in a Target parking lot near my house. While I wait, I run inside, order two pumpkin spice cold brews, and watch the barista float cold foam over the top like a soft cloud. When I step back out with the coffees, Oliver is hovering by my car, peering through the windows like a raccoon inspecting a trash can.

I laugh out loud. He jumps and spins around, hand to his chest.

"Oh jeez, you scared me," he says, eyes wide, "I thought you were some creep running up behind me."

"Oh, I was the creep?" I say, grinning. "You were the one peeking into my windows."

"Well I didn't know where you were."

"I texted you that I ran inside for these," I say, holding up the cups. I pass him one and we both take a sip. "Mmm, that is yummy."

He laughs, looking up at me with a dot of pumpkin foam on his nose. I lose it and laugh harder. He catches his reflection in my window, wipes his nose, and fakes a serious face that doesn't fool me anymore.

"So, ready to hit the mountains, Miss Fashionista?" he says, eyes flicking to my boots.

I laugh because of course he says it. I already knew he would and was just waiting to see how long it would take. For the record, it took less than five minutes.

"It's the best I have, and yes, I am very excited," I say, nudging him with my elbow. "Now will you please enter the name again, so I know where to go."

He leans in, types the trail area into my maps, and the route pops up, a thread of blue that promises switchbacks and views. A little over an hour. Not bad.

We drive through the middle of nowhere for half an hour, farm fields and peeling barns, then the road coils up a steep, curvy hill. My hands settle higher on the wheel and Oliver hums along to the radio, drumming on his knees. When we finally pull into a gravel lot, the world opens. We park along the edge of a mountain ridge, the horizon a long breath of layered blue and russet and gold.

"Wow," I say, shoulders dropping as if the view presses the tense parts of me smooth.

Oliver takes my hand and we walk toward the welcome board. A covered map is posted beside a rack of paper copies, and a wooden post holds a box of folded trail guides. On a nearby oak, a blue circle is nailed to the bark, a small badge of direction.

"So, all the paths are marked with a shape and a color," I say, tilting my head, squinting at the legend.

"Yes," he says, confident and warm, "and if I remember right, it is easy to follow, you just look for the symbol as you go. The blue circle trail is the easiest, so we should start with that one."

"Easiest," I tease, bumping his shoulder, "you don't think I can do anything harder? That one says fifteen minutes. We drove an hour. The next one is longer and has a sight seeing spur. You said the tree markers are not hard, so I vote we do that instead."

He watches me reading the complicated map, his smile crooked like he is half amused and half impressed.

"Okay," he says after a beat, "if you believe that will be fine, we can try it. I have done the longest path, and it stopped being fun after the three hour mark, so second difficulty sounds perfect. About an hour, maybe an hour and a half if we go slow."

I lace my fingers into his fingers and tug him toward the trail head, red triangles painted on the trunks like tiny flags calling us forward.

The first stretch is easy, pine needles softening the dirt, the air cool enough to wake up my skin. We pass a family pushing a jogging stroller, a couple with matching beanies, two friends with a dog that looks part cloud. After half an hour the trail narrows along a ledge. The trees pull back and the land falls away to our left, a spill of color so wide it looks painted. Someone has arranged a bench from a flat rock right before the narrowest part, and we sit for water, legs swinging over nothing.

I pull a bottle from my small book bag while Oliver reaches into his camera sling, the movement so automatic now that I smile before he even speaks.

"You should know the drill by now," he says, spinning the lens cap off with one hand.

I roll my eyes and stand, walking a few careful steps toward the edge.

"I am still not fond of this whole model thing," I say, side stepping a root, "and you better not even dare push me off this cliff."

The drop looks steeper from here, the kind that makes your stomach flip. I turn back and he is staring at me with one eyebrow raised.

"You really think I would push you," he asks, hand at his heart, "come on now, I cannot push the thing I am about to take pictures of."

"It would be an interesting photo, wouldn't it?" I ask, grinning, "a girl flying."

"I mean sure, but it is not the best escape plan when I literally photograph the evidence."

We both laugh, and the sound slips away on the wind. He lifts the camera and I twist away from it and look out across the mountains because the color is too much to ignore. Yellows and oranges and reds burn through miles of trees, the kind of palette that makes you think there is a fireplace inside the hills. The crisp air brushes my hair, and I take a small step back, careful and happy. He clicks the shutter a few times, drops the camera, and comes to me. His hand finds mine and then my waist.

"I could never imagine pushing you," he says in a voice that has a smile in it, and he pulls me in for a kiss, soft and warm as sunlight on a porch.

We stand there for a moment and look out together, tiny humans on a big edge. Then we keep going, the path stony, our feet finding a rhythm.

Time loosens. We walk and talk, other times not talking at all. We pass more families and couples, a pair of riders on calm horses, a group of college kids with a trail head speaker playing a song about summer. We stop for water, a handful of trail mix, and a quick photo when the light gets caught in the gold leaves and turns them into stained glass. The red triangles continue, then seem to skip a couple of trees, then return. At some point the path splits and we choose left because it looks like it will lead to another view. After a while my calves start burn and my toes ache against the fronts of my boots. My Target fashion choice starts to feel like a joke the trail is telling back to me.

I check my phone and pause.

"It is already five," I say, a small alarm moving through my chest, "the sun sets in an hour hours, and we are in the depths of this path."

I turn in a slow circle, searching for a symbol, any symbol. Oliver understands immediately and scans the trunks too.

There is nothing. No red triangles, no blue circles, no yellow squares. Just trees, beautiful and indifferent.

I pull the folded map out of my bag and try to match the squiggles to the world. Oliver pulls out his phone and climbs onto a slight rise to hold it higher, which is sweet and useless.

"No service," he says, quiet and a little defeated.

"Oh no," I say, my breath coming faster, "oh no, oh no."

My heart hammers like it wants out of my ribs. I take a slow seat on a nearby rock because the ground is steadier than my legs.

Oliver kneels so his face is level with mine and sets his hand on my shoulder.

"We still have an hour," he says, even and careful, "there is no way we are that far from the car."

"Compared to the time we have been walking, I am not sure an hour is enough," I say, and it comes out smaller than I want it to.

He looks around again, measuring something invisible, then stands and extends his hand.

"We will head back the way we came," he says, voice finding confidence, "we follow the ridge, stay left at the fork, keep the sun on our right, and we will hit familiar ground."

I take his hand, and we start. For a while it feels right. We recognize a fallen hemlock, a slanted boulder that looks like a whale, a stretch of birch that peels in curls. Then the trail dips, the soil changes, and the markers do not reappear. The trees press closer, and the leaf litter looks untouched.

We step into a small clearing and freeze. An old house sits just beyond a stand of pines, weathered boards and a front porch that leans, the kind of place that could be abandoned or occupied depending on the day. The porch holds a rocking chair and a stack of buckets. The nearby garage is a low concrete box with the door open, a graveyard of rusty, half dismantled cars inside.

"This does not seem right," I say, lowering my voice without deciding to, "I do not remember this, and it is not on the trail guide."

Beyond the house, a narrow paved road appears like a lifeline, cracked and moss edged, but real. It leads away from the property and curves out of sight.

"It is better than walking back into unmarked woods," Oliver says, shrugging the camera bag higher on his shoulder.

We choose the road, because a road is a promise, and follow it for thirty minutes. The silence between us grows because we are saving our energy for our feet, for our eyes. We finish our water and our snacks, and my body starts to feel like it weighs more. The air cools another notch.

At an intersection, Oliver stops so quickly that dust swirls around his shoes.

"Wait," he says, peering up the steeper branch of the road, "this is the intersection we drove through. Our car is up there."

He points toward a climb that looks like it goes forever. The sun is slipping toward the ridge line, the edges of trees turning to ink.

"Up we go, I guess," I say, and I hear the long sigh in my own voice.

We start. Cars pass, downshifting for the hill, and the breeze of their speed touches our arms. Couples stride by with trekking poles and cheeks flushed from the good kind of exertion. I am carrying the tired kind. Oliver keeps pace with me, shoulder close, steps steady. The slope tests every muscle in my legs and the blisters blooming at my heels. We climb for thirty more minutes, and then the gravel lot appears like a miracle. Our car sits exactly where we left it, which feels like a small kindness the universe finally decided to send.

We collapse into the front seats at the same time. I turn the car on and blast the air conditioning, cold sweeping our faces in sharp relief. Oliver jogs to the restroom building and fills our bottles from the outdoor fountain, then jogs back and hands mine over before dropping into his seat again like a puppet whose strings were cut.

"Well, we made it," he says, voice rough and satisfied.

"Mmm," I manage, because my body is an empty battery and words cost energy.

We sit in the humming cold for ten full minutes, eyes closed, hands wrapped around plastic bottles like they are warm mugs even though they are not. Slowly, we stitch ourselves back together. I stretch my ankles, flex my toes, tuck my hair behind my ears, and shift the car into drive.

The road down the mountain feels kinder. Trees arch over us and the last light breaks through in slants, and we ride the curves like we have earned them.

"We will not be coming back here any time soon," I say, half groan, half laugh.

"Agreed," Oliver says, the word long and exaggerated.

By the time we reach the Target parking lot and pull beside his car, the stars are out. The parking lot lights hum and make small halos on the asphalt. We sit for a minute and look at each other like we are making sure the other one is truly okay. Then we smile because the worst part is already funny.

We say goodnight with an easy hug, and I want to go inside the store for something small and sweet, but it is too late. I decide to stay at my parents' house because an extra two hour drive back to campus, in the middle of the night, after today, sounds like a bad idea. The road home is a quiet ribbon, and when I pull into the driveway the house looks like a patient animal waiting.

I tiptoe down the hall to my room, kick off my boots, and sigh at the relief that rushes up from my feet to my scalp. I change into shorts and an oversize shirt and slide into bed. The sheets feel cool and familiar. I text Oliver to check that he made it to wherever he is staying.

No response.

I jerk awake to my phone ringing on full blast. The room is dark except for the small screen burning my eyes. I fumble, tap, and press the phone to my ear.

"Hey, I called you like three times," Oliver says, voice startled and loud in the quiet, "are you okay."

"I was asleep," I say, a low chuckle inside the words, "it is so late, why are you just now calling me."

"I had to drive all the way back to campus," he says, talking fast, "the people I was going to stay with bailed on me, and there was a massive storm, so it took forever. I finally made it, but I missed your texts, so I wanted you to know I got here safely."

A thunderclap booms through the speaker, big enough to vibrate the air between us.

"Are you outside in the storm," I ask, sitting up, picturing him.

"Well, yes," he says, almost sheepish, "I just got out of my car but I was worried."

"So you are standing in the pouring rain," I ask, already smiling.

"Well, yes," he says again, like this is perfectly rational.

"Go inside, Oliver," I say, laughing, "you are ridiculous."

"I just wanted to make sure you are okay."

"I am great, just exhausted, so please go inside, and I am going back to sleep. I will talk to you in the morning."

I can see him in my mind, freckled face tilted up, rain running off his hair, smiling like the storm is part of the plan.

"Okay," he says, softer, "well, goodnight, Brianna."

"Goodnight, Oliver," I say, and hang up.

I slide back into the warm spot my body made and let the mattress take my weight. Outside, the storm moves across someone else's sky. Inside, sleep finds me like a blanket being pulled up to my chin.

Chapter 12

It's Halloween!

Although it is not my all-time favorite holiday, I still love the excitement that spirals around the day. The warm tree leaves and the pumpkins on porches, the cool, breezy air, costumes drifting across sidewalks, the classic movies, and, of course, the candy.

Halloween is stereotypically a very big deal in college. That is when everyone goes to the giant party in the skimpiest costume they can find. There are bunnies, cats, cheerleaders, and for some reason there is always a pool outside. People get ridiculously drunk, then dive into the frigid water like it is a rite of passage.

It seems great, except that is not me. At all.

It is a Tuesday, which means a full day of classes and homework before I fall back asleep. Oliver even has two exams today. Partying is not even a thought in our minds.

The dance company, however, allows dancers to dress up for class. In true me fashion, I am not going to dress up, at least that is the plan. It does not feel practical, and it feels embarrassing. What if no one else dresses up? Except, after class on Friday, everyone started discussing their elaborate plans. I caved, sprinted to Target, and built a last-minute costume. A deer.

I have always liked deer. Elegant and hidden. Timid and shy, yet startling when you finally see one. Picking the costume is not that deep, it is simply what the store had, but I decided the thought still counts.

I slide on a brown, high-neck leotard from a Christmas performance in high school. I add the deer accessories and head out the door. The costume includes a tiny velvet tail, a velvet headband with ears, and two small gloves. It is far from elaborate, but it makes me smile.

When I step into the bustling studio, my jaw drops. Yes, there are classic cats and bunnies, and there are ballerinas, which is ironic since that is our daily life, but there are also the wild ones. A full-body Spider-Man suit covers a dancer from head to toe. Next to her stands a girl in a full traffic light costume, boxy and bright, somehow already flashing. I am not sure how that is danceable, but it is hilarious. Every new entrance sets off a fresh wave of laughter across the room that usually looks so composed.

Class is even funnier. Watching Spider-Man complete triple pirouettes and grand jetés feels like a fever dream. The traffic light blinks after every small jump, green to yellow to red, like it is giving a grade.

After the ballet technique class, we file into the large open studio next door for the costume competition. I have no idea this is a thing, but I follow along with everyone else. Inside, the other three years of dancers stand in separate groups, cheering for us like we are a parade.

Each class gathers in its corner until the head ballet teacher calls us. Then we strut in a circle around the room, showing off our marvelous costumes while the rest of the dancers cheer and laugh. When it is our turn, another girl dressed as a deer slips her arm through mine. We prance, heads lifted, a little herd of two. We finish our lap, curtsy to the room, and hurry back to our corner.

The teacher picks one costume from each group, then the whole room votes. Spider-Man wins, of course. He bows in a way that makes the mask grin.

We drift back to our normal classes, only now there is a bowl of candy on the piano and the accompanist sneaks in a few bars of spooky themes. The break from the usual intensity feels like a breath my muscles needed.

"Do not forget there is a dance education meeting tonight," my teacher calls as we gather our bags. "All dance ed majors are required to attend."

"On Halloween," one of the girls groans.

"Yes," the teacher says, kind and firm, "as dancers you need to know your priorities. Attendance is required and will be taken. If you do not go enough times, you will not be able to graduate with an education certification."

I look at a few other dancers, their whispers tight with annoyance. We all know we will be back here later.

As a dance education major, I know I have to go. I return to my dorm, take a quick shower, and lie down for a short nap before I have to cross campus again.

By the time I leave my room, it is dark and windy. I am not sure why the meeting is so late, and so far, but that is not up to me. Campus is strangely silent. The streets have no cars, the sidewalks have no people. Everyone is at parties, or hiding from parties. I am alone on a dark, empty street, my breath making a small cloud in front of me.

I try to call Oliver for the comfort of a voice in my ear, but he is either asleep or still taking an exam. I try a dancer who said she would go to the meeting, but she only texts back, "partying." I guess she gave up.

The walk feels long and colder by the minute. Leaves scrape along the pavement and skitter past my shoes. Finally I reach the big bridge before the dance building. The studios glow like a lighthouse across the field. I pause at the top of the bridge and take a deep breath. It really is beautiful from here. The practice field is empty, lit by dim streetlights that make everything look like a quiet stage. After another breath, I take the tight, spiral staircase down toward the entrance.

I open the door and, for the first time in twenty minutes, I hear voices. The girls who made it are wearing sweatpants and hoodies, and someone has opened three bags of chips and a family-size chocolate bar.

Only seven people show up.

"Hello, dance ed majors," a girl calls, waving with a friendly bounce. "I am Susie, the president of NDEO."

There are four of us that are freshman. We glance at the three upperclassmen standing behind her with clipboards and matching enthusiasm.

"I know this looks bad," Susie says, smiling and wincing at the same time, "I told everyone they needed to come, but you know how it is. Anyway, welcome to the National Dance Education Organization. We advocate for dance in public schools. It is a dying art form as a class, and we want all students to have access, so that is what we fight for."

She is genuinely excited. She passes around forms, talks through requirements, then moves into introductions.

"I am a current student teacher for dance in an elementary school," she says, clapping once, "the kids are adorable. Some absolutely hate dance, but the ones who are curious make it worth it. Some days are rough, but it is great to share our passion."

She speaks for another thirty minutes about lesson plans and rubrics and grant proposals. I listen, but what I want to hear about is the university program itself, and the regular classes, and how people carve their path if public school is not the dream. I went into dance education because I have always pictured my own studio. I want to share my love with kids who choose to be there, kids with that same bright spark. I did not realize how public school focused this track would be. The thought sends my mind into a spiral, fast and loud.

When the meeting ends, I step back into the windy night and call my mom. I need to let the worry out, or it will make a nest.

She picks up excited but nervous, she knew whatever I was going to say probably wasn't about how magically happy I now am here.

"This is not what I thought it would be," I say, trying to keep my voice even.

"Give it time," she says, gentle as a blanket, "that is their focus, but it does not mean you cannot use what you learn for what you want."

"I have to student teach my senior year in a public school," I say, the words catching, "that is not what I want. Maybe I should just be a dance major, or pick something different. This is not what I expected."

"You have to give it time, my love," she says, steady, "you will figure it out. I believe in you. Do not rush. Stay in the major this year, and we will revisit it later. You might end up loving it."

I take a long breath and say goodnight. As much as I wanted

to keep talking, I also didn't want to start crying. I do not know what I am going to do, but I know this: teaching a room of teenagers who do not want to stand up is not my dream. Trying to pour a spark into students who are not ready for it might burn me out faster than anything. I do not want to extinguish the flame I have been tending since I was five. Switching majors now feels like too much, but the thought will not leave. I tuck it into the back of my mind for later.

On the way back, I stop at the cafeteria for a quick dinner. I put in my headphones and walk home beneath trees that sway and whisper. Campus is still eerily empty. Earlier it scared me. Now it feels like the break I needed.

Before going in, I sit on the low, brick half wall outside my dorm and tilt my face up. The stars are out. On a busy campus night, that almost never happens, but tonight they look clear and close. I stare and breathe. I think about the nights at home when I sat on the step and did the same thing, the quiet settling over our street like a quilt. The dark sky has always been a comfort, a wide roof I can trust.

I take one more deep breath, let it out slowly, and head inside for warmth and rest.

Chapter 13

It is the beginning of November. Thanksgiving sits right around the corner, and the end of the semester waits right after that. The trees have finally committed to their colors, a quilt of warm oranges and reds stitched across campus, and a cool breeze keeps brushing the paths clean of leaves that cannot hold on any longer.

Today is the fall dance concert. I am not in it, but I am excited to see it. It will be my first time attending a college performance as an actual college dance student. Weeks ago, the minute tickets went on sale, I bought two. I already planned my outfit and the whole timeline for tonight.

Two weeks back, I texted Oliver and asked him to go with me. He said yes right away, said he would not miss it for the world.

"So it is a date," I told him, grinning to my phone.

We have been on a couple of dates since we met, but nothing that feels as special to me as this night. It is everything I love in one place.

I start the day by finishing homework for my education class, which, surprisingly, I love. The behind the scenes of public schools fascinates me, the scaffolding that holds the day together, the way teachers choreograph movement through a building without anyone noticing.

After an early lunch in the cafeteria, I come back to my room to start getting ready. A maroon dress waits on its hanger, with the soft wedge boots I set under it last week. I plan to curl my hair, paint my nails, and slow down long enough to make my makeup feel like it belongs to an evening.

When I finish eating, I call Oliver.

"Hey," I say, "I hadn't heard from you today and wanted to check in. How are you?"

There is a pause, dead air that stretches.

"Oh, sorry," he says finally. "My mom called late last night saying I needed to come home, so I was busy packing and driving."

I sit up straighter.

"What?"

"Yeah," he says, voice flat, "something about her not feeling well and me not passing my classes. She is forcing me to come home this weekend and do work with my granddad on his car as punishment or something. I'm too old for this, but you know how it is. I do what Mom says."

"What about the concert tonight?"

"The what?"

I shut my eyes. I can tell he is not really here with me, even through the phone. I felt a shaky breath escape my mouth as my hands began getting clammy.

"The dance performance," I say. "I bought tickets weeks ago. I was going to make a big night out of it."

"Oh, I totally forgot. I'm sorry. I am already almost home and there is no chance my mom lets me go. I can pay you back for my ticket. I'll make it up to you later, I guess."

"It's not about the money, Oliver. I've been planning this for weeks. You not only forgot but didn't even tell me until just now."

"Look, Brianna, it is not my fault." He began to raise his voice, irritated. I felt myself and my feelings shrinking smaller and smaller. "My mom called and I had to go, it is what it is. I can make it up to you later, but it is not worth you freaking out about. Just chill out. I have enough going on with my mom and I do not need you mad at me too."

The words land heavy and cold.

"So you do not even care that you just crushed my plans for tonight."

"That is dramatic, Brianna. There will be more shows. Just chill out. Let me deal with my mom and I can deal with you later."

I paused before barely whispering, "Deal with me?"

"Yes, I mean... you know what I mean," he stammers.

"Sure," I say, my voice steadying the way a blade steadies. "Goodbye, Oliver. I hope you figure it out."

I hang up.

I am dramatic? He has to deal with me? The phrases bounce around the room until they sting.

I let myself cry for a few minutes, the kind of quick, hot tears that come more from shock than anything else. Then I call my mom and tell her everything. By the time I finish, she has already grabbed her keys.

Within minutes she is on the road. "Girls' night," she says, voice bright through the speaker. She is taking me to the show.

I get ready exactly the way I planned, the same dress, the same soft curls, the same careful mascara, only now there is a thin line of anger and disappointment under the surface. By four o'clock she texts that she is outside. I still have not gotten a single message from Oliver. I breathe it out, then run downstairs and fold into my mom's hug like I have not seen her in months.

From this point forward it was about me and my mom tonight, not him.

After a short debate, we choose our favorite pizza place in town. It is not fancy, but it is ours, and it is always delicious. We order an appetizer we do not need and two small pizzas. We share everything like we are celebrating something. We walk down the block for ice cream, and the wind has just enough bite to make the first cold spoonful taste sharper.

The performing arts center stands at the edge of campus like a lantern, a glass building cut into squares that catch the late light. Inside, you can see four levels of mezzanines with tables and chairs like a stacked cafe. We ride the escalator and step into the main hall, and both of us take a breath without meaning to, because the room itself asks you to.

We find our seats on the top row of the first floor, high enough to feel tucked away, close enough that the stage still fills our eyes. When we sit, my mom threads her fingers through mine and squeezes.

"I am proud of you," she whispers. "I know this was a rough day, and I know I am not who you pictured sitting here, but I am here, and I am proud. You have come so far already. You will take care of yourself with whatever comes next."

I look over at her and smile, a single tear slipping free. She brushes it away with her thumb, then pulls me into a quick hug. The house lights dim. The stage glows.

The first dance begins with one dancer sprinting silently across the stage, pointe shoes barely whispering. She stops like a breath held. Then ten more run in and peel out to places, the lines clean as cut paper. Their dresses float around their ankles, pale and weightless, a little old-world, a little dream.

The music is a variation on Vivaldi, Four Seasons threaded with a low, long orchestra line that carries it forward. It swells and thins and swells again, quick and slow layered together in a way that feels like weather rolling in. My eyes sting. I close them for a heartbeat to listen, then open them to watch the dancers match the music's tide. Every sweep of an arm lands in the exact pocket of sound that belongs to it.

A modern piece follows, bright and grounded, sweeps of floorwork and quick exchanges. It is not my favorite language, but there is something satisfying about how the bodies carve the space and then leave it clean.

After that comes a Broadway-style number that folds character into classical lines. The costumes hint at a Midwestern film set, small-town storefronts and smiles that may or may not be real. The ensemble sells the story so well I catch myself leaning forward, ready to see how a scene ends even though there are no words at all.

The closer is ballet again, but set to a pop track that makes the whole audience sit up. Pointe and pop should fight, but they do not. The choreography proves that ballet is not stuck in a museum. It is alive. It is allowed to be current and still be itself.

When the curtain falls, the room exhales, and the applause gathers like rain. We make our way out to the lobby where the dancers line up to meet the people who came to support them. The moment someone spots a familiar face, they break out of the line for a hug that lifts both feet off the ground. I see a few freshmen from class and tell them how beautiful they were, and their smiles make me feel like I am in the right place even if it still feels new.

It is different from my home studio, more professional, more advanced, but close enough to touch. I am at that level, I tell myself. I can be in these shows. I decide, standing there with my program folded in my hand, that next semester I am going to audition for everything I can and get myself into at least one piece. Dancing for a mirror is fine, but dancing for an audience is the reason I am here. The costumes, the heat of the lights, the quiet before music cracks open the room, the perfect second when you land a jump and feel the whole theater land with you. That is the reason I dance.

On the walk back to the car, I cannot stop talking. I list every small moment I loved, and by the end of the sidewalk I am basically floating.

"See," my mom says, laughing, "I knew you just needed some time. This school is amazing, and you made it in. You are one of them. You just have to go all in."

"I know," I say. "It is just not like me. It takes a lot."

"You can do it."

She drives me back to my dorm and parks in the quick drop-off lane. I hug her tightly and promise to text when I am upstairs. In my room, I shower away the hairspray and the day, put on pajamas, and climb into bed with my hair damp on the pillow. The clock on my desk clicks from 9:59 to 10:00. I realize I still have not heard from Oliver, not a single word.

I stare at my phone for a long minute, debating. Then I send the smallest message I can.

"You okay."

I wait

and wait

and wait

Midnight slides in. Nothing. I set the phone face down on the nightstand and decide I am not going to be a lost puppy on a doormat. I turn out the lamp, pull the covers up to my chin, and let the memory of the music play back to me until I fall asleep.

Chapter 14

It is over.

We are officially done.

No more dates, no more texts, no more growing into something soft and careful.

Just silence.

My phone lit up this morning with a single gray bubble.

"I need to focus this semester," it read. "I am sorry. I cannot do this right now."

That was it. No good morning, no call, no meeting under the tree. A period at the end of a sentence I did not write.

I stared at the screen until my eyes burned. I read it again, and then again, as if the words might rearrange themselves into something kinder.

He needs to focus.

I am too much for him.

How dare I ask for a hand to hold when midterms are here.

He is busy.

He is a student.

He has a life.

He does not have time for me.

We are done.

I set the phone face down on my desk and listen to the room.

The air conditioner hums. A door closes down the hall. I hear my own breath, shallow at first, then slower. I count like I do at the barre. In for four, out for six. I tell my body to unclench, but my body does not listen right away. That feels fair.

I pick the phone up again, open our thread, and scroll. The photo of the tree with the lights in the small park. The picture he took of me spinning. The coffee in his hand, the pumpkin we swore would be our secret. A pinky promise, small and serious, curled between our fingers. I save the photos to a folder I name and then rename three times. I will not delete them, not yet. I also will not let them live where they can jump out at me without warning.

I tap the three dots beside his name and stare. Block, delete, mute. I do not press any of them. I change the contact to his full name and remove the little heart I put there the night we left the theater with butter on our fingers. A small ritual, a quiet undoing.

The light outside my window is pale, the kind of cold morning that makes the campus look like a photograph. Even just the thought of photographs made my breath catch and my hands shake. Leaves collect along the sidewalk like a border. If I walked to the dance building right now, I could press my palms to the cool studio floor and feel it hold me. I could stand at the barre and remember who I was before I added someone else's shape to my days.

I pour water into my bottle, the one with a chipped corner from the first week. I wash my face and notice how swollen my eyes look, and I decide not to hide it. I am allowed to look like what I feel, at least for a day.

I think about what he wrote, the way the sentence sits there like a closed door.

"I need to focus."

I whisper back to the empty room, "Me too."

I need to focus on the classes that make my brain spark, on the ache in my calves that tells me I worked, on the friends who wave me over to a crowded table, on the music that fills the studio until I remember what breath is for. I need to focus on calling my mom back and telling her I am okay, and also not okay, a ball on an emotional roller coaster that never stops. I need to focus on the girl who moved here with a list of things she wanted and who is allowed to still want them.

I pull on my warmest sweater and sit on the edge of the bed. I let the quiet stretch. I watch a single leaf spin down past the window, slow and sure, like it knew how to fall long before it let go.

I pick up my journal and add a small but purposeful note. "Audition next term, at least one piece." It is not just a thought or a hope. It is a promise I have made to myself before, written again in a new hand. Writing it makes it feel so real and permanent. It was written in pen and cannot be undone.

My phone is still on the desk, face up now, silent. I do not wait for it to light. I do not beg it to. I tuck it into my bag, between my novel and my notebook, and I stand.

It is over.

We are officially done.

No more dates, no more texts, no more growing in the same direction.

Just silence.

I hear my own footsteps in the hallway, steady and even. I hear the door close behind me. I hear the campus, ready and indifferent and mine.

We are done.

I am not.

Chapter 15

Sunday morning arrives quietly, and my phone is still empty of any messages from Oliver. Worry started as a small knot and continues to tighten until I finally decide to call him.

He hangs up after the first ring. A text flashes onto my screen.

"I'm busy. Don't call me. Just leave me alone."

My fingers move before my thoughts catch up.

"Oh, okay. I'm sorry. I didn't mean to upset you. I just wanted to check that you were doing okay. I miss you and wanted to chat with you."

His reply lands almost instantly.

"I'm fine. I don't have time to talk. Please just give me the space I need."

I swallow and try again.

"Okay, I'm sorry. Is your mom okay?"

"Fine, just stop texting me."

I close my eyes. My thumbs keep going.

"Okay, well I miss you. When will you be getting back?"

This time he takes longer. When the message arrives, it feels like a door slamming.

"Brianna it's enough. Stop texting me or I will block you. I don't have time for this. I have screwed up enough already this semester and 'dating' you was just another one of my mistakes.

You are selfish and immature and won't just leave me alone. I can't hold your hand all the time and walk you through life. I don't have time for you right now so please just back off."

I type two words, because I cannot think of any others.

"Oh, ok."

No response.

I sit very still. Apparently I am immature and needy and an all around bad person. He has never said any of this to me before. I take a screenshot with shaking hands and send it to my mom.

"I'm so sorry, Bri," she replies. "He's wrong. Be grateful he showed his true colors now instead of leading you on."

"I guess," I text back, and the two words feel thin.

I lie back on my bed and sob. It is not graceful. It is not quiet. The tears come fast, like I have been holding them in a dam that finally cracked. I do not know what I did to deserve words like that from someone I thought I was falling in love with. I can feel myself sliding toward a spiral, so I try to put a railing up in my mind. It is the holidays soon. Exams are coming. I should not be focused on a boy right now.

I whisper to the ceiling, "I will be okay."

I say it again.

"I will be okay."

Every time I repeat it, my belief wanders a little further from the sentence. We were not together long, but I let myself imagine a future anyway. I pictured our lives braided together into something bright and ordinary. I planned a life with him while, apparently, he was planning a way out.

What made him think any of that was true, let alone okay to say? He seemed kind. He seemed calm. What changed? I try to find a reason to excuse him, but my chest tightens. I am hurt. I trusted him. I believed he was good for me. I believed he liked me and cared for me.

And here I am.

Alone in my room.

Again.

The rest of the morning drags. My phone stays silent while my head fills with noise. I decide to give myself small tasks, anything to keep my hands busy and my brain from looping. I pull on a cute outfit, something that makes me feel like I still recognize myself in the mirror. I walk the mile to my car in a steady rhythm and drive to the shopping center.

Target is quiet. I wander the aisles with a cart I do not need and let the calm of fluorescent lights and neatly stacked rows settle over me. That is when I remember the boots. The black pair with the sweater knit around the ankles, the ones that are always out of stock. The ones Oliver once said did not fit my style. I turn into the shoe aisle and there they are, waiting on the top shelf like they climbed there to be found by me. They do not have my exact size, but they have a half size up. I reach for them without hesitating and carry them to the register.

Breakup boots.

They make me feel confident, independent, in control of at least one small thing. In the car, I peel off my old Converse and slide on the new boots. They fit like I knew they would.

I go to a couple more stores with my head held a little higher, then decide to take myself to lunch. I have never eaten alone in a restaurant before. It makes me feel exposed and a little brave. I pick the place I want. I listen to my music softly. I sit by the window and let the sun warm my hands. I do not have to perform for anyone. Lunch is peaceful. It is calming. I am anxious and I am content at the same time, which feels possible in this small pocket of day.

After lunch, I search for a bookstore. The map takes me to a large brick building attached to an almost empty, aging mall. Inside, the bookstore looks like any other. The low music, the coffee smell, the soft thud of a stack of paperbacks set down on a counter. I walk slowly, trailing my fingers along the edges of spines. Near the back, the wall opens into a wide window that used to be a doorway. Beyond the glass, the abandoned mall stretches out, dim and strange. Old store signs hang crooked over empty spaces. A child's play area sits still and dusty. A plant in a concrete pot has given up. The hair on my arms rises.

For a second I think, Oliver would love this. He would take a dozen photos through the glass, all angles and echoes.

Then I remember.

Oh.

Right.

Not Oliver. Maybe someday I bring my brother, Cole. Maybe my dad. Not Oliver.

My thoughts start to slide again. I try to catch them. I pick up a book. I set it down. I flip through records. I study magazine covers and people's faces. Nothing helps. The quiet of this place makes my mind louder. I choose to leave before I start crying between New Releases and Staff Picks.

As soon as I shut the car door, I let go. I tip forward and rest my forehead on the steering wheel and sob in the parking lot of an abandoned mall. I check through the blur of tears to see if anyone is around. No one is. I let the ugly cry finish its run. He knows my soft spots. He knows where I feel small. He used those places like levers. The realization hurts in a clean way. I breathe. I wipe my face with a napkin from the glove compartment, the kind that always lives there for takeout emergencies.

I start the car. I queue up the best breakup music I can find, which is Taylor Swift, always, and I sing all the way back, loud and off key and exactly right.

By the time I pull into the lot near my dorm, I have gone through the entire playlist. The sun hangs low and turns the brick buildings the color of warm honey. Tomorrow is Monday. Classes will resume like nothing happened. Nobody will know what my Sunday felt like unless I tell them. I do not have to carry this everywhere. I can set it down to go to class and pick it back up later when I have time and space to feel it.

Today I wallow. Tomorrow I show up.

The rest of the day continues slow. I make easy food and eat it in bed. I watch movies that tell me the ending before they start. I answer my mom's check ins with small hearts and I am okay, mostly. When the sky turns dark and the room cools, I crawl under my comforter and let the weight of it press me into the mattress. I set my alarm. I put my phone face down. I close my eyes and tell myself one more time, out loud, that I will be okay.

I do not fully believe it yet.

I say it anyway.

Chapter 16

Friday finally arrives, and I decide I am driving home. I need a break from campus, from the crowded hallways and the silent room and the way my chest tightens when I think too far ahead. Home is the most comforting place I know. Farm animals, dogs, open land, and the people who love me without needing a reason.

As soon as my only class ends, I grab my bags and head for my car, as far as it may be. Thirty minutes later, the windows are down, Taylor Swift is blasting, and the hills are rolling past like a movie I have seen a hundred times and still love.

I pull into the driveway just after lunch. My parents meet me at the door and fold me into a hug that smells like laundry soap and home.

"I'm glad you're here," my mom says into my hair.

"Me too," I say, and I mean it.

I spend the first hour in what my family calls "animal therapy." I sit in the grass with the dogs and watch the goats blink slowly and unimpressed. Chickens peck in small, decisive steps. The breeze lifts the hair at the back of my neck. With every breath, a little more tension loosens from my shoulders. The thought of going back to campus still makes my stomach knot, so I practice staying right here, in this moment, where the only thing that matters is the sun on my skin and the sound of the wind moving through the trees.

A shadow falls across me. Someone clears their throat.

"Hey, Bri," my dad says softly. "I'm leaving in a few minutes for a meeting at your old dance studio."

I push up onto my elbows, then sit all the way up. "You're going to the studio? Oh, right. Youth arts committee." I smile. My dad is a people magnet. He is on every committee within a twenty-mile radius and somehow knows everyone's birthday. At the studio, he used to be "celebrity Bri's Dad," and by extension, I became "celebrity Bri's Dad's daughter." They don't even realize that I'm Bri. Its a joke my class made that stuck, but they no longer even understand it. Sometimes I still wonder if they remember me for me.

Then I remember who is teaching ballet tonight: Miss Pink, my favorite ballet teacher.

"I'm coming with you," I say, already halfway to my feet.

Inside, I change fast. Tights, leotard, warmups. Hair into a bun, spray, pins, done. I grab my shoes and my bag, then slide into the truck beside my dad.

I have not taken a ballet class at my home studio since the summer, and the ache of missing it has been living under my ribs. My teachers told me to come back anytime. I do not know why it took me this long. Dance is my favorite kind of therapy. It lets me feel everything and forget everything all at once.

As we pull into the lot, nerves prickle, then a warm rush of excitement takes over. Nothing has changed. The same picnic tables. The same cluster of cars. The soft leak of classical music through the door. Dancers moving in pairs toward the entrance, hair in buns, sneakers scuffing on concrete.

I breathe in and out, then grab my bag and go in.

Familiar faces line the lobby, and they light up when they see me. Hugs, quick questions about college, laughter that smells like rosin and hairspray. In the hallway, I drop my bag in a corner, slide into my flats, and peek into Studio A.

Miss Pink is finishing a younger class. She sees me and lets out a joyful little shriek, then rushes over and pulls me into a tight hug.

"I'm so glad you're here and taking class," she says, breathless and beaming. "We'll chat right after this, okay?"

"Okay," I say, and the relief that floods my chest feels like warmth.

I turn, still smiling, and run straight into a glare.

Lori.

We grew up together in this place. First grade pliés, sleepovers, homemade dances in empty studios, whispered dreams of stages and spotlights. I left for college. She took a gap year to keep training for company auditions. The last time we talked, we were both assistant teachers and seniors taking the advanced classes, still calling each other best friends, still excited for each other's next step.

Now she looks at me like she would prefer I vanish.

"Lori," I say, stepping forward. "Hey, it's great to see you. I've missed you so much."

"What are you doing here?" she says, flat and sharp.

"I'm in town this weekend, and I wanted to take a class. I missed the studio."

"You shouldn't be here." She glances around, as if she is searching for an ally.

"This is my second home," I say, gentler than I feel. "We grew up here together. It's been a rough week, and I just wanted to take a classic ballet class."

"This is not your home," she snaps. "You do not belong here. You left. I don't understand why you think it is okay. You need to leave."

"Lori," I say, stumbling a little. "It's a public studio, and the owner just told me I'm welcome anytime."

"Well, you're not." Her face flushes a bright, blotchy red. I can see her fighting tears. "I'm leaving," she blurts, grabs her bag, and bolts out the door.

The studio owner peeks her head out of the office, catching only the end of it. I meet her eyes, shrug with my own tears threatening, then turn and hurry outside.

My dad is already on the sidewalk, talking to Lori near her car, his hands gentle but firm in the air between them. I keep my head down, pass them both, and make it to the truck. I close the door, lean forward, and let myself cry, palms pressed over my face.

A few minutes later, a soft knock on the window. I roll it down.

"I still have to go to the meeting," my dad says, voice tight with controlled anger, "but you can take my car. Drive safe. I talked to Lori. I'll talk to the owner after class. Her reaction was not okay. She says it's because you left her. I think she's jealous, but it was ridiculous."

"Thank you," I say, shaky, and switch seats when he opens the door. The keys are warm in my hand.

At home, I tell my mom everything. She pulls me in and holds me until my breathing slows. Then she pops popcorn, cues a movie, and tucks a blanket around my legs like I am seven again.

Too many people are upset with me at the same time. It makes me feel like a burden, like I am walking through rooms, bumping into things I cannot see. I scroll through my last texts with Lori. All summer plans and shared excitement. Ballet tips, audition notes, nothing sharp that I can find. I try to thread together where the path bent without me noticing.

My phone buzzes.

A text from the studio owner:

"I am so sorry about what happened tonight. People say Lori has something going on at home, but that is no excuse. This will always be your home. It is my studio, and I say who is welcome. You, my dear, are always welcome. I will make sure she hears from me and knows her behavior was unacceptable. We love you here. Let me know if you need anything."

I read it twice, and the knot in my chest loosens. Not everyone feels like Lori. I am not a burden here. I am myself.

I send a thank you, simple and sincere, and put my phone face down. I sink deeper into the couch between my mom and the warm bowl of popcorn. Two more days until I have to go back to campus. I plan to use every minute to rest, to breathe, to put myself together again.

I do not know why my life feels like it is falling apart into small, sharp pieces. I only know that tonight I am home, and that has to count for something.

Chapter 17

November moves fast, and suddenly I am driving home for Thanksgiving. All but one of my classes are canceled, so I leave before the worst of traffic. Parents clog the curb outside my dorm, minivans tilted on the steep hill, students hauling bins and duffels, the whole place buzzing like a hive. I carry my bag down the steps two at a time and slide into my car before someone else decides the curb is theirs. The farther I go, the busier the roads get, but I make it into my driveway before five o'clock frees everyone else. No white knuckle back roads in the dark, no brake lights stretching for miles, just the familiar crunch of gravel and the feeling that my shoulders finally drop.

Inside, the house smells like veggies softening in butter and something sweet in the oven. My mom meets me at the door with open arms, and my dad stands up from the couch with that smile that is part proud, part amused. The dogs bark like I have been gone for years. I kneel to let them put their entire bodies into my lap. My mom laughs and says, "Brianna is home," like an announcement on a loudspeaker. I say, "Hi, I missed this," and my voice does that wobble that gives me away. We stand in the kitchen and talk in that quick way families do when they are happy to be in the same room again. My dad asks about classes between stirring a pot and checking a timer. My mom asks if I need anything washed before tomorrow. I say no, I did it already, and they both look at me like I just told them I bought a house.

Thanksgiving at my grandma's is as predictable as the pie. My mom's side brings their assigned dishes, we push dining chairs up to folding tables, and we eat until the room feels smaller. I balance a pan of green beans on a folded towel while my mom wraps bread rolls in foil. My dad carries a pecan pie like it is a trophy. The drive next door is filled with anticipation; the house is already loud when we pull up. The porch light glows, and the storm door creaks. The air inside is warm and full of voices.

"Look who it is," my aunt calls from the kitchen island, and she wipes her hands and pulls me in for a hug that smells like cinnamon and hairspray. My grandma is at the stove with a wooden spoon, completely in charge, wearing the same apron she has worn since I was five. She pats my cheek and says, "College girl," and I feel both ten feet tall and very small.

The cousins pile in behind me. There are nine of us. I am the second oldest to youngest, and the littlest ones still treat the hallway like a racetrack. I miss being one of them. When we were small, we played family in the shed, the girls pretending to cook on dusty boards while the boys invented villains. I can see us in my mind, bare knees, dirty hands, summer hair. Now the oldest two are in college, the next three are in high school, and the littles are racing through the years. The games live mostly in stories.

I put the green beans on the warming rack and try not to get in anyone's way. My grandma taps the counter and says, "Tell me about your teachers," and I do. I talk about the pianist in ballet who can make a plié feel like an apology and a promise. I talk about modern and how I am learning to let the floor hold me. My uncle asks about the football team, and I say I have never made it to a game, which makes him shake his head like I am missing a crucial part of college. Someone asks about dates. I shrug and say, "Nothing to report," and my aunt lifts her eyebrows like she knows there is a story I am not telling. I am not ready to unwrap it here, not with the turkey still resting and the gravy almost thick.

We sit down in that beautiful chaos of mismatched chairs and cloth napkins and paper plates, and the prayer is quick because people are hungry. The first bites are always the best. I pass dishes and laugh and try to answer the same questions in slightly different ways. How are classes? How is the dorm? Anyone special? I talk about my teachers again. I talk about the library bell that sounds like a warm wave. I talk about a funny moment in modern when half of us rolled the wrong way and turned into a pile of limbs. I run out of stories faster than I want to. Their faces soften into polite smiles, and they pivot to their own news, and I do not blame them. I am the college kid now, which seems to mean I am supposed to carry stories like confetti in my pockets. I have a few paper scraps, not a party.

Halfway through pie, the sky cracks open. Rain hammers the roof so hard that the porch is out of the question. Twenty people stay in the living room breathing the same air. The littlest cousins press their faces to the glass to watch the gutters overflow. My grandma brings out another pot of coffee. The grownups settle into clusters, and the conversation loops back to me because there is time to fill. I am honest in a careful way. I tell them I am finding my feet. I tell them I miss home. I tell them I like my classes more than I expected to. For once, nobody suggests I should be having the time of my life every second. The rain is good for that. It makes the house honest.

After we help wash the last dish and tuck the leftovers into plastic containers, the living room shrinks back to its normal size. We hug our way out the door one by one. My grandma pushes foil-wrapped rolls into my hands as if I might forget how bread works in a dorm. On the drive home, my mom says, "You did great."

I say, "At what?"

She replies, "At being you," which feels like a compliment I do not quite know how to hold.

Two months ago, I bought last-minute tickets to a Zarm show, plus a hotel room within walking distance. It was a surprise for Oliver, our first small trip, and I was so sure it would be perfect. I sent him a screenshot, and he wrote back a line of exclamation points and a promise to buy dinner. I saved the confirmation email in a folder called good things. Now I am in my room staring at the digital tickets on my phone and trying not to cry. My mom offers to go with me, because she loves him too, and I say yes. It is not the same, but it does not have to be sad. It can be different and good. It can be ours.

Friday morning, we pack the car and head for Charleston. We roll the windows down and sing along to blasting songs, then we talk the way you only talk when the road is steady and there is nothing else to do. We gossip, we laugh, we share the parts of the month we did not type in texts. I tell her the truth about how the first weeks felt like walking on marbles. She tells me the truth about how quiet the house is after nine at night. We cry a little, and it does not feel like a problem. It feels like rinsing something out.

We stop for lunch at a place with metal chairs and lemonade in glass jars. We wander through two record stores that smell like paper and old glue. We flip past albums with covers I have seen since childhood, and we hold up one or two for the other to judge. We do not buy anything. The browsing is the point. We duck into Target because we always do. We find travel-sized shampoo we do not need and a candle that smells like oranges and clean laundry. The sky holds, bright and thin, and the city opens like a postcard.

We check into the hotel three hours before doors. The room has two queen beds that look like clouds, crisp sheets that crackle when we pull them back. We drop our bags, set alarms, and sink into the covers. Sleep slides over me like it has been waiting nearby all week. When the alarms chirp, we get ready and walk next door to the venue.

Inside is a small theater, not a standard concert hall. The stage is close, the seats top out around a hundred, and everything hums with a quiet kind of anticipation. The lights are soft and the room is warm. People speak in low voices, the way they do in places that ask you to listen. Zarm steps out with a guitar and a microphone, thanks us for coming, and says it will be an acoustic night, mostly his favorites. My mom squeezes my hand, and I can feel her smile in the way her fingers press mine.

The music settles me in the places nothing else reaches. He sings about love and loss and the messy middle where you decide to heal. He tells a story about writing a chorus at two in the morning because he could not sit with a feeling any longer. He sings a song that used to play in my car on the way to last year's rehearsals, and I feel that version of me looking across the room at this one. He sings about moving on, about not wasting time wishing for a different past. The guitar sounds like a heartbeat under it all. I laugh at the stories he tells between songs, the ones where he makes himself the punchline. I wipe tears when a melody lands in a tender spot and stays there. When he bows, I feel full in a way I have not felt in weeks.

We step back out into the night, and the air feels cooler, like the show changed the temperature of the city. Back at the hotel, it is midnight. We slide into our beds, and the pillows know our names. I did not imagine the night like this, but it is somehow better. Oliver would have missed the point, or he would have stood and listened and not felt it the way I did. My mom understood every chord.

When the room goes quiet, my mind does not. I lie on my side and think about Oliver anyway, about our dates, the way he looked at me under the lights in the courtyard, the plans I made in my head without asking permission. Music is medicine, but it also loosens the lids I screw on tight. The love songs tip me toward my phone. I roll over and see it on the nightstand, black and tempting, the screen a dark mirror. I reach, the bed creaks, and my mom shifts in the other bed. I freeze, hand hovering in the cold air, then pull it back under the blanket.

"Why text him?" I whisper to the room, and the room has no answer. "What would I even want him to say?" I am here, with a full heart and a clean memory of a show I loved. I do not need to invite him into this room. I hum one of the lighter songs and let it nudge me away from the edge. I list the good things out loud in my head. I am in a pretty city. I spent the night with my favorite person. I felt something beautiful. I can keep that.

I finally drift, and morning arrives soft and ordinary. We have a whole day ahead of us, outlet malls, vintage stores, and coffee we do not need. We split a gluten-free cinnamon roll that is too big and say we will walk it off. We try on sweaters we will not buy and hats that make us laugh. At a vintage shop, I find a worn ballet print tucked between two landscapes, the paper foxed at the edges, the lines delicate and sure. I bought it for six dollars and feel like I won something no one else noticed was a prize.

On the drive home, the sun lowers in the rear view and turns the road gold. My mom puts a hand on my knee at a stoplight and says, "I am glad it was us."

I say, "Me too," because I am. We tell the story of the show again, the way it already feels like a memory we will keep. We stop for gas and snacks, and I pick the gummy bears that are all one color because it feels like a small, funny choice I get to make.

Back at my grandma's on Sunday, the leftovers come out like a second holiday. We make plates and sit at the table with the newspaper spread out under everything. My aunt asks for a full report on the concert, and I give it to her, hands moving like I am conducting. My grandma says she knew it would be good because it was just guitars and words. My aunt says we need to take her next time. The cousins drift in and out, hungry again already. Someone brings a deck of cards, and we play a fast game that I lose on purpose so the littlest cousin can win. She beams like she climbed a mountain.

Back in my room that night, I laid my new print on my desk and leaned on my elbows to study it. The dancer in the sketch is all line and intention, her face tilted toward a point I cannot see. She looks like she knows where she is going, not because the path is easy, but because she decided she would walk it. I want that for me. I say it out loud to the empty room, which makes me feel a little foolish and also brave.

Monday morning will come, and the week will do what weeks do. I will pack my bag, drive back to campus, and walk across the courtyard that always feels slightly too big. I will stand at the barre and remember what to do with my hands. I will take modern and try to let the floor hold me again. I will eat in the dining hall and look for faces I know. I will study, and I will sleep, and I will wake up and try again.

Before I turn off the light, I choose a rule I can actually keep. I am allowed to be happy right where I am, with what I have, without asking anyone else to sign off on it. I put my phone on the dresser, screen down, slide under the blanket that smells like home, and let sleep find me.

Chapter 18

It's the awkward week between Thanksgiving break and winter break, the quiet stretch before finals. I still have not heard from Oliver. No contact is difficult but also strangely freeing. For the first time since I moved in, I am starting to feel like I belong here a little. I pick my head up when I walk to class. I look people in the eye. I give small smiles on the sidewalk, and sometimes they smile back at me.

On Wednesday, right after ballet, my phone rings. I excuse myself from a conversation about travel plans and step toward the big windows that look over the practice field. The players are tossing a ball between themselves in the pale afternoon sun.

"Hey, Bri," my mom says, her voice bright.

"Hi, Mom," I say, watching a perfect spiral drop into waiting hands.

"I have exciting news," she says. "I know you felt like you did not really have the full college experience yet, and I heard the disappointment at Thanksgiving, so, drum roll."

"Drum roll," I echo, smiling.

"We are coming to take you to a football game on Friday. Your dad, your brother, and I. We got seats way up high, so you can show us around first, then we will drive to the stadium together."

"That sounds great," I say, loud enough that a girl walking past looks over and grins. I know how hard tickets are to get here. When you go to a school with thirty-five thousand students, four seats feel like a miracle.

"I figured we would get pizza at your favorite place, walk a little, see your dorm again, then head over. I hope that is okay. I got excited and might have gotten ahead of myself."

"It will be perfect. Thank you. Everyone says the games are a blast."

We talked for almost an hour. When I hang up, I feel both light and focused. I still have homework, but now I want the room spotless before they arrive. I put on music and start cleaning the way you clean when you care who will see the space, fold the blanket at the end of the bed, line up my shoes, wipe the desk, and make the brown and yellow leaf string lights sit just right.

Friday comes fast. I wake before my alarm. I have one morning class, then I grab a coffee and sit outside on a low brick wall to wait. The air has that soft winter taste without the bite, and the sun feels like a warm towel. At noon, my mom texts that they are ten minutes away. I jog to the main road so I can wave as they turn in.

The reunion is five full minutes of hugging. My mom grabs my shoulders and leans back to look at me like I am taller than last time. My dad squeezes me and says, "There she is." My brother bumps my shoulder and smirks like we share a secret. I take them to my dorm, even though they have seen it before, because the leaf lights do change the whole room in my mind. Natalie is out, as usual, so we sit and make a plan before the hunger takes over.

Five minutes from campus, on the softer edge of the city, is my favorite pizza place. The host recognizes me, and it makes me feel like I live here for real. We order nachos to share and two pizzas, one with gluten-free crust, so I never feel left out. We eat too much and then wander to the ice cream shop that we do not need but definitely want. My mom and dad chose chocolate, my brother chose something with rainbow sprinkles, I chose raspberry, and we all pretended we weren't going to try everyone else's.

On the walk back to the car, we see lines of students boarding buses to the stadium. The sight of all those jerseys and phones already recording sets off a small panic in me and in my mom. We hurry to the car and join the stream of traffic that leads in one direction like a river.

We are all in matching red and black shirts. I have never felt more loved or more stereotypical, and I am happy to be both. Then we hit the wall of cars. The line starts miles from the stadium. Tailgates pop up along the shoulder like tiny parties. Music thumps from truck beds. Smoke rises from grills. People weave across the road in groups with folding chairs and coolers on wheels. In the stop and go, my brother rolls the window down so we can people watch.

The confidence some people have in what counts as clothing amazes me. Shorts that do not cover anything. Tops made of what I would consider a headband. We laugh, kind and not cruel, because it feels like watching a parade. "Good for them," I say. "Could never be me."

By the time we crawl past the first gate, less than an hour remains before kickoff, and we are still a mile from any parking that looks possible. We have a brief family debate, the kind with layered voices and waving hands. Then my mom says, "Go," and my brother and I jump out with her and start walking. My dad stays to hunt a spot.

The crowd outside the stadium is a living thing. People press and part and press again. Vendors shout. The drumline echoes off concrete. The air smells like kettle corn, hot dogs, charcoal, and a little bit of spilled beer. My mom checks our tickets, points us toward our gate, and we keep our hands on each other's elbows so we do not lose each other. I see two girls from ballet in the flood of faces and wave, then keep moving. They are headed for the student section, that wild rectangle by the field where everyone stands and screams, shoulder to shoulder. The idea of the heat down there makes me sweat just thinking about it.

We get through the gate and security, then start climbing. And climbing. And climbing. Our seats are almost as high as you can go, one row from the top. The field looks like a bright board game. The players look like small pieces someone is moving with careful fingers. Our section is almost empty, which makes it feel like a private balcony. I love it.

My dad appears thirty minutes later, flushed and triumphant. "Parked," he says, holding up the keys. By then, my brother had already acquired two hot dogs and a bag of popcorn. He hands me a handful without looking away from the field.

The lights pour down. The band swells. When the first notes of the rally song hit, the whole stadium shakes. It is a physical thing, the way sound can make concrete vibrate. Towels spin. People jump in place like they are charging their own batteries. The team bursts through the banner, and the sound doubles. I cannot stop smiling. I do not understand football, but I understand this.

I thought back to the soccer game I went to at the beginning of the year. The one that was a surprise date from hell. But also the one where I met Oliver. I felt a sting rising up my back and shook my head. That game was so different from this. There were ten times the number of people here and more than ten times the amount of energy. This felt like a completely different school. The school spirit blew me away as I waited in suspense for the game to start and drift me from my thoughts.

Kickoff looks simple and violent at the same time. The ball arcs, bodies collide, and then the chess match begins. I decide the crowd will tell me what is good and what is not. It works. When the noise rises, I cheer. When it dips to a groan, I groan, then laugh. My dad and brother try to explain as the plays unfold.

"That is a blitz," my brother says.

"Watch the coverage," my dad adds.

"We need third and short," one of them says, and I nod like I understand, but I really only understand the mood in the air and the way the band hits a note and the way the student section never sits down.

Between plays, I look around. A kid three rows down keeps trying to start the wave, and when it finally reaches us, we raise our arms and laugh at how slow it rolls up this high. Behind us, the sky fades through three versions of blue, then slips into that in-between color that belongs to stadium lights and winter evenings. The air cools, then sticks again with the heat of thousands of bodies. The smell of nacho cheese and sugar drifts by and settles in the back of my throat. My mom leans her head on my shoulder for a second and says, "This is so fun," and it is.

The game is tight. The score seesaws, three points this way, seven that way, back to a tie, back to a narrow lead. I love how every second matters. I love how people sing the rally song chorus even when it is just drums. I love the way the stadium inhales together when a long pass leaves the quarterback's hand.

At halftime, we stand to stretch and point at the tiny ant band making letters on the field. My dad buys water and a second bag of popcorn because the first one is gone, and we pretend not to know how that happened. A couple in front of us asks where we are from, and we do the small talk of sports strangers, the kind that lives only in places like this. When the third quarter starts, the temperature has dropped just enough to make me pull my sleeves down and rub my hands together once for warmth.

Then, before I knew it, it was the last minute. We are down by three. The stadium goes quiet in a way I did not know a stadium could go quiet. You can hear the band holding its breath. People who were halfway to the exits stop in the aisles. I grip my mom's hand, and she grips back. My brother leans forward with his popcorn forgotten in his lap. I prepare myself to lose and still feel grateful, because the night is already perfect.

The snap, clean. The pocket holds. The quarterback turns and places the ball in the running back's stomach, and he is gone. He finds a seam that did not exist a second ago and slides through it like light. He breaks one tackle, then another. He cuts to the sideline. He is flying. The sound tears loose from the crowd and climbs as he runs. I am on my feet, and I do not remember standing. He crosses the goal line, and time breaks open. The roar lifts the hair at the back of my neck. The anthem blares. Strangers high-five. People scream words that turn into sound because joy stops needing vocabulary. The scoreboard flips, and all the numbers lean our way.

I look around and try to take a picture with my eyes. The lights, the towels, the band, my family with their arms in the air, the way my mom laughs with relief, the way my dad smiles like he built the stadium and always believed. This, I think, is what people want when they ask for college stories. This is the thing they imagine. I was here for it.

We file out slowly with everyone else. The walk is long, the traffic is longer, the air is full of sweat and sugar and spilled soda, and I do not care at all. My voice is already hoarse. My legs ache in a good way from the stairs. Back in the car, windows cracked for the breeze, we move through the dark maze of tail lights and celebrate the ridiculous luck of that last minute. My mom squeezes my knee. My brother hums the rally song off-key. My dad taps the steering wheel in a rhythm that matches the drumline in my head.

We won, and I was there, and all the way back through the traffic and the night, I could not stop smiling.

Chapter 19

I stare at the giant wooden door the same way I did on the day my parents dropped me off. The hallway hums with that end-of-semester quiet, and my almost empty room sits behind me like a paused scene. It is not required to take everything home for winter break, but I want to wash my clothes and my bedding, so my side of the room looks like I am moving out.

Natalie left three days ago. I heard her on the phone mumbling about going to the mountains with friends. She packed most of her clothes and makeup, and then she was gone. We still have never even a word to each other, not even "have a nice break." I am not sad about the silence. I am relieved that we will not be sleeping five feet apart, staring at opposite walls, for a few weeks.

My dad drove down early this morning to help me pack what I need. He steps back through the door and stops, like he walked into a memory. He can tell I am having a hard time. He knows what this semester has been. He understands that endings and beginnings sit in the same place and press on my ribs.

His arm finds my shoulders and pulls me in. I turn and bury my face in his shirt and let out a shaky breath I didn't know I was holding. He hugs tighter as my body finally lets go.

"It will be okay," he whispers, his hand moving up and down

my back in slow lines.

"I just did not expect my semester to go anything like this," I say into his chest. "What happened to the movie version of college? It went so slow, and it also flew by."

"I know," he says, and he means it.

We stand like that for a while, until I peel away and wipe my face with my sleeve. There is a dark wet spot on his shirt.

"I'm sorry," I say, half laughing at myself.

"It's okay," he says with a small smile. His eyes are glossy too, not as much as mine, but enough to tell me he feels what I feel. Maybe not in the same way, but close enough that I can see it.

I grab my purse and the final bag. We check the drawers one last time, unplug the lamp, and take down the leaf lights that made the room feel softer. The key clicks in the lock, and we carry everything to the truck. When the last bag thumps into the bed, I climb into the passenger seat and we pull away.

We don't stop. The drive starts quiet and turns easy. Halfway home we point out small things on the side of the road and joke about the posts we have seen online. The sky is a clean winter blue. The brown fields slide by like pages. For long stretches there is nothing to do but breathe.

Home smells like butter and sugar the second I step through the door. Warmth rolls out of the kitchen and wraps around my shoulders.

"Hi," Cole and his girlfriend say together, voices bright. My brother has been dating Lilly for about a year. She is between our ages, which made it simple for me to talk to her at first, and now we share a handful of favorites, books and movies and music. Her dirty blond hair is pulled into a loose ponytail, and she is in leggings and a band shirt.

"I made gluten free cookies," Lilly says, proud and sweet at the same time.

"Yum, they smell amazing," I say, dropping my bags in the entry. I walk into the kitchen and she slides the plate toward me. I reach for a glass from the cabinet, fill it with ice, then add vanilla almond milk. My dad and I have always done it this way. Cold milk tastes colder with ice. I dip a cookie into the glass and take a bite.

"These are delicious," I say around a mouthful, and everyone laughs because it is rude and real.

It feels like a pocket of air after holding my breath underwater. We unload the truck, make a small mountain of laundry by the washer, and then the four of us go to a movie. My mom is still at work and promises to meet us for dinner after.

On the way home we pick up burritos and burrito bowls, the whole car smelling like cilantro and lime. When we walk in, my mom drops her purse and hugs me like she did on move-in day, arms tight, cheek against my hair.

"Tell me everything," she says, and we talk while we eat. I give her the play by play of the day, the tiny details, the small wins, the tired parts. She listens the way she always has, with her whole face.

After dinner, Lilly heads home and Cole goes upstairs to play video games. I change into leggings and a big T-shirt, grab the book I am working through, and slip out the back door. The covered porch is a soft drum of rain and the kind of chill that feels clean. One of our dogs, Briella, pads over and sits pressed against my leg. She is a therapy session all by herself. She knows when I am tight with worry. She knows where to sit to make me feel steady. I tuck a blanket around my legs and open my book.

A few minutes later my dad comes out with his own book.

He does not say anything. He settles on the other bench, opens to his dog-eared page, and we read in the kind of silence that makes sound. The rain thickens. The wind shifts. Mist sneaks through the gap between the roof and the yard and cool drops find our sleeves.

"We should probably go in," he says, smiling.

"Probably," I say, and we both stand at the same time and carry our books inside.

We read a little longer in the living room, lamps warm, house quiet. Then I climb the stairs and slide into my bed. Briella jumps up and curls into a perfect comma at my side. The sheets are cold at first, then warm. I stare at the ceiling and let memory move through me. Maybe today and this semester did not go how I thought they would, but there were bright parts. There were new muscles I did not know I had. Before August I had never stayed away from home for more than a weekend. Now I live away and come back for a weekend when I can. College is not what the movies promised, but maybe that's okay. Maybe it's better when it is honest.

I think about what I want next. I want to feel like myself in my own life. I want to find my people, or be fine by myself until I do. I want to keep dancing, keep learning, keep getting stronger. For now I want to be here. I want to rest and read and fold warm laundry with my mom and talk to my dad about his book and play a game with Cole and take the dogs around the pasture and feel simple again.

Winter break lasts the next month. I do not have to move back until the first week of January. There is time to decompress. There is time to breathe.

I lie still and count my breaths. The house settles. The rain slows. Briella sighs in her sleep. Thirty minutes slip by and then my thoughts thin out and float. I let my eyes close. I let the dark feel like water.

Everything will be okay. I am home now.

Chapter 20

I had been home for three days when I felt the ache for ballet start to creep back in. Ballet is like an addiction for me. It is my exercise, my therapy, and the one way I can let emotions out without having to make sense of them first. Time away is nice, but after a few days the itch starts, then the restlessness, then the sudden urge to stand in first and breathe like music is already playing.

I kept telling myself to take the whole break off and let my body rest. It sounded smart in theory. In practice it would make me crazy. I knew what would happen if I stopped for too long: that first week back at Raylon would feel like moving through wet cement. Dancers do not really get "off." If you do, you pay for it.

So I started hunting for a way to dance. My old studio felt complicated after what happened with Lori. I could picture walking in and feeling every set of eyes slide over me, waiting to see if there would be another scene. Renting a room somewhere else was too expensive, and no one around here runs adult or college classes over the holidays. My parents' garage is concrete and narrow and terrifying for turns. The living room is a minefield of coffee tables and dog toys.

That left one option: ask Miss Pink if I could come back,

gently and with a plan. I pulled up her number and stared at the message box so long my phone dimmed itself twice. Then I typed.

"Hi Miss Pink! I'm home for winter break. I'm hoping to keep moving while I'm here. Would there be any chance I could rent studio time for some private practice? And, if it's okay, maybe pop into one of your classes? Totally understand if not."

I hit send and immediately regretted not adding more context, less context, more apologizing, fewer words. An hour later my phone buzzed.

"Of course! Although you owe me a class with you in it. I know last time was a lot, but I truly believe it will be okay. This is your home as much as anyone else's. A few alumni are coming to classes this week, so the spotlight won't be on you. I also spoke with Lori. Please come."

I read it three times. The part about Lori made my stomach knot, but the part about "home" landed exactly where I needed it. I gave myself the afternoon to think, which really meant I stared out the window and rehearsed conversations in my head. By evening I had decided.

I was taking class.

I stood in the bathroom mirror and checked everything the way I always do. Slicked back low bun. Black leotard, pink tights, warm ups over both because the studios run cold in December. A faded blue T-shirt on top. I pressed my fingers into the edge of my bun and felt the pins hold. My face in the mirror looked like me and also like the youngest version of me, the one who loved this place without thinking.

Walking into the lobby felt like stepping into a photograph I had carried in my pocket. The same scuffed gray marley squares, the same bulletin board with curling posters, the same perfume of rosin, hairspray, and lemon cleaner. A couple of younger dancers spotted me and ran in for hugs, breathless and warm. A few teens waved and asked about college like it was a distant city. I tucked my bag into a cubby, slid on my flats, and sat on the floor to stretch. My hamstrings argued for the first minute and then sighed open.

I peeked into Studio A. Miss Pink was finishing a younger class. She saw me and practically squealed, then crossed the floor in three long strides and wrapped me up.

"I'm so glad you're here," she said into my shoulder. "We'll catch up right after, okay?"

"Okay," I said, already lighter.

I took a corner spot at the barre, safe and out of the way. Dancers trickled in, whispering and laughing, shaking out arms and rolling ankles. More hugs. More waves. It felt like stepping back into a stream I had stepped out of for a second.

Two minutes before start time, Lori walked in.

She did not look at me. She was mid laugh with a girl who glanced between us like she had missed an important episode. Lori's chin lifted when someone else hugged me, and in that tiny movement I could feel the old friendship and the new edge of it, sharp and tired. Every time someone squeezed me hello, she squeezed someone too. It was almost funny if it did not bruise.

Class began. The old sound system vibrated as the chords played. The room clicked into its old rhythm. Barre felt like a language I could still speak. Miss Pink's voice was the same calm bell it has always been, specific, kind, impossible to ignore. "Soft ribs." "Present neck." "Let the tendu finish its thought." I could feel the corrections land and shift me. When she walked past I got the lightest tap under my scapula and instantly everything lined up. For ten minutes I forgot the lobby and the text and the tightness under my ribs. It was just body, breath, music, and a thin line of sweat at my hairline.

Center was generous and hard in exactly the right ways. Adagio that asked for patience, a petit allegro that asked for feet that never stop talking, and then across the floor.

"Quarter, half, full if you have it. Spot, breathe," Miss Pink said, clapping once.

I had it for two passes. On the third, I did not. My supporting foot slid an inch on the marley and the inch was enough. I went down hard, a surprised thud that echoed. The room gasped. I bounced up so fast I looked like a bad magic trick, bolted to the side, and pretended to tie my shoe. My tailbone rang like I had sat on a doorbell.

Miss Pink caught my eye. I gave her a thumbs up and an "I'm fine" smile I did not quite feel. She nodded and sent the next group.

The rest of class moved on. The ache in my tailbone settled into a dull complaint. I tuned it out as best I could. When we curtsied and the room clapped for Miss Pink, I knew I would be carrying a bruise home the size of a saucer, but I also knew I had needed this hour. Even the fall. Maybe especially the fall.

I slid my flats into my bag, pulled on warm ups, looped my sweatshirt around my waist. That was when I felt eyes on me, close enough to feel like a weight.

I turned. Lori stood there.

"Are you okay?" she said, quiet, eyes flicking around the room to make sure no one was watching us watching each other.

"Oh. Yeah," I said. "Mortified, but okay. Thanks."

She nodded once. "Okay." And she was gone.

A tiny thing, but a thing.

I said goodbye to a few girls and slipped out. Winter air hit my face and felt honest. I walked to my car, put my bag in the back, and sat for a second before turning the key. It is strange how being the dancer who comes back for break can turn every moment into a test. You feel like you are supposed to be new and improved after twelve weeks of studio hours and seminar notes. Growth is real, but it is also quiet. The pressure to make it loud made me sloppier, not better. It is hard to remember that when a familiar face is pretending she cannot see you and your brain is making charts in the corner about who hugged whom.

I drove home with the windows down and my favorite songs up. The sky was milky and low, and the air held the kind of cold that clears your head. By the time I turned onto our road, I could feel the tightness unwinding.

The front door opened before I got my key in it. My parents stood there like they had been listening for the car.

"How was it?" my mom asked, reading my face in one glance.

"Did you punch Lori?" my dad asked, perfectly straight.

I laughed then, the kind of laugh that shakes something loose. "No punching," I said. "Just a very dramatic lesson in gravity."

They both made the same face, lips pulled back and eyebrows up. The universal oof.

"It means you were working hard," my mom said, practical and kind.

"And I am relieved I did not have to chase Lori," my dad said, still straight faced.

We all laughed, and the worst of it fell off me. I told them the short version, good class, hard moment, small olive branch. They nodded in the right places and then shooed me toward the kitchen.

"Food first, then ice," my mom said.

I ate standing at the counter, leftover pasta and a handful of grapes, then took a bag of frozen peas to my room like a person with a plan. I changed into sweats and lay on my side with the peas tucked under my hip. My brain tried to replay the fall in slow motion. I told it no. I opened the notes app instead and typed *Why I'm dancing* at the top of a blank page. Under it, I started a list.

Because music builds rooms and I want to live in them.
Because breath feels different when my feet are talking.
Because performance makes the work make sense.
Because I do not want comparison to be louder than joy.
Because the clock is not the point.

It helped. It always helps to write it down where I can see it. When I got to the last line, I stopped and read the list again. Then I reached for a sticky note and a marker and wrote *Dance for me* in block letters. I took it to the kitchen and stuck it to the fridge beside next week's class times. The magnet holding it up was crooked and shaped like a lemon slice. It made me smile.

My phone buzzed on the counter. The screen showed Lori's name and three messages. My heart did the thing where it forgot what to do for a second.

"Hope your butt feels okay. That was a rough fall. I'm sorry for the past. I know we need space. Just wanted to say I'm sorry."

I stared at the words until they went a little blurry, then typed back before I could second-guess every letter.

"Thank you. I'm sorry too. College has been tricky. I just want to go back sometimes. I miss you."

The minute I hit send, I wished I could reach into the air and grab the last part back. It was true, but it felt like handing her something breakable.

"Yeah, same," she wrote. And that was all.

I stood there with the fridge humming and the sticky note crooked and felt something shift half a degree. Not fixed. Not even close. But different.

I did not want the night to flatten into replaying things I could not change, so I looked for small ways forward. I set an alarm for the next class. I tucked my flats by the door. I pulled my hair into a loose bun and walked to the hallway mirror. Just once, I marked the pirouette slowly, prep, spot, passé, down, feeling the mechanics click into place without the world watching. My tailbone complained, and I smiled at it in the mirror like, yes, I know.

Before heading back to my room, I paused by the back door. Rain had started, a fine mist tapping the porch rail. I stepped out for a minute and let the cold sit on my cheeks. The yard was black and silver, the kind of quiet that feels like a reset. I said the old note from my teacher into the dark, "Full out, no clock," because I needed to hear it out loud.

Inside, I grabbed my notebook and wrote one more line under the list: *Show up again.* Then I closed it, clicked off the kitchen light, and left the sticky note shining by itself on the fridge.

Chapter 21

On Sunday my dad invited me to lunch and to one of our favorite stores for a little retail therapy. He was really just planning to go to the store, but he knew I would want to tag along, so he asked, and I said yes before he could finish the sentence.

The sky had that washed winter blue that makes everything look a little sharper. We parked in front of the Mexican restaurant across the street from the shopping center and stepped into warm air that smelled like cumin and grilled corn. A server set down a basket of chips still hot from the fryer and a steaming bowl of queso that looked like melted sunshine. We broke as many chips as we ate because we kept reaching for the same ones at the same time, and we laughed every time our hands collided. When the chicken tacos came, the tortillas were soft and the cilantro tasted like a cold garden. It all helped, but the talking helped more.

"I'm sorry everything has turned out this way, Bri," my dad said, voice soft enough that the music from the speakers could have swallowed it if I were not listening. "I know how much you liked him and spending time with him. There will be other guys. I know that is a cliché and you have heard it a thousand times, but you are young and kind and beautiful. Do not let his words live in your head."

"Thanks, Dad. I know I need to move on and that there will be someone else." J paused and took a deep, shaky breath. "It just feels hard." I twisted the paper straw wrapper into a tight rope and then straightened it again. "First there was my messy high school breakup and now this. I feel like I cannot get anything right when it comes to dating. I just want to be happy."

"You will be. Trust me. I know it is hard, but be patient."

"I hate being patient. You know I am obsessive about things like this." I tried to smirk, and he gave me the matching smirk I have seen in the mirror a hundred times.

He let the quiet sit for a second. "Really though, Bri. I know he was sweet at times, but I also know he was the opposite at other times."

"I know." I pulled out my phone like I could prove anything by scrolling. "He said some upsetting things. I thought he would turn it around. I do not even know why we broke up in the first place. It felt so quick. It felt stupid." I could feel myself tipping into a rant and made myself stop. My dad just watched and listened, eyes warm and a little sad because he hates when he cannot fix something for me.

"I miss him," I said, smaller. "We were having fun, and he pushed me out of my comfort zone."

"Maybe that was his role," my dad said. "He helped you start, and now you keep flourishing on your own. He was the bit of sunshine you needed to begin growing."

"Now he is the rain that will make me grow faster," I mumbled, and the corner of his mouth lifted.

"There you go. That's my smart girl. Do not let him hold you back. I trust you and the choices you make, but promise me you will keep yourself first. Take care of yourself, because not everyone else will. Start there."

"I will, Dad." I looked down at my plate. It was not often that his protective side stepped out like this. It showed how much he cared. It almost scared me, until I remembered who was talking and why. He wanted me happy. He wanted me treated like a princess. Oliver did not really do that. I needed to admit it out loud, if only to myself.

"Ever since you left him you have seemed happier," my dad said, taking another bite.

"It was less that I left him and more that he left me, but I guess so. I am doing my best to keep my head above water. Distractions help."

"Well, it is working. I love having my daughter back, even if it is only until January."

We finished mostly in comfortable silence, tossing in small jokes and pointing out funny details in the wall art. When the check came, he snatched it faster than I could reach, which felt like its own kind of hug.

Across the street, the shopping center buzzed with the lazy energy of a Sunday afternoon. We wandered the aisles of the bookstore first. I traced my fingers over the spines in the new releases and then drifted to the poetry shelf I always pretend I do not like. He held up a hardcover with a ridiculous title and read the blurb in a mock dramatic voice until we both had tears in our eyes from laughing. In the record store the hum changed. I flipped through alphabetized rows, the plastic sleeves squeaking against my thumbs. The cover art felt like doorways. A camera shop on the corner had used lenses lined up like little galaxies. I thought of how Oliver would have stayed at the glass, how he would have tested every button on the old film bodies, how he would have looked up and grinned when he found the one that clicked right. I let myself have the picture for ten seconds, then filed it away.

We drifted through a craft store for no reason except that we always do, fingers sinking into stacks of yarn, noses buried in candle lids we had no intention of buying. In a global foods shop we stood too long in front of the spice wall, trying to imagine what we would cook with a jar of something deep red and smoky. By the time we reached the checkout of our last stop, our feet hurt in the best way. We each had three small things: he chose a paperback with a blue cover and a tiny jar of cardamom and a silly mug, and I chose a blank notebook with speckled edges, a record I could not leave behind, and a candle that smelled like orange peels and rain.

Back home I went straight to my room and sank onto the floor beside the bed, resting my head on the edge of the mattress. Briella knew the cue. She came and tucked herself into my side like a living weighted blanket, warm and steady.

I stared at the ceiling fan and watched it turn. The conversation with my dad stretched out in my head like a road I had just driven. It helped, and it also brought Oliver closer. I pictured him in those stores. I pictured his hand in mine. I pictured his hugs and his eyes that made me feel seen and also confused.

I missed him. More than I wanted to admit.

It was so different from my high school breakup. That ending had been clean in my mind. Sad, yes, but clean. I did not look back after the first day and ask why I did it. This felt wrong. It felt fast, thin on reasoning, like a sentence missing its middle.

Maybe I should text him.

Briella lifted one eyebrow and gave me the side-eye that has judged me more fairly than most people.

"Do not look at me like that," I said. "You do not get it."

She huffed and put her chin on my leg. Maybe she did get it. Maybe she was saying don't do it.

I picked up my phone anyway. I typed, "hey, can we talk." I deleted it. I typed, "I hope you are okay." I deleted it. I typed, "I miss you" and felt my face heat, and deleted it so hard the screen shook. I tried drafting in the Notes app like that would make it feel safer. Every version sounded either too small or too much.

After an hour of circling, I tossed my phone onto the rug and let the silence spread. The text stayed unsent.

I kept thinking that if future me could walk in, she would tell me the ending and I could breathe. Do we end up together? Do I meet someone else? Do I end up alone and weirdly happy with seven cats and stacks of paperbacks? I wanted any answer. Life refused to hand me one, which felt rude and also correct.

The quiet started to feel loud, so I crawled across the floor, grabbed my headphones, and opened my music app. I hit shuffle on my favorite artist and climbed into the chair by the window. The first few songs slid past like water. Then a guitar line I knew by heart showed up and I smiled before the words even landed. I turned the volume up until the bass felt like a second pulse.

When the chorus arrived, I paused and rewound. Then I did it again. And again. Sometimes a lyric clicks into the exact shape of your life. It did that. I mouthed, "If this was a movie you'd be here by now," and it sat in my chest like a truth and like a joke. This was not a movie. He was not going to show up at my door, pull me into a hug, and promise me things he could not promise. I was in my room in the middle of a quiet afternoon, and he probably did not even remember my street name. If this were a movie, the knock would come right on the line, the score would swell, the camera would push in. I slouched deeper in the chair and felt like a puddle waiting to become a person again.

Later, while I was in the kitchen talking to my mom about what to make for dinner, someone knocked on the front door. No one ever knocks here. Our road is long and quiet, and the neighbors are too far away to wander over without a reason.

Oliver.

No. Definitely not. Still, my heart jumped like it had practiced.

My mom opened the door to a man in a floral shop polo holding a vase so full of flowers it looked precarious. Pink and cream and a splash of deep red, eucalyptus spilling over the edge.

"These are for delivery to this address," he said, checking the name.

"Thank you," my mom said, lifting the arrangement like a newborn and setting it carefully on the counter.

Flowers. Maybe not Oliver at the door, but could these be from him? They were gorgeous, heavy with scent, the kind of bouquet that makes a room look richer.

"I have no idea who would have sent flowers," my mom said, hunting for the small card tucked between leaves.

I held my breath without meaning to.

"Your father," she chuckled, reading. "Of course. There is no reason for him to send me something this fancy on a random day like this."

Oh. Right. Not a movie.

I laughed and kept the smile on my face until I made it to my room. Then I slid down the wall to the same spot on the floor. Briella pressed into my side like a warm comma.

At least she loves me.

This was not a movie. He was not going to show up. He was not going to send flowers. I was not his girlfriend. He did not want me or have time for me. My mind spun the facts like a top and then watched them wobble.

The first tears came quiet, then faster. I pressed my palms to my eyes until colors bloomed there like fireworks. It felt ridiculous and also necessary. How could I be this delusional, I asked myself, and then I let the question pass through because shame was not going to move me forward either.

When my face felt puffy and my chest finally untangled, I stood up and grabbed a glass of water. I took Briella outside and walked the edge of the yard. The pasture was winter-brown and soft. The air smelled like cold hay. Far off, a crow called and then called again, annoyed at something I could not see. The sky was clear enough to count a handful of early stars. I pulled my hands into my sleeves and let the night do what it does best. It steadied me. Not all at once, but enough to make the ground feel more like ground.

Inside, I lit my new candle and watched the flame settle into a small oval of light. I stacked my record, the book and the notebook neatly on my desk and wrote a single line on the first page. *Keep showing up.* I underlined it twice. I sent Lea a quick text that said, "hi from home, hope your break is good," and she sent back a picture of her cat sleeping on her dance bag with three heart emojis. It was small and it helped.

When my mom called me for dinner, I tucked the notebook under the record sleeve and turned the candle off with the lid. We ate leftovers and told the kind of stories that are mostly inside jokes. After, I stood at the sink and washed dishes while my dad dried, the two of us moving in practiced steps we have had since I could see over the counter.

In my room again, I stuck the Keep showing up note to the corner of my mirror. I did not have answers, but I had that. I put the headphones back on and made a new playlist called Forward, then lay on the rug with Briella's head on my stomach and let the first song play all the way through without rewinding. It was not a movie, and maybe that was okay. I could still write my next scene.

II

Part Two

Second Semester

Chapter 22

I woke up on New Year's morning to my phone dinging non-stop. I groaned, rolled over, and slapped it silent, eyes still heavy with sleep. The house was quiet in that special way after a late night; even the heater sounded like it was tiptoeing. I told myself whatever it was could wait, pulled the blanket up under my chin, and let the dark hush pull me under again.

Last night we hosted my aunt, my cousins, and my grandma for a New Year's Eve party at my parents' house. We had scrubbed the garage until it didn't look like a garage. We pushed two couches against a bright white wall and set up the projector to catch the New York City countdown. Someone dragged out the pool table and a stack of board games. The folding table sagged under chips and queso, three kinds of wings, two pizzas, pigs in a blanket, and every finger food known to man. A second table was all sugar: cookies, brownies, and a pie nobody sliced until midnight because everyone kept "saving room."

We played endless games of pool, sang along badly to whatever music my brother queued up, and told the same stories we always told this time of year. When the countdown hit, the whole garage turned into a drum of voices.

"Ten, nine, eight…"

We screamed numbers like they were magic words and then

cheered when the ball made it all the way down the pole on a screen hundreds of miles away. There were hugs and cheek kisses and confetti poppers that smelled like burnt paper. Everyone drifted out with sleepy goodbyes and paper plates balanced on foil-covered leftovers. I brushed my teeth, fell into bed, and slept like I had been poured into place.

Seven hours later I couldn't fall back asleep. The quiet tick of curiosity kept tapping my forehead. I flipped onto my back and flung one arm out of the warm cocoon to feel around on the nightstand. My fingers found the phone.

One notification.

Just one. That didn't match the chorus of pings that had dragged me out of sleep. I frowned and hovered the screen in front of my face. Face ID blinked its little lock at me and refused. I tried again, squinting like that would change my features. No. The phone did not recognize the swamp-creature version of me. I typed my passcode with stiff fingers and swiped up.

A follow request.

From Oliver.

I stared at the screen until my eyes watered. My heartbeat kicked, then stuttered, then sped up so fast it made my hands shake. The boy who had told me to leave him alone, who had blocked me like I was spam, who had disappeared, was suddenly right here again, like the world had skipped a track and started a different song.

But what had set off the flurry of sounds earlier if this was the only notification left? He couldn't message me unless I accepted. I imagined him requesting, panicking, un-requesting, and requesting again, rapid fire. It was the only explanation that made a weird kind of sense.

I didn't know if I should let him back in. Part of me wanted to hit accept and pour out everything I hadn't said. The other part remembered every sharp word and every quiet absence and wanted to protect the small peace I had built. I needed air.

I slid out of bed, pulled on a sweatshirt, leggings and thick socks, then tiptoed downstairs. The dogs lifted their heads from their beds as I passed, ears cocked. I opened the back door and cold air pushed into the kitchen like a body. It wasn't just chilly. It was a slap of frigid air. I grabbed my coat and boots from the bench, shrugged into them, and stepped outside.

The wooden stairs were icy under my soles. I crossed the patio to the back gate, my breath a pale cloud. The dogs started barking that happy bark that means adventure. My fingers had already gone pink by the time I unlatched the gate. The dogs exploded into the yard, tails high, noses down.

Our usual loop cuts behind the garden and skirts the small pond, then climbs the hill that runs along the fence line. In summer you can hear frogs under the algae and the cattle lowing in the neighbor's pasture. Today the pond was a flat, dull mirror and the trees were bare fingers against a pale sky. My boots crunched frost. The dogs ran ahead and doubled back like elastic.

I walked slower than I meant to, trying to think and trying not to think. Why was he doing this now. Why was I so ready to fold myself back into the shape that fit his hands. My thoughts ran circles so tight I made myself a little dizzy.

The dogs yelped and I jerked my head up. A rabbit shot from the scrub by the fence like a thought, and both dogs launched after it, barking with joy.

"No," I yelled, pounding across the grass.

By the time I reached the fence, the rabbit had slipped through to the neighbor's field and vanished into the brown. I stood with my hands on my knees and laughed once, breathless. The dogs loped back toward me, tongues out, eyes bright, covered in a dozen grass seeds like tiny medals. I collapsed backward into the cold grass and let them clamber over me, licking my face like I had done something heroic. The ground was wet through my coat, but the shock of cold cleared my head. For a few minutes I forgot the small rectangle of panic waiting for me on my nightstand upstairs.

When I stood and started walking again, I put in my headphones. Upbeat music filled my ears and pushed my thoughts into the background. I walked the rest of the loop with my hands tucked into my sleeves and my gaze on the line where the field met the sky. By the time the house came back into view, my cheeks hurt from the cold, but my chest felt looser.

The back door was locked. Of course it was. I knocked, then banged with the side of my fist, then stamped my boots on the mat to keep feeling in my toes. After a minute my dad leaned around the hallway corner with a confused, mildly annoyed look.

"It's locked," I said, over-articulating through the glass like that would help.

He hurried over and twisted the deadbolt, pulling the door open so the warm air hit me like a blanket. The dogs barreled in past my knees.

"Sorry," he said. "I thought you were upstairs. It's freezing. Where were you?"

"Just went for a walk." I pulled off my boots and lined them up on the mat. "Needed air."

"In the cold?" He raised his eyebrows. "Everything okay?"

"Mm-hmm." I bobbed my head, not trusting my mouth. He held my gaze for a second, then nodded once and stepped back, giving me space like a gift.

I made coffee the way I like it when I need comfort: too much cream, too much sugar, a swirl that turns the surface the color of warm sand. I carried the mug upstairs and curled into the chair by my window, the one that catches the morning light. Steam fogged my glasses. I wiped them with the hem of my sweatshirt and brought the phone into my lap like it might bite.

I opened the app. The request still sat there, patient and impossible. I scrunched my nose and tapped accept. The button flipped to follow back. I tapped that, too, quick like ripping off a bandage, then tossed the phone onto my bed before I could watch it turn into anything else. I picked up a book and made myself see the words.

Two hours later I gave in. The book lay face-down in my lap, and my coffee had gone cold beside me. I reached for my phone. One message waited.

"Hey."

I blinked at the single word. No question. No explanation. Just a thin line cast into the water to see if anything tugged.

"Hey," I typed back.

His reply landed almost immediately, like he had been holding his breath.

"You okay?"

"Uh, sure. What's up?"

"Just wanted to say Merry Christmas and Happy New Year."

My stomach tilted. The small talk felt like a disguise pulled halfway over something else.

"Oh. Um. Okay."

I watched the gray bubble appear, disappear, appear again. A full minute of it. My breath sat high in my throat. Then the next message arrived.

"I miss you."

The words hit like a physical thing. My hands started to tremble so hard I had to set the phone on the arm of the chair. Tears slid before I could bargain with them. I pressed my lips together and tried to breathe around the thud in my chest. A dozen answers charged the gate at the same time. I miss you too. You hurt me. Where were you. Why now. I want to talk. I cannot do this.

Another bubble. Another line.

"Well anyway I have to drive now. Bye and sorry I guess."

I stared at the screen, my face hot and my fingers cold. He had to drive. Why send the grenade and then walk away? Sorry for what? For texting me? For leaving? For the whole crooked mess of it?

My brain did what it always does. It ran scenarios like trailers. He is on his way here. He is driving past the exit to my town without stopping. He is sitting in a parking lot talking to me between classes. He is two hours down the highway before he realizes what he typed. The truth is he probably had an errand or a shift or a class and decided to write the thing before he lost the nerve. The truth is I do not know.

I set the phone face-down on the windowsill and wiped my cheeks with my sleeve. Outside, a bird hopped along the top rail of the fence, light and unconcerned, its feet barely denting the frost. The sky was the color of paper. Somewhere downstairs a cabinet door thumped and my mom's voice floated up the hallway, cheerful, calling to the dogs. Life kept moving in the same rhythm as before the message.

I pulled the blanket tighter around my shoulders and let myself sit in the feeling without trying to fix it. The coffee was cold, but I took a sip anyway. It tasted like the end of a long night. I didn't write back. Not yet. I pressed my palm flat on the notebook by the chair, felt the familiar texture of the cover, and flipped to a clean page. I wrote the date at the top and then wrote one line, steady and small.

I get to decide.

The words looked simple there, not dramatic or brave, just true. I closed the notebook and put it on the sill beside the phone, the two rectangles side by side, one heavy, one light. Then I stood up and went to find my parents. There were leftovers to eat, and a puzzle spread on the dining room table, and a long dog walk we could take when the sun slid a little higher. The day was still mine, even with his words humming at the edge of it. And for the first time since I woke up, that felt like enough.

Chapter 23

"Meet me at the Walmart near my house tonight at seven."

What? That is easily the sketchiest text I have ever received, and it does not help that it's from my ex, the same ex who decided he "missed me" out of nowhere on New Year's Day and then disappeared again. After that flurry of messages there has been nothing, and now suddenly he has more to say.

"I'm sorry, what?" I type.

"Please just do it and I'll explain once we are there."

"Umm, yeah, no way. I'm not sure how stupid you think I am, but I have seen movies and heard horror stories. Why in a million years would I meet you at Walmart on a dark Saturday night?"

"Fine I get it. I just need to see your face. It's not very often I go out alone while home for winter break and tonight I will be. I know it's not the best meeting place but it's the only place I'm going before meeting my family at a party. I just wanted to see you and explain some things, in person."

My body answers before my brain. The same symptoms slam the switch: shaking hands, heart rolling into a sprint. It makes me mad that a boy who hurt me still has that power.

If I were in my right mind, I would say no. I know my parents would hate this. I never go out alone at night, and I definitely do not meet people in parking lots.

"Sorry, I don't think I can. My parents aren't going to let me and it just doesn't make sense to me."

"Come on Bri. Please, I am begging you."

Desperation leaks through the screen. I sit and stare at the bubbles and weigh things I cannot measure. Part of me wants to see him. My mom is at work. It would only be my dad to get past. I do actually need shampoo. A store run would not be a lie.

I want to see him.

I want to talk to him.

I want it to make sense.

I want back what I thought we were building.

I want Oliver.

At seven I am walking across a dimly lit lot under humming lamps that turn everything a tired yellow. Automatic doors breathe warm air into the cold night. Through the glass I catch the back of his head, the dark brown hair I could pick out of a crowd. My stomach drops, my forehead beads, and yet my feet keep moving. I leave a generous space between us, in case my spine suddenly decides to turn me around.

It does not. I catch up.

"Hey," I say, just above a whisper.

He turns and folds me into a tight hug that concentrates every weird feeling at once. I don't move. I stand like a coat rack while he wraps his arms around me.

"Um, sorry, hi Bri," he says, stepping back when he feels my stiffness. He reads the room. He always has.

"Sooo," I say, easing forward into the long aisle of fluorescent light and gray tile.

"Right. I know this is weird, and I already tried to explain myself, but basically my mom needed me to pick up a few things, and I agreed, and then I realized I would be closer to your house, and I am really ranting here." He exhales and looks at me. I look away at the floor, which is clean only in theory. "I miss you, Bri. I know I messed up, and I know you probably do not want to see me, but I wanted to see you and talk to you, and I was wondering if you would give me a second chance? I mean I am begging you to. I have been miserable without you."

I stop walking, and he stumbles to a stop too. The look on my face tells him to pull back from the edge, and he does, turning his shoulders so he is half facing away, like he is giving me room.

"Just think about it," he says quietly.

"Okay."

"Okay?" he repeats, like the word is fragile.

"Okay. I will think about it. I need better convincing than an awkward Walmart date with an intense hug in the doorway though."

"I know, I know, I'm sorry. I got excited. I will show you what you need to see. I promise."

We wander. The store is a collage of odd silences, squeaking carts, and the soft voice over the intercom that nobody truly hears. We drift past bins of discounted slippers, past a shelf of candles that all smell like vanilla in slightly different costumes, past a wall of Gatorade that looks like stained glass. He tries, here and there, to crack a familiar joke. I offer the ghost of a smile, and the shapes of our old inside jokes float between us like they belong to other people.

At the end of an aisle, while we look at a rack of dog toys that squeak if you breathe near them, his hand brushes mine. I jerk away and lift a rubber bone like I meant to examine it.

Five minutes later it happens again. This time I do not jump.

I do not move at all. I can feel his eyes on the space between our hands, measuring. He lets his knuckles touch mine a little more intentionally, as if to prove to both of us that contact is real. I glance down, then let my eyes fall to the floor and keep walking.

I want to be here with him; I also feel like I have stepped into the wrong scene and forgotten my lines. We have not seen each other in weeks. He is acting like we can pretend nothing happened, and also like we must keep this a secret from the world. Does he want to be back with me or only erase his guilt? If we cannot talk without flinching, how could we even hold hands?

We turn into a quiet aisle of clearance Christmas, red stickers slapped onto snowmen that blink, candles that never found a December table, face masks shaped like penguins and reindeer. The shelves feel like an afterthought. I point at a snowman mask marked down to twenty-five cents, ready to make a joke, when he catches my hand and steps into my path. He is suddenly the whole horizon.

For a second all my old alarms blare. Then I meet his eyes.

It is Oliver. Not the version that said mean things and vanished. The boy who brought milkshakes to the movie we both pretended we had not seen a thousand times. The boy who learned my schedule because he liked walking the same sidewalks at the same time. The boy who took care of me when the homesickness hit so hard I could not breathe. My shoulders stop bracing.

"I am sorry, Bri. I am really, truly sorry for all of it." He glances around the aisle and laughs once, nervous and genuine, then looks back at me. "I know this is not where you bring someone when you are trying to win them back, but you have to understand how badly I want you in my life. It's not even a want. It's a need. I have been miserable without you. I know you have been too."

I tilt my head, lift one eyebrow. He winces a little.

"Not to put words in your mouth," he adds quickly. "I just mean I have missed you."

His eyes are green and wide in the store light. A smile tries to crawl across my face and almost makes it.

"I am not saying yes, and I am not jumping into anything, but I will think about it."

His smile flashes and then he looks around like he needs the shelves to confirm this is happening. The space between us tightens by an inch. His breath warms the air between our faces. I close my eyes and lean in because my body is faster than my brain.

"Oh, crap." He jumps back and fumbles his phone. "It's my mom. I have to take this." He edges around the end cap and disappears while I stand there with my mouth half open, staring at three glass angels that sing if you tap them.

I'm not sure why he couldn't just answer right beside me. I'm not sure why I almost kissed someone in the clearance aisle of a Walmart. Is this really what I want my new standard of romance to look like?

I pivot toward the front of the store. Maybe I should leave. Maybe this is a sign that I am confusing momentum with meaning.

His footsteps catch me before I pick a direction.

"My mom needs me there earlier than I thought, so she can frost her cupcakes," he says, rolling his eyes at himself. "Sorry. We should head to checkout."

The awkward chill returns and settles on our shoulders.

We walk side by side, not touching, like kids trailing after a babysitter. He loads his few items onto the belt. I add my shampoo and a pack of cotton pads I do not actually need. The cashier makes light conversation about the weather and hands over the receipt like a peace offering.

Outside, the lot feels colder, the sky flatter. We discover our cars are only a row apart and end up walking the same direction. He lifts his trunk and sets his bag inside, then closes it with his forearm.

"Thank you for meeting me," he says softly.

"Sure. I mean I am not fully sure why I did, but here we are."

"I thought it was nice." He gives me a look like he is genuinely confused by my skepticism.

"It's a Walmart," I say, laughing once despite myself.

"But it was with you," he says, and the corny line somehow lands. The butterflies that have been sulking all night lift their heads. "I meant what I said. I hope you will consider giving me another chance. A real one. Not just Walmart."

"Okay. I will give you one more chance, but that is all. The next date better be nice."

"It will be. Maybe I will take you to Target," he says, and winks.

"Stop," I say, smiling. "Although you know me and Target." I turn away and start toward my car. "I will see you. Somewhere. Sometime."

"I will text you incessantly until you agree," he calls, amused. "Since you promised, you better be careful."

"All right, all right," I say, opening my door and sliding in. He lifts a hand and steps back. I connect my phone to the car and glance up, expecting to see his taillights leaving.

He is still there. He taps on my window and twirls his finger to ask me to lower it. I press the switch and the glass slides down with a soft shiver.

"Everything okay?" I start to ask.

He leans in and kisses me.

Electricity tears down my arms and settles as warmth in my ribs. For one suspended second the parking lot is nowhere and the fluorescent lamps are stars. I kiss him back before I can decide if I should.

"You forgot that," he says, eyes lit, and steps away. He walks toward his car like he did not just detonate my plans. I sit with my hand on the steering wheel and my mouth an impossible temperature and my thoughts trying to stand up.

It was not our first kiss, but it felt like it. New, bright, and wrong in all the ways a person like me notices. A Walmart parking lot. After a month of silence. After the words that still live under my skin if I poke them.

He pulls out of the space and turns toward the exit. I watch his blinker flash against the asphalt. My phone buzzes once with a new text from someone else reminding me the world is still the world.

Oliver just surprise kissed me in a Walmart parking lot after not seeing me for over a month. I sit there and breathe and let that sentence exist, whole and ridiculous and true, while the heater clears the fog from my windshield and the radio mutters the end of a song I was not listening to. Then I put the car in reverse and decide I will not make any other decisions tonight.

Chapter 24

Not even a week has passed and somehow I am unironically waiting at Target for Oliver. We joked about our next date being here, a step up from Walmart, but I never thought it would actually be the very next place we met.

Earlier he sent a message like the one from days before, the kind that tells me to meet him at a specific store and promises to explain later. I guess we are still pretending this is a secret mission and not two people trying to figure out what we are.

I drift through the dollar section, trailing my fingers over felt hearts and tiny ceramic birds, trying to look occupied and not like someone whose heart rate doubles every time the automatic doors sigh open. Warmth hovers behind me. Before I can turn, a hand slides around my forearm and laces through my fingers.

"How are you doing?" he whispers close to my ear.

I step forward and turn to face him. "I'm all right." The words come out calm, but I keep my shoulders square and my hands loose. I want him to notice that I am not sure about the sudden touching. "What does your mom need today?" I ask, and I let the sarcasm show.

"Actually, today I am shopping for a gift exchange with my friends. I could really use your help. Her name is Gracie, she is a nursing major about our age."

I blink up at him. "So you brought me to Target to help you buy a present for another girl?"

"For a group exchange. I drew her name out of a hat. I wanted one of the guys, but that is not how it works." He lifts both hands in surrender. "Will you help me or not?"

I stare at him, then angle toward the exit on instinct. He reaches for me with a soft, almost sheepish voice. "Bri, please? It means nothing. I mostly wanted to spend time with you. Just walk with me."

He sticks out his bottom lip in that exaggerated pout he knows is ridiculous. I sigh. "Fine. I will walk."

We move down the main aisle, past end caps stacked with blankets and water bottles in candy colors. Every few steps his shoulder brushes mine. Then our hands bump. Then he tries to take my hand outright. I let it happen because the almost-holding feels more awkward than the real thing, and also because my chest is already busy with a million other thoughts.

My feelings are split clean down the middle. Part of me likes being near him again, hearing his voice, watching him try. The other part keeps replaying what he said to me and how it felt, and how my body remembers that hurt. I want it to work. I also want to protect myself. Both are loud.

We pause at a display of mugs with barely funny sayings. "Would a mug be too basic?" he asks.

"For a nursing major who probably lives on coffee," I say, "a mug is a perfect. Maybe add something small so it feels thoughtful."

We pick up a heavy white mug with a small red heart painted inside the rim. He turns it in his hands like he is testing its story. "What about a blanket too? Cozy?" he says, glancing at me.

"Cozy is good." I reach for a knit throw the color of oatmeal and set it in the cart. "Maybe a sheet mask or lotion? Nurses wash their hands a million times a day."

We wander into skincare. He defers to me without pretending he knows what he is looking at, and I appreciate that. I choose a gentle hand cream and a tiny tube of peppermint lip balm and tuck them in beside the blanket. For a few minutes it feels easy. Normal. Like we are just two people picking out a gift.

His phone buzzes. He glances down and answers fast. "Hey. Yeah. I am at the store," he says into the microphone, and I recognize the tone he only uses with one person. He lifts a finger in the hold on gesture when I lean in to say he can go if he needs. I step away and pretend to be deeply interested in a shelf of candles.

"Vanilla Birch," I read off a label, and I lift the lid and inhale a scent that tries too hard to be a forest. "Sugar Cookie," which smells like a kitchen in December. "Clean Cotton," which smells like laundry and a memory I cannot place. I hold one to my nose and take slow breaths, letting the wax and the idea of it fill the space where nerves want to live.

He reappears at my shoulder. "My mom is getting paranoid and wants me home soon. Sorry. You know how she is."

"Well, actually," I begin, and before I can finish, he leans in and presses his mouth to mine. Quick. Certain. Public. Apparently he is committed to the surprise kiss in a store theme.

"I have to go," he says, already backing away. "I'll text you. Promise."

Then he is gone, and I am still standing in the candle aisle with a jar in my hand and a heat in my face that does not belong to the store lights.

I swallow. My throat feels dry, like I have been running. Tears prick, and I blink hard, refusing to let them fall in a Target next to a display of wick trimmers. I set the candle back and start walking with purpose even though I don't know where I am going.

I push the cart to the home goods section and make myself read price tags. Picture frames. Dish towels. A small lamp with a ribbed glass base that looks like it came from a nicer store. I circle to stationery and pick up a pack of gel pens I do not need. I ended up putting them back. I pick up a notebook with thick paper and no lines that feels like a clean page in more ways than one. I keep it.

I tell myself I can let this lift my mood, even if only by a thread. I check my list. Shampoo. Conditioner. Cotton pads. I go back for the mint lip balm, not for Gracie, but for me. I add a travel size hand cream and toss it in the basket like a promise to take care of myself, at least a little.

By the front of the store, near the dollar section where I started, a little girl in pigtails turns to her dad and holds up a glittery pencil cup like it is treasure. "This one," she says, sure and bright. He smiles and says, "Good choice." It is the smallest thing, but it steadies me. Everyone in here is choosing small things. I can choose small things too.

At self checkout I scan the blanket and the mug and the lotion and the lip balm for a person I do not know. I scan the notebook and my own balm and the shampoo I came for. The machine chirps and tells me to place items in the bagging area in that chipper voice that never matches the moment. I pay. I tuck the receipt into the pocket of my coat.

On the way out I pause under the blast of warm air from the vents above the doors and watch rain that I wish was snow drift through the lights. I pull my phone out and see no new messages. My chest tightens and then loosens again. I put the phone away.

In the car I sit for a minute with the engine off and the radio low. I do not want to cry. I do not want to pretend nothing hurt. I let both truths sit beside me. Then I turn the key, check my mirrors, and drive home slowly, as if slowness could teach my heart to be careful.

At a red light I glance at the bag on the passenger seat. The ribbon on the mug box has slipped loose. I tighten it and smooth it flat. "Good luck, Gracie," I say into the quiet car, and I smile at myself for being ridiculous.

By the time I pull into the driveway I have decided one thing. If this keeps happening, if we keep meeting under fluorescent lights with other people's lists in our hands, then I need to say what I need. Not in a fight. In a sentence. The same way I chose a notebook and a mint lip balm for myself. Clear. Small. Honest.

Inside, the house smells like dinner and something sweet. I set the Target bags on the counter, take the mug and the blanket out, and fold them neatly so they look like care, even if they are for someone else. I wash my hands, tie my hair up, and help my mom stir a pot on the stove. Steam fogs the kitchen window, and my day settles, quiet and warm, like it finally has a place to land.

"Target successful?" my mom asks, peeking at the blanket. She does not have to ask who I met there. She knows my face too well.

"Mostly," I say. "We picked gifts for a girl from his friend group. It was fine, then his mom called and he had to leave."

She lifts one eyebrow. "And you?"

"I bought a notebook," I say, and it sounds small, but it feels like more.

After dinner I carry the notebook upstairs and sit on the floor by my window. The paper is thick and soft. I uncap a pen and write a title at the top of the first page. What I need. I make a short list, not a manifesto. See me on purpose, not accidentally in a store. One real plan at a real time. Talk to me, do not surprise me, especially not with your mouth in public and your phone in your hand. If you need to leave, say it before you kiss me. I add one more line. If you cannot do this, let me go.

I copy the list in smaller handwriting on a sticky note and press it into the back cover. Then I open a second page and write what I like about him, because both truths can live side by side. He notices when I am cold and rubs my arms without making it a show. He loves cameras the way I love music. He looks at the sky like it is a friend. He laughs with his whole face. The page looks balanced. I feel steadier.

Chapter 25

The rest of the night moved in slow motion. After I got home from the so-called date, I sat on the shower floor and cried until the water slid from hot to lukewarm. I dried off, pulled on an old T-shirt, and lay flat on my back staring at the ceiling. My eyes burned. My face felt tight. My head throbbed in that hollow way that says you cried past the point of usefulness. I felt crushed and, at the same time, so very stupid.

Why did I think it would go any other way. Why did I let hope climb into the car with me. In the light of the sunset it felt obvious that it would end with me in tears and him sounding untouched.

Maybe it is time to actually let him go.

I should have done it weeks ago, but I wanted it to work. I wanted the version of us that lived in my head to win. I gave him another chance, then one more, then a handful more I did not name out loud. Now I could see it was not going to work. For my own sanity I needed to move on.

If I was going to let go, I wanted him to know it. Not to be cruel, not to score a point, but so I would stop being the person who waited on texts that did not come. I rolled toward the edge of the bed so I could reach my phone. Briella groaned and lifted her head as my arm stretched over her. I scratched behind her ear. She thumped her tail once against the comforter, as if to say she was still here even if the rest of the world was unstable.

It was the next day and already past midday. All I had done so far was lie around and rehearse the same conversation with myself. I unlocked my phone, opened Messages, and Oliver's thread rose to the top like it had been waiting for me. Blue and gray bubbles from the day before glared up at me. I read and reread until the words felt printed on the inside of my skull. My heart pounded. My palms went damp.

I typed slowly so I would not backspace the courage away. "I just wanted to let you know that I need to let go. I am no longer interested in trying to figure this out. I am ready to move on. I am sorry for how it all went down and I wish you the best."

I stared at the screen, squeezed my eyes shut, and pressed send. The whoosh sounded louder than it should have.

I waited. I stared for dots that never appeared. I set the phone down. I picked it up again. I scrolled without seeing anything. I set it down and went downstairs because the room felt too tight.

In the kitchen I made tea I did not want and sipped it anyway. The house was weekday quiet, the kind of quiet where you can hear the heat turn itself on and off. I stood at the back door and looked out at the pasture. The sky was the color of recycled paper. The pond was a dull sheet of metal. I told myself a walk would be good, so that's what I did. Laps around the pond and large field, grass wet and cold under my shoes, dogs trotting a polite escort beside me like they were on patrol. Moving helped. Not much, but enough to keep my chest from locking.

By late afternoon the light went to that strange gray that comes before a winter sunset, and my hope of a reply thinned out with the day. I didn't know why I had expected him to answer quickly. I didn't know why I still wanted him to.

My phone buzzed just as the horizon picked up a thread of pink. One line lit the screen.

"Sorry, been super busy today. I'll call you tomorrow and we can talk about this."

Too busy? Doing what? Yesterday he said he had no plans. Heat climbed my neck and face. I set the phone face down and pressed my palms to the counter to steady myself. I did not want to spiral. I did not want to pretend I did not care. Both were true, and I had no idea what to do with that.

I loved him. I could not deny it. If it were up to me I would marry this man, name dogs, hang photos, learn how he takes his coffee without asking. I would have said yes to forever. But I do not live in that world. In my world I get invited to dim stores, asked to stand nearby while he runs errands, told it will make sense later, and sent home with a kiss I did not ask for. In my world I get half promises and the word busy.

There was nothing to do except wait for tomorrow. I washed my face hard and changed into leggings and went to the living room where my dad was reading. He looked up and studied my face like a doctor checking a pulse.

"You want to watch something dumb," he asked, "Or sit here and read next to me and pretend the dumbness is far away?"

"Sit here," I said, and I sank into the other end of the couch. He did not ask questions. He let the dog climb between us and rest her chin on my thigh. We stayed like that for a long time. I went to bed when my eyes began to blur, but I didn't sleep. I felt as if I was moving the ceiling around with my stare and waited for morning to prove it still knew how to arrive.

The next day was the same thick soup of time. I cleaned

the kitchen because it was something I could control. I folded laundry and tucked pairs of socks together like small reunions. I took a shower and braided my hair tight so it would not touch my face. I ate toast I did not taste. I set my phone on the table and refused to pick it up, and then I picked it up anyway because I am still a person who can be pulled by a small sound.

The sound came just after ten. His name lit up on my screen. I connected my headphones and answered.

"Hello?" I said. My voice sounded like I had been whispering secrets to myself all morning.

"Hey. Listen, I am super busy so we have to make this quick, but I figured I would call so we could get this out of the way." His voice was low and flat, like he was shielding it from people near him. I pictured him standing in a garage, or outside a door, or hiding in his car with the engine off.

"Oliver, I really do love you, but I have not loved where we are," I said. I wanted to begin in honesty so I could end in it.

"Whoa, Bri. Listen. We had a great time together, but as you have already said, we are done." He exhaled like it was a relief. "It did not work out and you need to take time to focus on yourself."

"Wait? When did I say all that?" My hand tightened around the phone.

"Bri, I do not know. I'm not some record keeper. I know you did though." His voice sharpened. "This is all just too much. You are way too much for me right now. I need to focus on my family and my classes and you are always trying to talk and hang out and I just can't do it anymore."

"Oh. I am too much?"

"Geez, Bri. Don't make me the bad guy here. You knew this was coming. Do not act naive."

"But Oliver, I—"

"Bri, listen. I think you need to go to therapy." He said it like he was offering directions to a store. "You are so anxious and worried and it is a lot. No one is going to be able to deal with all that until you deal with yourself first. I enjoyed spending time with you, but you have a lot to fix."

"I need therapy?" It came out flat, dry and cold as ice.

"Yes. Definitely. You went before, right? Just go back. I am trying to help you here. Please take my advice."

"Oh. Okay."

"Look, I have to go. Please don't get all bent out of shape or act hurt over this. We knew this is where we would end up from the start. I'm just being honest. It's not like I'm purposely trying to hurt you, so don't go throw me under the bus. Bye, Bri. I hope you figure all this out."

The line went dead. I sat in the quiet kitchen and stared at the bowl of oranges on the table like they could tell me what had just happened.

I am too much? I need therapy? He knew it would end here? I rolled each sentence around and none of them fit. Maybe he was in a horrible mood. Maybe I had been refusing to see what was there. The only solid fact was that the call did not stitch anything closed. It cut me in a new place.

I stood because sitting felt dangerous. I rinsed my cup and put it in the dishwasher. I wiped the counter even though it was clean. I opened the back door and waved my arm in signal for Briella to come walk with me. She wagged once, politely, like she knew this was not a joy walk but was willing to come anyway.

We walked the edge of the pasture. The winter air was sharp enough to make my eyes water, and I let the water stand in for tears. Frost clung to the grass in a thin white pelt. The sky was so pale it almost disappeared. At the pond a heron lifted out of the reeds and made a slow gray line across the water, legs trailing like a thought. I breathed until the pain in my chest eased from a crush to a pressure.

Back at the house Briella went to find a patch of sunlight on the rug. I went upstairs and pulled my notebook from the nightstand. The page where I had written *What I need* looked steady and simple. *See me on purpose. Make a plan. No secret errands. If you need to leave, say it before you kiss me. If you cannot do this, let me go.*

He had not done any of it. He had done the opposite. He had told me I was an assignment, not a person. He had handed me a prescription and hung up.

I turned the page and wrote myself a letter. Not to him. To me.

You are not too much. You are exactly as much as you are. You do not need to fold yourself into a smaller shape to fit inside someone else's schedule. You can love someone with your whole chest and still not be a place they can stay. That is not a failure. That is a fact. You are allowed to be sad. You are allowed to be angry. You are allowed to take care of yourself without asking permission.

I set the pen down and let the words rest. Then I did something that was both small and huge. I opened my phone, opened the thread, scrolled to the first bright hopeful lines we ever sent each other. I let them ache. I let them be what they were. Then I scrolled back to the bottom, tapped the little circle with an i, and turned off notifications. I did not block him. I did not delete him. I made a boring choice that was kind to myself.

Downstairs my mom was filling the sink with soapy water.

She looked up and paused, like she was measuring how fragile I was before she touched my day.

"Want to help me make soup," she asked. "We can chop things. Very therapeutic."

"Yes," I said, and I meant it. She handed me a cutting board and a knife and a pile of carrots and potatoes. We worked side by side, the steady rhythm of knife on wood marking time in a better way than my phone ever could. The kitchen fogged with warm smells. My shoulders lowered from my ears.

"What happened," she asked eventually, not prying, only opening a door.

"He called," I said. "He told me I am too much. He told me I need therapy. He told me we knew it would end like this."

She set her knife down and turned to face me fully. "Do you want to hear what I think, or do you want me to only listen."

"Both," I said. "Listen first."

So she did. I told her the whole thing, start to finish. I told her the parts I was embarrassed to admit. I told her about the hope I had carried like a candle cupped in my hands. I told her about the kiss in the store aisle and the way I felt stupid for wanting it and wanting more than it could ever be.

When I ran out of words she reached across and squeezed my wrist. "I am sorry he said those things," she said. "Sometimes people say the worst thing they can think of because it is easier than looking at themselves. If you ever want to talk to someone, a counselor, we can look. Not because you are too much. Because you are human, and humans sometimes need help sorting their hearts."

I nodded. The word help did not sting the way therapy had when he said it. It felt like a blanket instead of a label.

We finished the soup and ate at the counter with spoons and

soft bread. Cole came through and told a story about a video game as if nothing in the world could be wrong. The dog begged politely and then gave up. The afternoon slid by without drama.

Later I went to my room and put on music that did not hurt. I stretched the tight places in my back and legs until they let go. I pulled my hair into a bun and practiced tendus in socks on the wood floor, slow and clean, like I was teaching my body how to pay attention again. I counted in eights. I held balances until they trembled. I let the mirror be a mirror and not a judge.

When I sat down again the house had that blue evening glow that makes everything look gentler. I picked up my phone. No new messages. It did not feel like a verdict. It felt like quiet.

I opened my notebook and wrote one more sentence at the bottom of the page. *I do not want to be wanted like an afterthought. I want to be chosen on purpose.*

I underlined the last three words and closed the cover. Then I went downstairs to watch a movie with my family and eat popcorn from a big bowl and let the dog put her head on my knee. I was still sad. I was still bruised. I was also breathing, which felt like its own small victory. Tomorrow would come, the way it always does, and I would meet it without waiting for a phone to tell me who I am.

Chapter 26

Suddenly I was standing in the middle of my dorm room, watching the heavy beige door settle into its frame the same way it had on move-in day. Winter break was over. I was back at school, back on campus. Only this time everything felt different. I knew where I was and who I was here with. I was not scared anymore, but I was not excited either. As I had driven in earlier that day, the whole place looked pale to me, as if someone had turned the color down.

My mom knocked on the door. She had stayed to help me get settled. I had told her everything after the call with Oliver. She was gentle and practical, and I could still see in her eyes the thing she did not say out loud, the I told you so that belongs to mothers and meteorologists.

"Let's go grab lunch. I can tell we are both getting hangry," she said, looping her arm over my shoulders.

We drove in circles for half an hour and then chose a fast-food place we could have reached in five minutes. We ate mostly in silence while thoughts about the semester and Oliver tried to race each other in my head.

"You will get through it," she said.

"Huh," I answered, blinking at my half empty bowl.

"It will be all right. I know it's not easy or fun, but it's for the best. Everything happens for a reason." The classic lines. They are not untrue, just always early.

"Yeah, guess so," I muttered, scooping another forkful into my mouth.

"Hey, I have an idea," my mom said, standing up so fast her chair scraped.

"What is it?"

"Not telling you. Just follow me."

I followed her out to the car.

Before I knew it we were standing in a local pet store and staring at a wall of fish tanks. "A fish?" I said when we stopped.

"Yes. You are allowed to have a fish in your dorm. I remember reading it and thinking how strange it was, but I think it could be fun."

"Hmm. Okay."

"I know you are a little lonely and you miss the dogs at home. A fish could keep you company. It's something to care for."

"Wow. I'm pathetic," I said, cutting my eyes at her.

She picked up a bright blue and red beta and held the cup at eye level. "Hi, Bri. I am Mr. "Fishy and I want to come home with you and study with you and eat with you," she said in a fake deep voice, cheeks puffed, mouth poised like a fish.

"All right, all right." I could not help laughing. "He is really pretty. I guess this could be fun."

"Yay! A fish it is."

We spent too much money on that tiny fish. Tank, gravel, food, water conditioner, a filter, a silk plant, a small castle that looked like it belonged in a child's bathtub. Back at the dorm, I rinsed gravel in the bathroom sink until the water ran clear and poured it in, then arranged the decorations like a set designer. Night had fallen and the hallway had gone quiet.

"So does he have a name?" my mom asked.

"Winston."

"Winston?" She laughed. "What a proper name for such a little guy."

"He deserves it. It's from a show, but it also just fits."

"I like it. I'm sure you and Winston will have a great time. That being said, I have to get going if I want to make it home tonight. I love you, and you are going to be just fine."

"Okay. Thank you for helping and for everything. I will call you in the morning."

"I know you will. Take care of Winston." She hugged me tight. A few tears, not many. Then the door closed again and the room was mine.

I sat on the desk chair and watched Winston test all four corners of his tank. The little filter hummed. The small light made a pool of blue on my desk and threw a soft reflection on the wall.

My phone buzzed.

I figured it was my mom, a forgotten item or another goodbye.

It was not my mom.

Oliver.

My hands shook so hard I had to brace the phone with both palms to read it.

"I miss you."

I stared. He had told me I was too much. He had said we were done. Now this. The read receipt flipped on by accident. I didn't reply. I put the phone face down on the bed and stepped into the shower, hoping the water would rinse him out of my head. It didn't. Every tile was a question. Every drop of water was a memory. I got out, pulled on clean clothes, and stared at the phone again.

"I 'm sorry, Bri. I'm sure you don't want to hear from me, but I wanted to check on you."

Two minutes later: "This is stupid. Forget I said anything."

Two minutes after that: "I love you."

Then nothing.

He loved me? He missed me? My heart pounded so hard I could feel it in my teeth. I typed, fingers clumsy.

"Why?"

"I don't know. I tried to move on, but I couldn't. All I think about is you."

"You tried moving on?"

"Yes. I went on dating apps and on dates, but it didn't work. Please just give me another chance."

"It hasn't even been that long and you have already been on dates?"

"You said move on. I was listening to you."

"That was quick though."

"That isn't what this is about, Bri. I didn't text you to brag."

"Sure feels like it."

"Just stop and listen."

"Fine. What is it?"

"I love you. I messed up big time and I know that. I take the blame. I was being stupid and I'm sorry. I truly apologize. Please give me another chance."

"Listen, you know I love you too, but I don't know that I can. I already tried again once and it went so poorly. I felt weird and uncomfortable. I don't want that anymore."

"I will make it up. I promise."

"How? Costco this time?"

"No. Real dates. Nice dinners and walks like the beginning."

"Oliver, I just don't know."

"Oh come on, Bri. You know you want to."

"I don't know that. I know I'm hurt and tired and about to start classes. I know I feel alone and stressed and like I was pushed down and crushed until I was dust. So I don't know."

"Think about it then, and in the meantime I will prove it to you."

I didn't respond. I sat on the edge of the bed and listened to the tank hum. Winston drifted through the castle archway and flared his fins like silk. The tiny world I had made for him was clear and bright. My own felt foggy.

I'm tired of his games. I'm also a person who wants this to work. We are both back on campus, which should make things easier, but maybe it only makes them louder. I hate that I gave in to talking to him. I hate that my body answers before my brain can argue. It feels like standing on the shore and letting a tide pull at my ankles. The push and pull toward him is magnetic, even when it hurts.

I turned off the lamp and let the tank light glow. The room softened at the edges. Somewhere down the hall a door closed and footsteps faded. I wrapped a blanket around my shoulders and opened my notebook. On a clean page I wrote a line and left space under it.

If you want me, choose me in daylight.

I capped my pen and watched Winston test the surface of the water, curious, calm, moving because moving is what he knows how to do. I breathed in and out until my shoulders lowered. The phone stayed face down. The tank kept humming. I let the room be small and safe and mine.

Chapter 27

I woke to my alarm blaring at six o'clock Monday morning. It's the first day of the new semester. I was not ready. My schedule already looked like a mountain. Add my personal life to it and the whole thing felt like a slide covered in ice.

At least I had a goal. A real morning routine. That was why I was out of bed before the sun even made it above the horizon.

I pulled my yoga mat from under the bed and slipped into the bathroom with it tucked under my arm. Yes, I was doing yoga in the bathroom. Yes, it was a little gross. I clean it often and I refused to practice in the middle of the room while my roommate snored. This was the only door I could close.

I unrolled the mat, sat cross-legged, and queued up a ten-minute video. Breath in, breath out, slow neck circles, cat and cow, a shaky plank that made my arms wake up. By the end my mind felt calmer and my muscles were at least willing to negotiate with me.

Coffee next. I made it too sweet on purpose and sat at my desk while the steam fogged my glasses. I still had an hour before I needed to leave, so I opened my journal and emptied my head. A few lines about what I was afraid of. A quote I had saved about starting where your feet are. Three small intentions for the day. *Be kind. Be early. Keep breathing.*

When the mug was empty I pulled on my leotard and tights and slicked my hair into the tightest bun my hands could make. Layers over that, because the air outside was below freezing and the wind on campus does not care that you are a dancer. I packed lunch and snacks so I would not have to leave the warm studio once I got there.

Modern. Ballet. Pointe. Company. Ten to five in dance classes, with French in the morning and an education class in the evening. The line up of it looked impossible. The company class was new for me. That part I should have loved, since performing is the reason I can talk myself through the hard days. I love the stage lights and the feeling of a piece carried in my body. I do not love auditions. I do not love the way a room can turn into a mirror full of other people's thoughts, even if everyone is kind. I know I'm not a bad dancer. Auditions make me doubt what I already know though.

We started the day with quick versions of syllabi. Teachers cut their classes short to go over calendars and expectations. It was good to see everyone, but there was a small tug in the back of my mind that said something was off. Maybe it was me. Maybe it was the weather. Maybe it was the quiet that always comes before you do a thing you have been dreading.

By the time I moved from studio to studio, my body was already tired in the way a break makes you forget. Legs heavy, lungs loud, feet honest. The hours stretched and then snapped shut. Suddenly it was the part I had been bracing for all day.

Auditions.

We learned three combinations in an hour and then performed them in groups while the teachers watched. They would decide and email the cast lists later. I was already registered for company, so I knew I would land somewhere, but that didn't comfort me.

The first piece was a pointe ballet, a collage of classical themes. I felt like myself in it. Clear shapes, clean lines, music that let my breath arrange itself. The second was modern with a lot of floor work. Running, sliding, rolling, a spine like seaweed. Not my language yet, and I'm sure it showed. The third was a blend. Ballet flats, a ballet base with modern arms and small sections of weight and release. It sat in the middle of me. Not a no, not a yes, a maybe.

When we finished, I peeled off my shoes and stuffed them into my bag with that special audition shake still in my hands. I grabbed dinner on the way back to my dorm, ate fast, and showered even faster. Then I headed to my evening education class, where we did another round of syllabus and schedule and rules. The professor seemed kind, which helped. My wrist buzzed three times during the lecture. I snuck a look at my watch and could not tell what it was. After class I stepped into the cold and pulled out my phone.

The cast list. That was fast.

My fingers went clumsy. I opened the email. My name was in the third piece.

Not the pointe ballet. Not the floor-heavy modern. The blend. The one that had felt like a maybe.

I stood there on the sidewalk while the cold slid under my coat and read the names again. My stomach dipped. It was not my least favorite, but it was also not the one where I had felt that clean hit of yes. My brain did the thing it always does and ran ahead without me.

If my best audition did not get me in, then maybe my best is not good. Maybe I am not good enough. I scrolled to see who got the pointe piece and saw the same cluster of girls who always get the cleanest parts. They are good. They are also a clique. Both things can be true without effecting the other right? I told myself that and it still stung.

I walked back to my dorm as if the ground might move. Inside, I set my bag down, turned on Winston's tank light, and watched him flare his fins around the little castle. The room hummed. The window was a square of night.

I pulled my journal to the middle of the desk and wrote what was true without trying to dress it up. I'm disappointed. I'm also in a piece. I wanted the pointe ballet. I got the blend. The blend will make me stronger if I let it. The blend will ask me to stand in a place that is not comfortable and breathe anyway.

I wrote a list of what I could control.

I can show up to every rehearsal early. I can warm up before class and cool down after. I can keep my ankles honest. I can practice the modern arms in the mirror until they feel like they grew out of me. I can stop checking who is in which cast. I can remember that one email is not a verdict on my entire body of work.

My phone buzzed again. A group chat I barely read was already spinning about costumes and rehearsal blocks and who needed which shoes. I put the phone face down and took out my planner. I penciled in the rehearsal times and drew a small star next to the third piece. Not a gold star. Just a mark to say I saw it.

I stretched on the floor for ten minutes and felt the soreness settle in like weather. I drank water like it was medicine. For a second the old voice tried to start up again. Not good enough. Not invited. Not what you wanted. I sat up and looked at Winston. He made another slow circuit of his tank and paused to stare back at me like he had all the time in the world.

I stood and packed my bag for tomorrow. Pointe shoes and

flats. Extra socks. A granola bar. I laid out a fresh leotard and ran my hand over the fabric like a promise. Then I texted my mom a picture of Winston and the caption, "Say hi to your grandson." She sent back three heart emojis and, "You've got this." I believed her for a small second, which was enough.

I did not have to love the decision tonight. I only had to choose what I would do with it. I wrote one more sentence at the bottom of the page in my journal. *Show up anyway.* Then I closed the cover and sat in the chair by the window until my shoulders dropped and my breath felt like mine again.

Chapter 28

It was Saturday morning, and all I wanted was to go home. Instead I was in my dorm, waiting for a required dance rehearsal. The show was a few weeks away and we were officially behind on choreography. I sat in the quiet room with a cup of coffee cooling in my hands, watching the time and wishing one o'clock would hurry.

I was halfway through a sentence in my journal when my phone buzzed. I ignored it. It buzzed again. Then again. And again.

I gave up and reached for it.

Oliver.

Three missed calls and one short text blinking on the screen.

"I just need to talk. Please call me when you can."

I blew out a long breath and glanced at Winston. The little fish hovered near his castle and stared back, unbothered, a pearl of air slipping from his mouth and lifting to the surface. The ache that lives under my ribs returned, familiar and heavy, like a knot that never loosens.

This was exhausting.

I set the phone face down and tried to keep writing. My pen moved and my thoughts did not. I told myself to focus on the performance. I told myself I could wait.

I lasted five minutes. Then I picked up the phone, closed my eyes for a beat too long, and tapped the missed call.

It barely rang twice.

"I messed up."

His voice was thin and shaky. My chest tightened. I swallowed and waited.

"I thought I was choosing something that would make everything better. Choosing myself. Choosing you. But I do not think it was right."

I rubbed my forehead with the heel of my hand. The silence pressed close, like the room had taken a step toward me.

"My parents are furious. They are talking about kicking me out. I am screwed and I do not know what to do."

My mouth opened and nothing came out. I listened to him breathe, fast and uneven.

"Come on, Bri. Say something."

"What did you do?"

"I dropped out."

"You dropped out?" The words came out quiet and sharp. "Why?"

"I can't do it. I hate my major. I hate the people. I hate the whole idea of school."

"But it's college," I said. "No one loves everything about it."

"I thought you would understand. You always understood me."

A small, empty laugh escaped without my permission. It sounded like it belonged to someone else.

"Bri, please help me."

"Help you how? You already made the decision. I don't know what you expected from me."

"I know. I just thought maybe what we had could grow. I

would get a job and focus on that. You made me feel confident and now I've messed it all up. All the times I try to do something it ends up ruining everything."

"Oliver."

"No, you know it's true. I ruined what we had. I ruined my shot at a job. I ruined it with my family. I have really screwed myself."

I closed my eyes and let the heaviness sit on my shoulders. There was nothing I could say to stitch this together.

"I'm sorry," I whispered. "I'm not sure what to do. I'm sure you will figure it out."

"Bri, please?"

Another long stretch of air. He spoke first.

"I understand," he said softly. "I will start trying to figure something out."

The line clicked and went quiet.

I stared at Winston. Tiny bubbles rose and broke at the surface. My own breathing sounded loud in the small room. The call had ended worse than I expected. There was nothing left to do except keep my hands on my own life. I can't build a raft for someone who keeps jumping into storms.

And then, to my surprise, I felt almost nothing. No surge of guilt. No swell of sympathy. The blankness scared me. It also felt like relief.

Rehearsal was a lifeline. My body took over where my brain couldn't . I moved through phrases I knew by muscle and bone, the music washing like water over the thoughts that tried to pull me under. For a few hours I was only Bri the dancer. Not the girl caught in someone else's spiral.

Back in my room, the quiet met me at the door. My phone buzzed again.

Oliver.

I hesitated and swiped to answer.

"Can we talk? I just need to hear your voice. Maybe even see you in person."

I stood in the middle of the floor, phone pressed to my ear, staring at the scuffed linoleum. There was a time when this was all I wanted. His voice. His need. Proof that I mattered. Now it felt heavy, like a weight he wanted me to carry for him. It did not sound like he needed me. It sounded like he needed anyone.

"I don't know, Oliver."

My words settled between us.

"Okay. I get it," he said after a few seconds. His voice was soft and tired, like he had hoped for a different answer and knew he would not get it.

A small part of me cracked at the sound. The rest of me remembered the cost. I ended the call before he could speak again.

I set the phone on my desk, face down, and let my hand hover there. I didn't change my mind.

I peeled off my rehearsal clothes and walked into the bathroom. My muscles ached. My feet throbbed. My mind buzzed like a swarm. I turned the water too hot and stepped under it. The heat bit my skin and I let it. I rested my forehead against the cool tile and listened to the rush in the pipes, as if the water could carry everything away.

I pictured him sitting somewhere and waiting for me to appear. I pictured myself not going. Space is not unkindness. Space is oxygen. He needed it. So did I.

I thought I would feel guilty. I thought I would feel torn. Instead I felt lighter, and that terrified me more than anything else. I stayed until the water ran cold. Even then I stood a little longer, shivering, watching the last of it twist down the drain.

The dorm felt louder when I turned off the water. I dried off slowly and dressed like each small task was a thread holding me together. I didn't check my phone. I didn't need the confirmation of his name waiting there. I knew it would be.

I sat on the edge of the bed with my towel over my shoulders, hair dripping down my back. The heater hummed. The room smelled like steam and coffee that had gone stale. I used to crave his attention, to believe that someone needing me meant I was safe. Now I wasn't sure anyone ever had. A lump rose in my throat. I swallowed hard and blinked until my eyes cleared.

I wanted to feel nothing. Maybe that was the scariest part. Maybe it wasn't. Maybe nothing was the first quiet after a storm, the kind that lets you hear your own breath again.

I stood, crossed to Winston, and tapped the glass gently with one fingertip. He flicked his tail and turned, a flash of blue and red catching the light.

"I'm here," I said out loud to the room, and to myself. "I'm here."

Then I set an alarm for morning, braided my hair, packed snacks for the next day, and slid my journal onto the pillow. I didn't write a long entry. I wrote one line.

Protect your peace.

I left the book open so the ink could dry, turned off the lamp, and let the dark settle without asking it to fix anything.

Morning came clear and brittle. Sunlight found the crack in the blinds and drew a white stripe across the floor. I fed Winston a few pellets and watched him dart, small and certain, like this was the one part of the day that would go exactly as planned. I made tea and oatmeal and put on warm socks. My phone lay face down on the desk. I didn't flip it.

Lea texted first. She asked if I wanted to meet in Studio Three to run phrases before company. I said yes before I could invent a reason to stay inside my head. On the walk over the air stung my cheeks. The sky was so bright it made the buildings look flat and cut out. My breath rose and disappeared. It felt good to move.

In the studio the marley was cool under my flats. Lea and I ran the opening combination of our piece. The mix of ballet and modern had annoyed me at first, but today the seams felt softer. Plies held their ground while the torso asked to pour. We practiced the diagonal across the floor until our timing matched the piano cut in the track. Alexis and Zoe slipped in and stretched beside us. No one asked if I was okay. They said hello, then asked if I had tried the new coffee cart and whether I wanted to run the lift again. It was the kindness I needed.

Company started with notes. Our choreographer stood near the mirror with a notebook and a pencil that looked like it had been sharpened a thousand times. She talked about weight into the right heel and the breath before the turn, and how the last phrase needed less intention and more trust. When I danced, my body did not ask for permission. It knew where to go. I messed up counts twice and still kept breathing. I heard my name and a correction about my left arm. I fixed it and felt the phrase click like a key turning.

At the end of rehearsal she dismissed us early with a smile and told us to eat something green today and to drink water like we were plants. We laughed and promised to try. Lea looped her scarf and asked if I wanted to walk to the student union for cocoa. I almost said no. I said yes.

We sat by the big window that looks over the lawn and

watched people cross it like pieces on a game board. I told her a careful version of yesterday. Not all of it. Enough. She listened without making a face. When I finished she stirred the cocoa slowly and said, very simply, that she was proud of me for choosing myself. Then she told me a story about her own boundary, and how hard it was to hold, and how glad she was that she had. We made a pact to remind each other to eat dinner this week. It felt like a real plan.

Back in my room I watered the plant on my windowsill and straightened the stack of class readings. I put my pointe shoes on the heater vent to warm the glue and laughed at myself for how domestic it looked. Then I picked up my phone.

There were messages. Nothing dramatic. A missed call. A line that said he was around if I wanted to talk. A question mark. The urge to answer flickered and then steadied into something else. I opened a new message and wrote slowly.

I care about you and I hope you figure out what you need. I cannot be the person you lean on right now. I am focusing on school and my own health. Please do not contact me for a while. If there is an emergency, email me. Otherwise I need space.

I read it three times. I did not add a joke. I did not apologize for taking up room. I pressed send. Then I opened settings and turned on a focus mode that silenced his thread and moved it off my main screen. Small and boring. Kind to myself.

The afternoon slid by in ordinary ways. I did laundry and watched it turn in the dryer window like a soft cyclone. I highlighted a chapter for education and took notes in the margin where the author said learning happens in layers, not leaps. I stretched my calves against the door frame. I called my mom and told her I had eaten an apple and she cheered like I had won a prize.

At dusk I climbed the stairs of the parking deck and stood on the top level where the wind always feels a little stronger. Campus pulsed below, headlights tracing slow rivers between buildings. The sky was the color of steel and then, slowly, bruised purple. I breathed in until the air bit and let it out in a long line.

On the way back I stopped in the lobby and taped a small note to the bulletin board over the jumble of flyers. It said Free to a good home, one slightly used desk lamp, and my room number. Ten minutes later someone knocked and I gave it to a freshman who said she had been doing homework by the light of her phone. She thanked me like I had handed her the sun. I felt useful in exactly the way I had been wanting to feel, and it did not cost me anything I could not give.

In my room I fed Winston again and watched him flash like a secret. I turned on my string lights and sat on the floor with my journal. I wrote down the combinations from company so I could remember where my brain had let go and my body remembered. I made a list for tomorrow that was not just tasks but comforts. *Stretch after breakfast. Call Cole. Wear the softest sweater to lecture. Put peppermint balm in my bag. Take yourself for a walk if your heart starts to race.*

When I finally climbed into bed the room felt like it belonged to me again. The heater hummed. The hallway door clicked far away. Somewhere a siren wailed and then faded. I closed my eyes and let the nothing come, not as a void but as space. The kind you can breathe in. The kind that feels like choosing.

Chapter 29

I didn't have the energy to think about Oliver anymore, not after that last call. Ignoring him didn't mean I felt better. The silence left behind was heavy, like a weight sitting on my chest, squeezing the air out of my lungs. I wanted to push him out of my mind completely, but the memories crept in anyway, the sound of his voice, the way he looked at me before everything fell apart, the hollow space where I thought something real had been.

When nothing else made sense, there was dance. Not because it felt good, not lately, but because it was the only thing I knew how to do to cope. It was the one place that demanded all my attention and left no room for broken thoughts.

When the guest choreographer walked into the studio that morning, I let myself hope, just for a second, that this time it could be different.

She was a young modern dancer from New York, with wild curly hair thrown into a messy heap on top of her head, and an energy that filled the room the moment she stepped in. The fact that it was a modern class terrified me. Modern was so much more difficult than I thought it would be, and it typically made me feel awkward and out of place. That is, until she introduced herself.

"Good morning, dancers," she said with a warm smile. "I'm Malani. I'm so excited to start this class today. You'll have to bear with me, because I like my classes a little different than what you're used to, but you'll see hints of what you normally do in here."

And she was right.

We started the class by shaking out bad energy. At first, it felt stupid and awkward, but then I closed my eyes and let the music wash over me as I imagined all the tension and anger and sadness being physically shaken out of my body. It was freeing, even if just for a moment.

We moved on to running around the room, listening carefully to her commands. Sometimes we played games, sometimes we fell down, but there was an unexpected lightness to it all that slowly chipped away at the tightness inside me. It was no longer modern dance that made me uncomfortable, but this version of modern that opened me up to new ideas, one that invited me to let go of all judgment, of myself and others.

The disconnected feeling I had when I walked into the studio that morning seemed to drift away, replaced by a new energy growing inside me.

I quickly changed my mind about going straight home that day, deciding instead to stick around for the audition to be in Malani's piece. It would be hard work, but based on that one class alone, I not only wanted it, but needed it.

I walked into the studio with a few of the other freshman girls and started preparing for the audition. I had no idea what to expect, but I was thrilled, and better yet, Oliver hadn't crossed my mind once since Malani walked in.

There ended up being ten of us at the audition in total. I felt exposed, vulnerable even, but also like I was ready to pour all of myself into the dance.

I tried to keep from noticing how all the other girls laughed and complimented each other, how they seemed to fit so easily into this new group while I stood silently on the sidelines. I knew they had more experience with modern than I did, but I wanted this, I wanted it far more than I wanted to admit.

Even as I threw myself to the floor over and over, feeling a bruise already starting to rise on my hip as sweat dripped down my back, I wanted it with everything I had.

This had to mean something. I put all of my energy into it and prayed it counted for something. My ballet training had taken me far, but I believed that my interest and passion could take me the extra mile. Every time I hit the floor, every landing, every turn, I thought maybe Malani would see how much this mattered to me.

I left the audition exhausted but hopeful. I left everything out there, and Malani seemed pleased. Now came the waiting game, but my gut told me I was going to make it. There was no way I wouldn't.

Later that day, I sat at my desk, my fingers moving automatically as I refreshed my inbox over and over, like some kind of ritual that would change my fate.

Then I saw the subject line, *"Malani Guest Piece,"* and my heart caught in my throat. I stared at it, hoping that maybe if I didn't open it, the answer wouldn't be real.

But of course, it was.

I took a shaky breath and clicked the email open.

There it was, a list of names under the heading *"Cast Members."* Only eight names.

I scanned the list once, twice, three times.

My name wasn't there.

I squeezed my eyebrows together, feeling a tight lump grow in my throat. I wasn't in it? I scrolled back to the top, then all the way down to the bottom, searching desperately for any clue.

And then, at the very bottom of the list, after a long scroll of names that weren't mine, I saw it:

Brianna-Understudy.

I stared at the screen, tears spilling down my cheeks before I could stop them.

Understudy.

I read the word again, hoping it would sink in differently if I said it twice.

Understudy.

I told myself it wasn't nothing. I told myself I should be proud. After all, I was still going to get to work with Malani, just on the sidelines, while everyone else got the spotlight. There were only ten people; why not include us all? It was insulting to cut two and label them understudies. I was embarrassed and heartbroken all at once.

Sitting alone in my dorm, staring at my name at the very end of that list, all I felt was small.

I closed my laptop softly, like slamming it would make things worse.

Then I sat there, in the quiet.

Understudy. The word echoed endlessly in my head.

I called my mom, trying to hold myself together, but the moment I heard her calm voice, I broke. I poured out everything, my pain, my sorrow, my confusion, and she listened. She took in my hurt and tried to help me find the positives, even if I refused to see them at the time. Every part of me felt heavy.

And yet, I still showed up.

The days blurred together after that.

Studio, practice, bruises.

The music looped in my head, even when the speakers were silent.

I ran every part, not just mine, all of them.

My notebook was filled with pages and pages of other people's choreography.

I learned the steps for solos, the group transitions, and the lifts I'd never be part of.

I stayed late after everyone else left. My reflection in the studio mirror became my only company.

Every landing sent a fresh ache through my knees.

Every turn felt a little less sharp than the last.

But I kept going.

Because quitting would hurt worse.

Malani's voice echoed in my head like a second heartbeat.

"Push through," she said.

"Don't stop moving."

"Again."

She didn't watch me anymore, not like she did at the audition.

But I watched her, and I kept hoping.

I watched all the dancers grow closer on the weekends we were stuck in the studio. They joked and laughed during rehearsals. They had created bonds I could only admire from the sidelines. I wasn't sure if many of them even knew my name like I knew theirs.

I told myself that learning every part meant I mattered, that I was valuable. Maybe I was the only one trusted to learn all the parts, and that's why I was chosen as understudy.

No matter what, though, I felt like the one person Malani was embarrassed to put on stage, like the girl who didn't belong in the piece.

I put in more work than anyone else, because that's what was expected of me. That's what I had to do if I wanted to be seen as better, to maybe earn a spot in the future. Some nights, it felt like I was doing everyone else's work, carrying everyone else's steps.

I wanted to love the piece again. I wanted to feel the excitement, the motivation, the passion.

But right now, it just hurt.

One night, after a long practice alone, I looked at myself in the mirror, sweaty, exhausted, but still standing.

Maybe being unseen isn't failure. Maybe it's just the beginning.

Understudy was far from what I wanted, but it also meant I wasn't fully cut.

I wasn't sure how to feel pride, but I knew how to show up, and that was the one thing I had control over.

If I kept showing up and learning, maybe something would change, even if not anytime soon.

Chapter 30

The week after the list went up my life rearranged into a loop. Class, rehearsal, understudy notes, a quick dinner eaten on the floor, then back to the studio for a quiet hour with the mirrors. I started keeping a separate notebook just for Malani's piece. I drew tiny maps of the stage and marked where everyone entered, where the clump broke, which dancers crossed on count six. I wrote their names in pencil so I could erase and recast the pathways in my head. It felt like building a puzzle no one else realized I was solving.

The director emailed a rehearsal schedule that looked like a train timetable. I copied the call times into my planner and set alarms that hummed instead of blared. I showed up ten minutes early and stretched in the corner to stay out of the way. My shins turned into the colors of a storm as the floor work added up. I learned to tape my toes before modern the way I do for pointe even if it made me feel dumb. I bought a roll of kinesiology tape in a shade called blush and pretended it was an accessory.

The other dancers met for coffee before Saturday rehearsals. They posted photos with the same caption and tagged each other. When they laughed between sections, I smiled at the floor and worked on the transitions they got to practice full out. I noticed the tiny things. This one always trips on the marley seam and recovers like it was part of the phrase. That one forgets the level change before the canon and covers with a jump. The lift that scares me most works only when the base breathes out on the downbeat. I wrote all of that down like it mattered, then decided it did in attempt to make what I'm doing have some kind of meaning.

Malani surprised me sometimes. She would stop the run because a shoulder tightened at the wrong moment or because the energy dropped at a corner of the stage the audience never sees. She talked about weight traveling and how the body can decide to be a river or a brick. During one rehearsal she looked my way and said, to the room but also to me, that clarity is kinder than perfection. I felt the words land in my ribs and stay there.

On Tuesday I stayed after company and ran the opening phrase alone. The building had emptied down to the hum of the vending machine. I turned the music down and tried to listen to the floor. On my third run a girl I didn't know well poked her head in and asked if the studio was free. I said I was finishing and she hovered, then stepped inside.

"Can I ask you something," she said. "You looked like you understood the diagonal better than I do. What are you thinking about in the reach?"

I blinked. I told her I imagined the reach coming from my ribs and not my hand. I showed her how much space my elbow needed if I didn't want to get stuck. We did it together once. She tried the shift and smiled like something unlocked. She thanked me and left. I stood there with my heartbeat a drum in my ears and realized I had just taught someone the part I was not allowed to dance. It didn't sting the way I expected. It felt like proof I knew what I was doing.

Winston watched me when I got back that night. He hovered near the glass like he could read my face. I fed him a couple of pellets and he darted after them in little lightning bursts. I told him I had survived another Tuesday. He blew a bubble and I decided that counted as applause.

On Thursday, one of the dancers rolled her ankle in a petite allegro combination during ballet. She iced it and insisted she could still rehearse. By company she was pale and trying to act fine. The director made the call. Understudy in for the day. My stomach dropped and then steadied like a boat settling into water. I tied my hair tighter and warmed up my back with cat-cows while pretending my hands weren't shaking.

Jumping into a piece without ever fully running it is a strange animal. The room is bright and unforgiving. You feel the hallway traffic and the echo when a door opens. You have to find the invisible edges of a stage that is not there. Malani stood near the mirror with her pencil and gave counts. I moved when the person I was supposed to be moved. I kept the shape clean even when my lungs wanted to rush. On the first pass I missed the corner by half a foot and almost collided with the diagonal. On the second, I felt the diagonal in my peripheral vision like a school of fish and threaded through without touching anyone.

We ran the ending well. It is the part where the music drops and the bodies have to do the talking. I didn't think about who I was or was not. I thought about the weight traveling Malani talked about, how a body should be a river and not a brick. When the last chord cut, there was the tiny inhale right before the audience would take over, only there was no audience. Still, Malani wrote something in her notebook and flicked her eyes toward me for a second before speaking. "Good," she said to the room. "Groups three and five, mind your spacing on the exit. Understudy, keep the rib shift going during those counts."

I felt the word understudy tug at me and release. I put my hands on my knees and breathed. The next day, when the injured dancer returned with a tighter wrap and a stubborn smile, I told her where the seam was catching on the diagonal so she wouldn't trip. She nodded and squeezed my arm like we were on the same side.

The days kept stacking. I started to know which vending machine had decent granola bars and which drinking fountain was coldest. I learned the names of the janitors who taped new seams every morning and how they fold the tape on itself so it peels clean. I started saying hello to people I only recognized as shapes in choreography. Sometimes they said hello back with my name.

One afternoon Malani called a break and headed for the water cooler. I didn't move just yet. She looked at me over the rim of her bottle.

"Brianna," she said, the first time she used my name out loud in front of everyone. "You're learning all the tracks?"

"Yes ma'am, taking as many notes as I can to keep up with it all," I said. I tried to smile without looking like I needed anything.

She nodded. "That's what understudy means in my room," she said. "Not waiting. Preparing. Whoever goes on needs to know what the piece needs. That's a different kind of responsibility. Different muscle."

She didn't add anything along the lines of I chose you for that on purpose. She didn't have to. I heard it even if it was only in my head. I tucked the moment away where I keep corrections that actually help.

On Friday night I went to a small show on campus where the theater majors were doing scenes. Lea sat next to me and whispered the entire time in a way that somehow didn't annoy me. Afterward we walked back in the cold and I told her about the spacing run. She pumped her fist like we were at a sports game and told me I had to let that count for something. I wrote it down when I got home so I wouldn't decide later that it didn't.

After that day I found myself sleeping better. Not perfect but better nonetheless. I put my phone across the room so I had to stand up to turn off the alarm and by the time I got there I was already up. I did ten minutes of yoga every morning. I stopped checking my email while brushing my teeth because it made toothpaste taste like panic. These were embarrassingly small changes and yet they worked like wonders.

The first costume fitting happened on a Saturday morning. A rack rolled in with simple black, mesh tops and soft pants that would let the floor work do its thing. The costumer took measurements and pinned hems while people shuffled in and out of the makeshift curtained corner. When she got to me, she didn't ask if I was on stage or not. She measured me like I would be. She handed me an outfit that matched the others. I looked at myself in the mirror with the fabric skimming my knees and saw a person who could stand under lights and not disappear.

On Sunday, I stayed late to mark the transitions again. The building was emptying when Malani came back for her scarf. She saw me, took in the filled notebook on the floor, and leaned against the door frame.

"You work hard," she said. "That is not a compliment. That is a fact."

I laughed once because it sounded like her. "Thank you," I

said.

"Keep your curiosity," she added. "It shows and reads well for you."

When she left, I sat on the floor and let the words live in the room for a minute. Then I did the phrase one more time with the rib shift she had noticed because I wanted to feel seen by her.

I still craved more. I still wanted my name in the list without the extra word beside it. Some nights the longing made my skin itch. On those nights I wrote the feeling down and then wrote one counterweight next to it. *You are learning every part. You are useful. You are building a spine for the work.*

The email that week reminded us of tech week rules. Bring water. No scented products. No jewelry. No phones backstage. I copied it into my planner like a pledge. When I closed the book, I saw the scrap of paper I had taped to the inside cover at the start of the semester. The one that said *show up again tomorrow.* It made me smile because it was still true, and because I had.

Understudy didn't turn into a medal. It didn't hand me a spotlight. It did something quieter. It kept putting me in rooms where I had to pay attention. It made me stronger in strange places. It built a practice I could carry even when none of this looked the way I had imagined.

On a Wednesday after rehearsal I found a sticky note in my bag. It read *thank you for helping on the diagonal* with a lopsided heart and no name. I stuck it inside my notebook beside the map of the opening clump and let it be proof that I existed in this piece in more ways than one.

When I looked at myself in the mirror that night, sweaty, tired and still standing, I believed the thing I said in the empty studio a week ago. Maybe being unseen is not failure. Maybe it's the beginning. And maybe I was not as unseen as I thought.

Chapter 31

I did it. I applied to transfer.

After another grueling rehearsal, my feet blistered and aching inside shoes that had gone soft, I drifted toward the community room where a group of dancers were gathering. The meeting was supposed to be about the upcoming show, but the conversation slid away from choreography almost immediately. I hovered near the snack table and listened.

"Mrs. Dalton keeps granola bars in her desk for anyone who forgets lunch."

"The campus coffee shop writes affirmations on the lids on Fridays."

"The freshman dorm has a plant shelf where people swap cuttings. I killed three but it was still nice."

They laughed until their shoulders touched. Someone mimed the chaos of a pep rally. Someone else described a teacher who learned everybody's name on day one. Their stories were small and exact. No one bragged about triple pirouettes or complete 180 degree penchés. They talked about their classes and I felt a tug in my chest so sudden it startled me.

When they left, the room exhaled. I stood alone and realized how long it had been since I felt that kind of easy belonging, the kind that doesn't ask you to audition for it. I thought about home and the small-town streets where everyone knew your name, the way the grocery store clerk asked about your grandmother, the porch light that always burned after dark. Maybe going back, or finding a place like that, was not giving up on dance. Maybe it was choosing a life that made space for me.

That night I stayed after rehearsal and sat on the studio floor with my back against the mirror. Rosin dust floated in the air like the last flakes in a snow globe. Somewhere down the hall, a janitor's cart squeaked and a door clicked shut. My reflection looked back at me with tired eyes and a careful mouth. I counted the hours I had poured into this place and yet still felt very small in return. The decision rose like a tide I had tried to ignore.

I was going to apply to transfer.

I wanted to be closer to home, to my family and to the streets I know by name.

In the morning I called my mom. Dawn pushed a pale square of light across my floor and turned Winston's tank a watery gold. I wrapped my blanket around my shoulders and tried to keep my voice from shaking.

"You haven't even been there a full year," she said gently. "The deal was a year before any decisions."

"This isn't me leaving tomorrow," I said. "It's an experiment. I'm keeping options open. I probably won't even get in."

We both knew that was not true. The school near my hometown accepted most applicants who showed they could do the work. I hadn't settled on a major. They had dance and dance education, but it wasn't ballet based and the technical level was not near the level of Raylon. If I went, I would need a program that actually fit. Something they did well. Something that felt like a door opening instead of closing.

I remembered the dance education club meeting a few weeks back. It had been a checkbox on a list, but I left with a thought that would not leave me. The seniors talked about student teaching and lesson plans and the first time a child's eyes light up when a lesson clicks. I didn't fall in love with the idea of corralling kids through pliés they didn't want to do. I did, however, fall in love with the picture of a real classroom. Real books. Real projects. Real small humans who showed up because school is where their day takes place.

Maybe I didn't need to braid teaching into ballet. Maybe I could choose teaching on its own.

The school I was looking at was known for education. Their program won awards. Their professors published articles with titles about curiosity and care. The more I read, the more a path drew itself in front of me.

I opened my laptop and started the application. The form asked for dates and addresses and test scores. I filled the boxes one by one, each click like a tiny metronome. Then the personal statement box waited, a blank rectangle that seemed much bigger than the others.

I stared at the cursor until it felt like it was breathing at me. I thought of the boy in second grade who once whispered that reading felt like holding a heavy bucket, and how his teacher sat beside him and turned the bucket into a cup. I thought of my grandmother using a chalkboard like a magic trick and my aunt kneeling beside a desk to talk to a child at eye level. I thought of ballet and how it taught me to listen with my whole body, how to count without counting, how to read a room, how to offer corrections with kindness and take them without flinching.

I wrote about attention and care. I wrote that I wanted to help small people become brave readers and patient problem solvers. I wrote that dance had made me resilient and curious and that those are teacher muscles too. I wrote that I wanted to be the grown up who learns children's names on day one and keeps saying them.

I finished and read it out loud. My voice wobbled on the last line. I hit submit with hands that would not stop shaking.

Then I waited.

I didn't tell anyone except my mom. I moved through the days as if I had not pressed that button. Rehearsal. Class. The work kept me upright, but my mind wandered. I watched campus through windows and imagined belonging in smaller letters, in the way people looked up when you walked into a room, in the way a hallway could feel like a welcome.

I made a list in my journal to keep from spinning. Things to check if I am accepted. Credits that transfer. Program prerequisites. Options for a minor. Scholarships. Housing. Winston's travel plan. The list calmed me. It was a way to hold something that kept slipping.

Two days later, I went to the education building on our own campus just to sit in the lobby. I wanted to test the shape of the idea in my body. A student teacher crossed the tile with a stack of picture books and a tote bag that said Be Kind, Be Curious. A bulletin board held fliers for tutoring and reading buddies at a nearby elementary school. I scanned the QR code before I could talk myself out of it.

The sign-up form was simple. Name. Availability. Subjects. I chose early afternoons and checked the boxes for reading and math. When I walked out into the cold, I felt a thread of warmth move up my spine. It was small and stubborn, like a seed.

The tutoring coordinator emailed back the next morning. They needed volunteers right away. Could I come Thursday?

I could.

The school smelled like pencil shavings and hand soap. A mural of a giant octopus reading a book covered the library wall. The coordinator handed me a lanyard and led me to a small table in the corner. A girl with a purple headband and a tooth gap sat down across from me and introduced herself in a whisper.

"We are working on blends," she said, like it was a secret mission. "S and h."

"Sh," I said, and put my finger to my lips. She giggled. We read a book about a shy sheep. She ran her finger under the words and sometimes moved too fast and sometimes stopped to look at the pictures. When she got stuck, she looked up at me with big eyes, and I said, "We can work it out together," and we did. Thirty minutes went by like ten. When she closed the book, she looked taller.

On the walk back to campus, my face hurt from smiling in the cold. That thread of warmth had turned into a small flame.

I still went to rehearsal. I learned four understudy roles and wrote micro maps in the margins of my notebook. I stood on the sidelines and tracked the piece with my eyes, marking entrances and exits with my thumb on my palm. Some nights I stayed late and ran the transitions alone. The mirror became a friend again instead of a judge. When I caught my reflection laughing at a mistake, I realized something had shifted. I was still working hard, but I was no longer asking the room to tell me who I was.

The email arrived in the middle of a Tuesday night. I was in bed with my pink blanket bunched at my waist and the dorm finally quiet. Natalie was out with friends. I watched a video of my pointe variation and hummed along, the music a familiar path my brain could still walk. My phone buzzed.

Decision.

I opened it with the kind of caution you use to lift a hot pan. Confetti rained down the screen.

I was in.

I went very still. The room did not cheer. The ceiling did not change. I stared and felt a weight slide inside me like a book moving from one shelf to another.

What was I going to do?

In the days that followed, the world held its breath. I kept showing up. I ran phrases until my breath scratched my throat. I iced my feet and recited spelling words with the purple headband girl over Face-Time because her teacher asked if I could. I ate soup in the dining hall and watched light move across the floor and thought about a different campus where I could be seen before I proved anything.

I made another list in my journal. *Reasons to stay. Reasons to go.* I wrote them small and honest. *Stay, because I am stubborn. Because I worked for this. Because ballet has been my compass for years. Go, because I want to teach. Because I want to wake up curious. Because I want friends who know my middle name without a roster. Because I want to be a whole person who dances, not a dancer who is trying to be a whole person.*

I booked an appointment with my advisor. She wore bright earrings and had a calendar full of colored blocks. I told her about the acceptance and the tutoring and how my chest felt when the little girl read sheep without help.

"Do you want my practical advice," she asked, "or my person advice?"

"Both," I said.

"Practical. Ask for a preliminary credit evaluation. You don't want surprises in August. Ask about scholarships you may have missed. Get names. Get emails. Personally on the other hand, you are allowed to change your mind when you have new information about who you are."

I nodded and wrote it down like it was homework. She printed a sheet of transfer questions and circled the most important ones, then she hugged me at the door in a way that made me feel like I had grown an inch.

I told my dad on a walk that weekend after driving home. We crunched through frost along the pasture fence while the dogs zigzagged like elastic bands.

"Brave," he said, after I was done. "Also smart. You are both and should choose your next steps for yourself."

We didn't say much more. We didn't need to. He pointed out a hawk sitting heavy on a fence post, and we watched it open its wings and step into the air like the sky had always been waiting.

I waited one more week before I filled out the confirmation form. I wanted the decision to settle in me, not just on paper. I met the tutoring girl again. She read *Splash* without stopping and looked up like the sun had switched on. I walked back to campus and didn't feel like a ghost walking through someone else's life. I felt present. I felt awake.

The confirmation email arrived that night. I read every word three times. I set my laptop on my knees and walked myself through my reasons out loud. I want to teach little kids. I want a program that fits what I want to learn. I want to wake up excited, not exhausted. I want a hallway that feels like a welcome. I want to keep dancing because I love it, not because I have something to prove.

I clicked confirm.

My hands shook. Then they settled. I whispered into the

quiet room, "This is it. A new start." Winston floated near the blue plastic plant like he was listening. I told him he was coming with me, which made me laugh and then made me cry a little, which felt exactly right.

The weight in my chest didn't vanish. It rearranged itself. A fragile thread of hope stitched through the places that had felt scraped raw. I kept going to rehearsal because that's who I am and I wasn't going to give up just because I knew I was leaving. I marked one more exit and one more entrance. I learned a final understudy track because I still cared about the people who would stand in the light this semester. I walked across campus and noticed the trees had started to bud despite the cold.

I told the choreographer. I expected disappointment. She surprised me.

"Good," she said softly. "You look lighter just saying it. That is how you want to look when you walk into a classroom."

On a quiet afternoon I sat by the window and filled a page in my journal with the smallest reasons I was choosing this. A professor who remembers your pronouns. A campus that smells like cut grass in the spring. A school of education that sends students into real classrooms early. A town where the librarian learns your name by September. A fish tank on a dorm dresser that feels like a tiny lighthouse.

Sometimes I panicked. What if I miss this place the second I leave? What if I miss the ache in my knees and the way the studio smells after a long class? What if I am not good at being new. Then I remembered that I had already been new, and I had survived. I remembered the hawk stepping into the air.

I started a practical list on a sticky note and put it on my mirror. Request transcript. Email credit evaluator. Ask tutoring coordinator for a reference. Look up book lists for

Intro to Literacy. Call about housing. Buy a better planner. Buy band-aids for blisters anyway, because old habits die slowly.

The future stretched out in front of me, wide and unknown. It belonged to me. That was enough to keep me moving.

Chapter 32

It was Friday night, exactly two weeks until the show. The bruise on my hip still throbbed, every small shift sending a bright sting through my body. I sat on my bed with a bag of ice wrapped in a kitchen towel pressed to the spot and a lukewarm cup of coffee cooling on the nightstand. I watched the steam thin out and disappear. My feet, taped and tender, rested on a folded blanket that used to be pink and now looked the color of ballet dust.

The knock at the door sounded ordinary. I thought it was Natalie, probably forgetting her keys again. I pushed the ice aside and stood too fast. My sore foot snagged the blanket, the floor rose a little too quickly, and I caught myself with a graceless grunt that lit my hip on fire. I stood again, slower, and shuffled to the door.

I pulled it open and turned away at the same time, already reaching for the bed and the cold coffee and the small circle of things I could control.

It wasn't Natalie.

I stopped with my gaze on the dorm carpet, that institutional gray with darker gray flecks that tried to look like a design. My heart pinched in on itself.

"Bri," he said. Soft. Familiar. Dangerous.

My nails bit into my palms. For a breath I stood in the middle of the room, back still to him, unsure whether to turn and step past him and let the hallway swallow me or pull the door shut and lock it and pretend I was no one.

The silence between us stretched tight. We used to fit inside pauses like this. Now it felt like the kind of fragile that shatters if you breathe on it.

"Please come get coffee with me," he said. "We can go to that little shop I took you to. I will pay. We can talk, or I will talk and you just sip your coffee. Please?"

The words slid past my defenses. The memory of that shop pulled at me, the small round tables, the chalkboard menu, the barista who draws little hearts in the foam if you tip. I felt my chest cinch as if someone had tightened a strap. The sound of his laugh. The weight of his hand at the small of my back. The hollow click of the door the day he left.

Old wanting stirred. Not clean wanting. The kind that confuses being needed with being loved.

"I can't," I said. It came out steady, like a line I had practiced. It was for me, not for him.

"You can," he said. His eyes met mine and my ribs ached. Memory is a muscle and mine remembered him.

"You hurt me," I said. My voice snagged on the last word.

His mouth opened. No sound came out.

If I didn't shut the door now, the room would fill with all the ways we used to be, and I would let them talk me into forgetting. I reached for the edge of the door and closed it. The latch clicked with a finality that felt too loud in the small room.

I stood with my forehead against the wood until I heard his footsteps recede down the hall. They sounded slow and heavy, like he was carrying something he could not set down. I didn't move until the elevator dinged.

When I turned, the coffee was cold and my hip pulsed in time with the dull ache that had been living behind my sternum for months. I eased myself onto the bed and let the mattress take my weight.

I didn't have space for this. Not seven days before the show. Not with understudy written under my name in bold, black letters that had not faded no matter how I tried to rub them away in my mind. It was all too much. My body was tired. My heart was tired. My mind had been tired for so long I had forgotten what rested felt like.

I knew he would come back. Or maybe I only hoped that he would, because hope is a habit and mine dies slow. I had wanted to feel a spark at the door, the good kind that lights a room. All I felt was stale air, the sense of something left too long in a closed container.

I curled toward the wall. Winston drifted behind the dark green plastic plant in his tank, a small flame colored blur in the glow of the clip light. I watched his fins fan and settle. I listened to the heater hum. I let my breath count the seconds until the ache softened.

The weekend began to stretch in front of me, a slow blanket. Required rehearsals. Empty hours between them. The others would laugh and lean on each other and share snacks on the studio floor. I would rehearse alone in the gaps. I would mark counts under my breath and tape my toes and try not to think about what it would feel like to stand in light that did not belong to me.

By midnight the room caught that dorm quiet that is never complete. Someone in the hall laughed and then hushed. A door closed somewhere far down the corridor. The ice in my towel had turned to a small warm puddle. I tossed the towel into the sink and stared at my phone until the screen lit from my gaze alone.

I typed and erased. I told myself this was a mistake. I told myself it was closure. I told myself nothing and pressed send before I could watch my own hand and stop it.

"I don't have anything else to do. Want to meet for coffee tomorrow at 8?"

His answer came faster than I thought it would.

"Yeah. I will be there."

The next morning I was nothing but a ball of anxiety, switching between excitement and regret. I pulled on a sweatshirt and a pair of jeans that didn't press on the bruise and laced my sneakers with a double knot. Outside it was cold enough to bite. I walked with my hands in my pockets and my eyes on my breath. The coffee shop's windows were bright squares on the dark street. Inside, everything looked warmer and kinder than it really was.

He waited, leaning against a lamppost. Hands buried in jacket pockets. Shoulders hunched. A face that looked like my past and not my present.

"Thanks for coming," he said.

"I wasn't going to let you keep knocking forever," I said. "Natalie would have left a note on the door."

We went in. The bell chimed. The barista looked up and smiled because that's what baristas do. I ordered something with cream because black coffee would set my heart racing and I wanted it steady. He ordered black and pretended to like it. We found a corner table that wobbled until I folded a napkin under one leg.

For a long moment there was only cups and steam and the

soft clatter of other people's lives. He stirred his coffee even though there was nothing to stir. When he spoke, his voice sounded thin and raw.

"Bri, I'm sorry. I think we can fix this. I really do. I don't want to lose us."

The words found their old path through me. They didn't land the way they used to. I stared at the small comet of cream still spinning at the top of my cup.

"I don't hate you," I said. "But the spark is gone. The thing that made us us, it's not there for me now."

He flinched and then leaned in like the distance could be crossed by leaning. His next words came out heavy and harsh, "I am drowning. I fought with my mom last night about reapplying for college. She wants me to do something practical. I want to keep trying photography or just give it all up. I can't find a summer job. No one is calling me back. I am stuck. I need someone, Bri. I need you. If we could hold on to us, I could hold on to something."

His panic clanged across the table. It would've been so easy to reach for his hand and let that energy flow into me the way it always had. I held my cup with both hands and glued my fingers where they were.

"I'm barely holding myself together," I whispered. "I can't be your lifeline. I'm already bent under my own weight."

He swallowed. "Please don't walk away. We can lean on each other. We can figure it out. Push and pull. Give and take. I'm ready to fight for us. I know I messed up. I love you. I want to make this work. Stay with me a little longer. Please Bri?"

Tears touched the edges of my eyes. I blinked hard. "I stayed for a long time. I kept thinking we would turn a corner but we never did. I don't think we ever will."

He stared at a spot on the table, then looked up with a smile that was not a smile. "So what now?"

I set my cup down and watched a drop run down the side and make a small ring on the wood. "I'm leaving."

His mouth moved before sound came. "Oh. Why?"

"So many reasons," I said. "Mostly myself. I'm transferring."

He reached across as if the word itself might be pulled back. His hand found mine. It was warm and familiar. My fingers slipped away because they remembered, too.

"Bri, please? Don't do this. I'm working on reapplying and I'm going to get my life together."

"It's not all about you Oliver. Don't you get that?"

"I", he paused and looked up at me "I just thought maybe we could try again."

I stood because I couldn't say the same sentence sitting down. "Goodbye, Oliver."

I took a step. He stood and closed the distance and kissed me. It was soft and full of everything we had ever been. It was also empty of anything I could use.

No spark.

No flame.

Only the cold weight of goodbye settling in the space where love had been.

I stepped back. He searched my face for a sign that would let him rewrite the last six months. I didn't give him one.

Outside, the air cleaned my lungs and froze the remnants oi tears to my cheeks. I put my hands in my pockets and walked without looking back because looking back always invites a story to keep talking. My sneaker soles scuffed the sidewalk. The city hummed in that way it does on the weekend, full of other people's lives I will never know.

By the time I reached campus, the coffee had gone warm in my stomach and cold in my hands. My reflection in each window caught my face and handed it back to me, I couldn't look away. When I finally made it back to my room it was cold and dark. It smelled like laundry soap and the faint metallic tang of the fish tank. Winston ghosted from one side of his little world to the other and hovered near the glass like he recognized my shape.

I wrote one line on a sticky note and pressed it to the frame of the mirror where I would have to see it.

Choose the life that makes space for you.

Then I did small things. I emptied my bag and tucked extra Band-Aids into the pockets. I checked the rehearsal schedule and set two alarms because I know myself. I put my acceptance email at the top of my inbox and star-marked the credit evaluation questions. I muted Oliver's thread. Not blocked. Not erased. But silenced.

I texted my mom one sentence.

"Met him and said goodbye. I'm okay."

The heater clicked. The room settled. I lay back on the bed and stared at the ceiling and let my breathing find a rhythm that belonged to me.

Morning came with a pale light and the taste of resolution. My hip still hurt. My feet still ached. The bruise bloomed in that ugly yellow at the edges that means it will fade soon. I slipped a sweatshirt over my leotard and headed to the studio early, long before rehearsal time, because the quiet there soothed me. The building smelled like marley and dust and lemon cleaner. I set my bag down and stood at the barre that always feels like a hand on my spine.

I rolled through my feet and listened to the small clicks and pops that meant my body was waking up. I pushed into a gentle stretch and breathed past the first resistance. I marked the entrance I would not make on stage and the exit I would not take. I ran the counts anyway because being prepared is its own kind of dignity.

The others drifted in with coffee cups, sleepy jokes and the easy tangles of friendship. I smiled when I should and nodded when I meant it. I took my place at the edge and made myself a promise I could keep.

I will show up with my whole self for the things that deserve me. I will stop handing myself to people who only want something to hold on to.

They ran the piece. I wrote notes in the margin of my notebook with a stubby pencil.

"Push through", Malani said. "Don't stop moving! Again!" Her voice landed like a heartbeat. Mine kept time with it.

Between runs I leaned against the cool wall and pressed two fingers to the bruise on my hip, a careful touch that made me wince and then breathe easier. I thought of the coffee shop. I thought of the look in his eyes that used to unspool me. I thought of the way my hand had refused his on purpose.

On my way out I stopped at the bulletin board and read the flier for tutoring one more time, even though I already had a shift on Tuesday. Someone had added a bright sticky note that read, *Thank you volunteers*. The handwriting looked like a teacher's, round and certain. I pressed my finger to the paper like I wanted some of that certainty to rub off.

Back in my room I fed Winston two pellets and watched him dart to the surface and back down like a small comet. I put my phone on the desk and turned it face down without checking it.

I pulled out my journal and wrote what I wanted the week to

be.

Tape. Ice. Run till it's clean. Drink water. Sleep enough. Text the coordinator about Tuesday. Email the credit office. Pack a sweater. Choose the life that makes space for you.

I underlined the last sentence. Then I stood and stretched and felt the bruise complain and quiet.

The show would arrive whether I felt ready or not. The transfer would wait but not forever. The door had closed and it stayed closed. The future felt wide and unknown. It was mine. That alone warmed me more than any coffee could.

Chapter 33

A week and a half before the show, one of the dancers caught the floor wrong in a traveling fall and landed wrong on her wrist. The studio went silent except for the thud and the quick intake of breath that followed. She sat up slowly, eyes glazed, and the room shifted into that strange, careful mode that artists use when the work keeps moving even while your stomach drops. Someone fetched ice. Someone squeezed her hand until help arrived. The show would go on. It always does.

Malani gathered us and broke the fall into pieces. We practiced how to send weight into the palm instead of the wrist, how to spiral, how to aim the hip for the safe part of the marley. We took turns dropping and breathing and standing back up. The other understudy was all bright voice and fast yes, already sliding into the injured girl's line with a smile that flashed to everyone in the mirrors. I stood near the back with my notebook open and my mouth closed. I was still half convinced my name belonged in the shadows.

That lasted until the Monday before the show.

Five days until the performance. Two days until our first stage rehearsal. One of the dancers limped in wearing a medical boot, face paper white. "I tore a tendon", she said, trying not to cry.

Out.

Just like that, I was in.

I was going to be in the dance I had been learning from the back row for weeks. I had forty-eight hours of onstage rehearsal before the lights and the audience and the avalanche of sound. The truth hit hard, like a wave that knocks you down and still leaves you grinning when you stand.

We drove straight into long runs that blurred day into night. I doubled what I had been doing and then doubled it again. My quads burned on the third pass, my calves hummed on the fifth, my shins bloomed in green and yellow medals that I wore without apology. I reviewed counts while I brushed my teeth. I marked transitions on the way to ethics class. The music took up residence behind my ears and stayed there no matter what else I tried to think.

Malani thanked me for being ready. Her voice softened around the words, more human than usual, and for a second I felt the light angle toward me. All those hours in living rooms and quiet studios, drilling alone while no one watched, reached forward and pulled me to center.

I called home that night. My mom put me on speaker and my dad whooped and my brother asked which number I was in so he could film the right one. They reshuffled their entire weekend without a single complaint. I went to sleep with my phone face down and my heart beating like a metronome set a little fast.

Opening night arrived before I even knew it. There had been quick fittings and longer notes and a dozen reminders about spacing and spike marks. I spent hours practicing. Sometimes with the group and sometime on my own but I wasn't going to waste this opportunity.

Then suddenly I was in the dressing room with my hair pulled into tight Dutch braids that met in a ponytail down my spine. I had black pants, a mesh black top, and a plain sports bra. Nothing pink or glittering or swan-like. It was not ballet and that felt right. My bruises showed when I bent to warm up. For once they felt like part of the costume, medals I earned leading up to this moment.

I slid down the wall to the floor and pulled my toes toward my shins until my calves let go a little. The room buzzed with hairspray and low chatter. Bass thudded through the ceiling from the stage above, a slow heartbeat under everything. Maya, a freshman like me, sank into a side stretch at my shoulder and spoke to my reflection.

"I still don't get how you pulled this off," she said. "You had what, a week?"

Olivia rolled her ankles at the barre, ponytail sliding forward when she tipped. "I have been here since day one," she said with a small laugh. "I still miss the turn to the floor. That transition is brutal."

They smiled. Warm, and edged. It landed like both a compliment and a test. I felt their eyes on me and wondered if they saw me as an outsider who got lucky or a teammate who had earned a square of floor.

"I practiced every second I could," I said, keeping my voice even. "Usually it was after everyone left each day."

Maya rolled her eyes in a way that didn't feel mean. "Good for you," she said. "I would have cried in a bathroom."

Olivia folded in half and placed her palms on the floor, voice muffled by hair. "That last turn bites. If you wobble, don't freeze. Keep going."

Their words hovered somewhere between advice and warning, a reminder that this room is always both community and competition. It wasn't like my old studio where backstage was a whirlwind of inside jokes and shared bobby pins and someone always singing the wrong harmony. Here, the laughter was careful and the alliances sat under the surface. Here, kindness arrived with a guard.

I flexed my feet and felt every place the floor had kissed me too hard over the last week. I thought of the way Malani's voice had settled into me.

"Push through. Do not stop moving. Again." Those lines had become the drum I moved to. Every late night, every ache, every time I almost said it's not worth it and then kept going anyway, pointed to now.

The ceiling trembled with the last bass drop from the number before ours. Somewhere a headset crackled. A stagehand ran. I breathed in the smell of rosin, hair spray and old wood. Maya stood and stretched tall.

"Break a leg, Bri," she said. "You earned this."

Olivia's smile went all the way up this time. "You are going to crush it," she said.

I nodded and let the warmth of that sit where my nerves usually lived. The stage manager touched my shoulder.

Places.

The wings were dark and humming. The tape glowed under the sidelight. I pressed my barefoot into the marley and felt the slight grit catch my skin. The light opened in front of me and I stepped out.

Performing felt different than rehearsing. The piece woke up under the heat. The air had weight. The music crawled into my bones and shook them from the inside. The falls had intent now, not just mechanics. The reaches turned into sentences. I didn't think about who was watching or not watching. I didn't think about anyone I used to try to impress. I felt the other bodies near mine and trusted the hours we had stacked under this moment.

There was a moment near the end where the turn into the floor had always found me, the one Olivia warned about. My heel skated for a heartbeat and for once I didn't seize. I softened my knee, sent my weight forward, and the floor let me down easy. My palms found it. My breath landed where it should. I pushed up into the final shape with the rest and held still as the last note cut off.

Silence hit first. Then applause arrived like a wave that lifted the skin on my arms. It wasn't polite. It wasn't the kind that says we see you tried. It was full and loose, a sound that wrapped around my ribs and stayed there.

I walked into the wings, lungs burning, eyes stinging, not because anything broke, but because of the exact opposite. There was no Oliver in the corner, no sudden circle of new best friends. There was Maya bumping my shoulder, Olivia grinning in a way that made me like her more, the crew moving set pieces with quiet skill, and somewhere out there was a row where my family sat, probably blurry with tears on a phone screen none of them could hold steady.

This moment was mine. The long nights, the no's, the understudy lines on cast lists, the weekends everyone else used to rest, the mornings I came early and left late with no one to notice, all of it carried me to this square of floor.

I thought of the little girl who used to dance in the bedroom mirror and whisper counts like prayers. I thought of the first time I learned to fall and hated it, and the first time I did a landing correctly. I thought of the transfer email waiting in my inbox, a door I would walk through soon enough.

I didn't walk off as the understudy. I walked off as the dancer I had been building the whole time.

After bows, I slipped into the quiet hallway for a minute and leaned my head against the cool cinder block wall. My phone buzzed. A message from my mom: *We are so proud.* A second from my dad: *You flew!* A video from my brother that was mostly ceiling and cheering. I laughed out loud, alone, and it felt like relief.

Back in the dressing room I peeled off the sheer top and checked the bruise on my hip. It was ugly and honest. I packed my bag slowly, the way you do when you do not want to jar a good thing. Malani walked by and paused.

"Thank you for staying ready," she said. "That was clean."

"Thank you for trusting me," I said, and meant it.

On the sidewalk outside the theater the spring night had a thin chill to it. I pulled my coat close and looked up at the dark sky. Campus glowed in puddles of light. People laughed a street away, their footsteps quick and careless. I took one long breath and let it out.

Whatever comes next, I thought, I can meet it. I had wanted this stage and then I had it, not because someone handed it to me, but because I kept showing up when it didn't even make sense. When the door finally opened, I was already standing beside it.

I started walking toward my dorm room, shoes thumping softly in my bag, hair tight on my scalp, legs warm and tired. Each step felt steady. Each step felt mine.

Chapter 34

The roar of the applause still hummed in my ears hours later, not fading but circling, steady as a second heartbeat that refused to settle. For a breath I could not tell whether the crowd had really clapped that hard, or whether disbelief was replaying it louder in my mind. I had stood on stages before, recitals, endless rehearsals, but never like this. Never with the lights so hot they painted halos across my skin. Never with the silence before the first note so sharp it felt like my breath alone might shatter it.

I remembered the tremble in my legs as I walked into the opening formation, the certainty that the front row would see the shake in my hands and recognize me for what I feared I was, a girl pretending to belong. Then the music rose and my body stopped asking permission. It moved without hesitation, like it had been waiting all year to be trusted.

Images flickered through me in still photographs. The tight turn I had once rolled my ankle on, placed cleanly tonight. The leap that took hundreds of tries and bruises to make look easy. The breathless, suspended instant when the entire theater seemed to hold me in its gaze. In those frames I was not rehearsing anymore. I was not the understudy. I was not Bri the transfer who did not fit. I was a dancer, and for a handful of minutes I owned the air between the notes and left the audience no choice but to watch.

Backstage didn't match the ones I grew up in. My old studio had been cheerful chaos, someone tugging a costume into place, someone braiding hair on the floor, laughter spilling through the curtains until the director shushed us with a smile. A family stitched from sweaty bobby pins and shared snacks. Tonight was quiet and precise. Dancers warmed up in their own corners, polite smiles that dissolved before they could turn into something real. Respect, yes. Belonging, not really.

The thought stung, and still it thinned under the weight of what I had just done. I had survived every bruise, every lonely weekend, every night I cried into a flat dorm pillow when the ache of not fitting in felt too big. I had walked through a small fire and made it to the other side, scarred in places, stronger in others.

Malani's nod flashed in my mind. A small nod, quick and almost hidden. I knew her standards, sharpened by years in rooms that did not forgive laziness. Her approval lived in details. If she nodded at me, I had earned it. If she nodded at me, I had not been invisible.

That glow couldn't rewrite the year. It couldn't refill the quiet of my dorm. It couldn't erase how classes sometimes made me feel small. It couldn't blot out the shadow Oliver left behind.

My heart tripped a beat after that thought.

He was not in the crowd.

I had told myself I wasn't looking for him. I had told myself my eyes hadn't skimmed the rows as the lights dimmed. Then I stepped into the wings after the bow and felt the cooling air, and I knew I had searched for him without meaning to. I had been waiting for the promise he always made, to show up and call it love.

The emptiness where his face would've been ached harder than I expected. It felt ridiculous that after weeks of dragging myself through rehearsals alone I still wanted him to materialize at the end and make it easy. That was the way I had carried him, a safety net that frayed and still begged to hold me.

I thought back to the night he admitted his mother didn't believe in his path, to the way his voice thinned with shame. I had carried his fear in my hands and called it proof that I mattered. For so long being needed felt like being loved.

Tonight pressed a steadier truth against me. He was not there for the late night tears or the weekends when the quiet swallowed me or the bruises on my knees or the morning I almost quit. He was not here for the night I finally became the thing I said I could be.

Anger rose first. Then relief arrived behind it, low and solid. Relief that I had not tied this moment to him. Relief that my joy hadn't asked his face for permission. If he had been there, I know myself. I would've chased his reaction, measured my worth against his smile. Tonight I didn't need that. I felt enough in my own bones.

Maybe growth is not the absence of missing someone. Maybe it's the quiet recognition that you don't need them to stand up. That ache was not longing. It was a new kind of strength.

Oliver had been an anchor. Tonight I realized I don't want anchors. Anchors keep you still. I want to drift forward, even if the water is unfamiliar.

The thought of leaving rang louder now that the curtain was down. The forms were signed, the emails sent, the choice made. In the shine of my best night, leaving felt like betrayal. Like walking away from the thing I had chased since I could lace shoes.

The truth was messy. Leaving looked like defeat if I only counted the achievements. It felt like truth if I counted the living. This place built me and broke me. I didn't recognize parts of myself that survived here.

I remembered my first studio again. How joy came first, then discipline. Somewhere between then and now joy thinned into something sharp. I chased an idea that didn't belong to me anymore.

I also could not pretend this place had given me nothing good. It gave me discipline I can feel in my posture. It gave me strength I can measure by the way I land. It gave me proof that I can endure inside rooms that do not welcome me. I do not hate the way the year made me tough. I hate the toll and still respect the shape.

So leaving is both defeat and victory. It is grief for the friendships I did not make and the belonging I did not find and the spotlights that missed me. It is freedom to choose a place that wants the whole of me, not only my turnout and my pain tolerance.

Maybe dance is not forever. The thought pulled a thread that runs through everything I am. Who am I if not the girl who tries again. Maybe endings are not failures. Maybe they are invitations.

The transfer is not running away. It is rewriting. It is choosing a campus where I can breathe and speak at the same time, a department known for teaching that will let me build a classroom where kids feel brave and bright. It is trading one stage for another.

I told myself that as I peeled off the costume and scrubbed the last of the eyeliner away. I told myself that as I packed the sheer top like a relic and tucked my bruised hip under the towel on the bench. In the hallway a cluster of parents moved toward the lobby bouquet table, the air full of flowers and cologne and pride. I stepped out into that current and found my family in the middle of it. My mom's eyes shone. My dad lifted his phone and missed the first second of the hug. My brother handed me a cheap grocery store bouquet and apologized for the drooping snapdragon. I loved it more than the perfect ones.

"We heard you," my mom said into my hair. "Even when we could not see, we heard you."

I laughed, the kind of laugh that shakes something loose. We took a photo against the poster and it came out crooked and I did not care. We went to the diner on the corner and split milkshakes and fries because that is what we always do after big things. They made fun of the way I tried to sit without moving my hips. We talked about nothing and anything. The night felt lighter when we said goodbye in the parking lot.

Back in the dorm I set the flowers by Winston's tank. He swam close and stared like he always does, curious and unhelpful. I set my shoes on the windowsill, soft slippers with the sweat of the night still in them. I let the room be quiet, then let the quiet belong to me.

I texted Malani a thank you because I wanted her to hear it. She sent back three words that meant more than I admitted. You stayed ready.

I slid my notebook from under the pillow. On one page a list of corrections leaned into the margin. On another page a small declaration waited where I had written it weeks ago. I get to decide. I ran a finger over those words and felt their edges rise under my skin.

Sleep did not come quickly. I replayed the turn, the fall, the breath before the bow. I also replayed a hundred small ordinary things that will make up whatever comes next. Morning coffee in a different dining hall. A classroom with miniature chairs and bright name tags. Shoes that squeak on tile instead of Marley. A calendar with different circles on it. I thought about the first day at a new place where no one knows what you were before. I let fear show up. I let hope sit beside it.

When the sky went pale I laced up for a slow walk around campus. The theater doors were locked and still, the posters taped neatly behind the glass. I put my palm to the cool panel and said goodbye without saying the word. On the way back I took the long path past the studio. I watched a janitor mop under the exit sign and for once felt no tug to go inside.

That afternoon I wrote a note and taped it inside my understudy notebook. For whoever needs it next, the shortcuts that saved my knees, the count I kept with my breath, the way to land without fear. I left it on the piano in Studio C. I liked the thought that someone would find it and feel less alone.

Later, once the laundry spun and the flowers slumped their heads, I opened my email and sent the last confirmation for the transfer. My hands shook and then steadied. It felt like jumping from a place that had finally learned my name. It also felt like the only honest move left.

By evening my body hurt in a good way. The kind of hurt that says you asked for everything and gave it. I sat by the window and watched the campus fade to lamps and shadows. People passed in groups, laughing in little bursts. Somewhere music thumped through a wall. Somewhere a door shut and opened again. I felt the applause hum in me one more time, softer now, not a roar but a purr.

I do not know if I will dance on a stage again. I do know I

can. I do know I did. That night belongs to me, not as proof for anyone else, but as a light I can carry into rooms that do not yet know who I am. Dance has been beautiful. Dance has been brutal. Both can be true. Both can also be enough.

I tucked the memory of the stage into the place where I keep the steadier things. I let the rest of the evening be simple. I fed Winston. I answered a text from my mom with a photo of the crooked bouquet. I set an alarm for the morning. I turned off the lamp and lay on my back and felt my heartbeat slow.

This was the end of one version of me. It was also the beginning of another. I was not leaving empty. I was leaving with muscle and ink and a yes that I gave myself. The future was wide and unmarked and mine. That was enough to fall asleep to.

Chapter 35

It was the last week of classes, and I stood at the front of the room about to perform my pointe final for everyone. My palms were damp. I pressed them flat against the stiff skirt of my tutu and lifted my chin. I took a long breath and nodded to the pianist. Mira's fingers hovered for a beat over the keys, then the first soft notes slipped into the air like a secret I already knew.

This was not my first solo in front of classmates. It would however, be my last. That fact settled into my bones as I settled into my starting position, heel forward, ribs quiet, eyes soft. After this week, everything I had built here would fold itself into a memory and tuck away. I felt the thought land and then I let it go so the music could have me.

That morning we had sat in a wide circle on the marley for our final modern class. One by one people shared summer plans. Intensives, gigs, teaching jobs, a month with grandparents at the coast, a road trip with two friends and a dog. I picked at a frayed thread on my tights and waited for my turn. When it came I rested my hands on my knees and went for steady. My breath still caught.

"I will not be coming back next year."

The room went quiet in a way that made the air different. A few girls blinked, eyes quick toward each other as if to check that they heard correctly.

"Oh," my teacher said gently. "May I ask why?"

The true answers crowded my throat. I don't fit. The competition wore me thin. I have spent a year feeling invisible and louder inside than anyone knew. I swallowed them and offered the answer I had rehearsed.

"Personal reasons. I want to be closer to home. I'm changing my major. I hope to keep dancing at my new school though, just more on the side."

He nodded slowly. His face gave nothing away. The silence stretched a little longer. Heat climbed up my neck. One tear made its own path and I let it, then wiped it away and looked down at my hands. It was bittersweet, heavier than I wanted, and still there was no turning back.

Hours later I was here again, center floor, with the whole class waiting. Maya stood near the front with my phone to record me. Our teacher perched on her stool, head tilted in that small angle that meant she was measuring everything.

The floor creaked as I stepped with the music. The variation lived in my muscles from weeks of practice, which meant I could have danced it on autopilot. I chose not to. I let the thought in that this might be the last classical variation I ever perform. I let in the memory of all the days I had hated this place and the truth that I had grown anyway. Then I decided to make it count.

Every breath had a job. Every arm was an argument for softness and control. My legs reached higher and stayed there. I felt the square of my hips when I needed it and forgot them when the music asked me to forget. A turn that had thrown me all semester landed without a wobble. I heard the quick snap of fingers from the corner, small and real. I let a smile lift the corner of my mouth and kept going. A year ago I couldn't have danced like this. The year had been hard and it hadn't been wasted. My body understood more. My mind had learned the specific skill of moving forward when quitting seemed like the only step.

The final phrase arrived. I felt the last note ring inside my ribs. I sank to one knee and stayed, chest rising and falling, letting the echo dissolve into the quiet. No one moved for a heartbeat. Then the room lifted into applause.

It had been clean and brave. It had been mine.

I stood and curtsied. My eyes found my teacher's. She smiled, small and steady, and gave one nod. I had been chasing that exact nod all year. It landed and I let it soak in.

Just like that it was over. My last final. My last class here.

There would be packing and check out lists and the final sweep of a half empty dorm room. None of it could touch this moment. I was not leaving with only disappointment. I was leaving with a win I had earned.

This was my closing bow.

I crossed to the corner and slid my shoes into my bag with careful hands. I tucked the ribbons in like they could break. The chatter behind me swelled, names and plans and jokes that did not ask for me. For once the sound did not sting. It washed past like a tide I had already stepped out of. I felt finished.

I walked the room slowly. I ran my fingers along the mirror where my breath had fogged shapes on long nights. I touched the barre where my forearms had ached and my calves had caught fire. Every square of this floor held a story. Some I wanted to keep. Some I was glad to leave.

At the door I paused with my hand on the handle. I let myself really see it. Marley with its scuffs and tape lines. The rosin dust along the edges. The stool where my teacher sat. The little chunk of paint missing from the door frame where someone once rolled a piano too hard and everyone laughed. The applause still hummed faintly in my ears and, for the first time this year, I believed it belonged to me. I had ended well.

I opened the door and stepped into the hallway. The heavy wood shut softly and made a seal. My time here had a boundary now. The corridor stretched long and bright, a runner of pale light under my shoes. I walked and each step felt lighter.

Halfway down the hall I heard quick steps behind me. "Bri." Maya held out my phone. "I sent you the video. You should watch it. It's really good."

"Thank you," I said. She hesitated like she might say more, then she smiled and jogged back inside. It was a small kindness but it's weight was much heavier.

At my locker I peeled off the tutu and slid into sweats. I loosened my bun and shook the pins into my palm. The smell of hairspray and warm skin sat low in the room. Another freshman asked me quietly where she could find stronger ribbon thread and I told her which shelf to check in Studio B. I wrote the exact brand on a sticky note and stuck it to the corner of her mirror. She looked surprised and thankful. I recognized the expression. I had worn it all year.

Outside, late light fell across the path like thin gold cloth. I texted my mom a photo of my pink shoes on the bench and three words. *It went well.* She sent back a row of heart emojis and a promise of dinner when I got home. My phone buzzed again. A message from Malani. *I heard you finished strong. Proud of you.* I didn't expect tears, but they came anyway, a quick sting then gone.

I took the long way back to the dorm. The theater posters

curled at the edges behind glass. The practice rooms lined up like little square secrets, each with a piano and a lamp. I peered into one and watched the empty air. For once I felt no pull to go inside. I had already said what I needed to say.

In my room I set my bag by the desk and fed Winston. He flicked his fins and stared, patient and nosey as always. I took my shoes back out and set them on the window sill to dry. The satin was scuffed to a soft gray. I smoothed the ribbons and let the light catch the frayed edges. It was strange and right to see them like that.

I opened my notebook and wrote a date at the top of a clean page. Under it I wrote three lines.

I learned to stay ready. I learned to end well. I get to choose what comes next.

I closed the cover and slid it into my backpack. Then I put on a hoodie and walked to the dining hall for a bowl of soup and bread I didn't have to think about. I ate at a small table and watched people drift in and out. I didn't search the room for a face that wouldn't appear. The quiet felt like mine.

Back in the dorm I started a load of laundry and took the trash out. I pulled the posters off my walls and folded the corners that had curled. I took one last photo of the room that had held me without holding me. When the dryer was done, I stacked warm clothes in a neat pile on the bed and sat beside them with my phone.

I watched the video Maya had sent me from start to end. Then watched it two more times. There were minor parts I would change but major parts I was impressed by. At times I forgot that it was me in the video and just stared in awe at the ballerina on my screen.

The sky went dark and then purple. Somewhere down the

hall a door shut and someone laughed. I set my alarm. I turned off the lamp. I lay on my back and felt my heartbeat slow, steady and tired in the best way.

I didn't know what my dancing life would look like at the new school. I didn't know what my days would feel like as I changed my major and stepped into classrooms that belonged to a different version of me. I did know this, I had finished what I started here. I had given myself a better ending than the year seemed ready to hand me.

Tomorrow there would be boxes. There would be people dragging plastic bins and hugging in clusters. There would be one last walk past the studio. There would be a drive home with the windows cracked and a list of things to do taped to the dashboard. I felt the weight of it but the lightness too.

I closed my eyes with the applause still somewhere inside me, softer now, less a roar and more a purr. It was enough.

Chapter 36

The next morning my dorm room was quiet, sunlight stretched across the wooden floor in golden stripes. The air felt heavy, as if the silence itself had been waiting for me to start the day. I thought about the way our teacher had clapped once, softly, and dismissed us with a smile that did not quite reach her eyes yesterday. A few girls had lingered to hug one another, promising to meet up over the summer, already talking about fall rehearsals. I stayed back, rolling my pointe shoes in my hands, waiting until the chatter thinned and the door sighed shut.

I thought about the way Maya squeezed my arm and whispered, "I will miss you," while most of the others looked at the floor and smoothed the wrinkles in their warm ups rather than say goodbye. I didn't blame them. I had been more of a shadow than a friend here, and sometimes I questioned if all of them even knew my name by this point. A shadow can share a room and still stay unseen.

I slid to the edge of the bed and pulled my suitcase over. The zipper rasped as I opened it, too loud for the stillness of the room. I started folding leotards into neat stacks, tucking tights between them. A safety pin clinked against the frame. A ribbon trailed across my thigh like a loose thought. Each piece of fabric held a memory, some I wanted to keep, some I wanted to forget. The lavender bag of rosin left a faint dust on my palm. Sweat, perfume and hairspray, the year had a smell and it rose up around me while I packed.

As I shoved loose papers into a pile from my desk drawer, a folded scrap slipped free and fluttered to the floor. I bent down and recognized Oliver's handwriting immediately, the messy scrawl I knew by heart. My stomach dropped. My hands turned clammy. I thought I had thrown this away. I thought I had erased everything he had touched. Yet here it was, staring up at me from the floor.

You've got this. You are stronger than you think. I will be in the crowd cheering for you.

My chest tightened. I remembered that day, the way he grinned sheepishly when I found the note, the way I folded it and kept it like proof. I carried it like a promise, convinced it meant he would always show up. But he hadn't. Not then, not tonight, not for so many nights when I needed him most.

It had been foolish to even hope he would come tonight. Yet part of me admitted the truth I hated to face. If he walked through the door right now, I might have let him back in. The thought ached in my chest and left me guilty. I imagined how easy it would have been to hug him, to feel his arms around me and pretend that everything could be tied neatly into a red bow. I imagined the relief of postponing the work of leaving, the soft lie that love could be simple if we wanted it badly enough.

I sat with the note for a long moment, smoothing the crease with my thumb until the paper grew soft, before I slipped it back into the drawer. Not to keep, but to leave behind. I didn't need promises that had already been broken. The drawer shut with a small wooden click. It felt like setting down a glass I had been clutching for too long.

Still, the memories rose up around me. The first time he walked me home after rehearsal, carrying my bag even though I insisted I could manage. The late night conversations where his voice cracked as he confessed how lost he felt, how small under the weight of his mother's disapproval. The dinner he set up for my birthday, a whole night spent convincing me I mattered. There had been sweetness in it. There had been care. None of that was a lie, but it also was not enough to keep me afloat.

The sweetness had been tangled with silences, absences, and hollow spaces where I reached for him but found nothing. What I clung to with Oliver hadn't been love. It was loneliness disguised as love, a desperate need to feel wanted, to prove I mattered by keeping someone else from falling apart. I thought that if he couldn't live without me, then I had worth. But love shouldn't feel like drowning so someone else can breathe. Love should be two people treading water together and still seeing the shore.

Why had someone like that held so much power over my life, and why had I never been able to take it back? I knew we were wrong, and still I wanted it anyway. Even now, I found myself scanning sidewalks and cafeterias, my pulse quickening at the sight of dark curls or the slouch of familiar shoulders, only to realize it was never him. The hope flickered anyway, sharp and uninvited, like a porch light that forgets to shut off.

Why could I not just let him go? The boy I dated before college slipped out of my life like water through my hands. I never think of him. But Oliver clung to me like hardened molasses, impossible to scrape away no matter how much I tried to shake him off. Maybe it was the timing. Maybe it was the way we fit when everything else felt foreign. Maybe it was only the story I told myself to make the ache make sense.

I had hoped leaving would close this chapter, but part of me feared otherwise. What if I carried him with me, even into the new school? What if every classroom and every quiet dorm room still ached with his absence? I thought of the first night I slept here, the walls pressing in on me, the silence loud enough to make me cry into my pillow. That loneliness had felt unbearable. And still, even after all these months, a piece of me worried I would never escape it. Loneliness has a way of learning a person's address.

I wanted the bad memories to outweigh the good, to crush them until all I felt was anger instead of longing. I wanted him gone. I wanted to be free. Wanting has its own gravity; it pulls and pulls even when you know which direction you should walk.

The sunlight shifted across the floorboards, dust floating in the golden air. A tiny thread of music drifted from a room down the hall and then faded. I realized how long I had been sitting there, bent over an open suitcase. My throat burned, but not with tears. With clarity.

I closed the suitcase and tugged the zipper until it clicked into place. The sound echoed in the room, final and certain. I gathered the last bobby pins from the windowsill, wiped the rosin dust from the desk, and opened the drawer one more time. The note lay where I had left it. I slid the drawer shut and didn't look again.

I remembered the words he had written, the promise he never kept. *I will be in the crowd cheering for you.* For too long I had waited for that moment, scanning faces, holding my breath. But I knew now he never would be, and that was no longer mine to want.

"Goodbye, Oliver," I whispered, the words soft but steady. I let them land and then let them go.

This time, the silence didn't feel empty. It felt like breathing again. I stood, lifted the suitcase by its handle, and the room shifted in the light as if it had been holding its breath for me too.

Chapter 37

I looked around at the small room, filled to the brim with boxes and trash bags full of bedding and clothes. The space already felt foreign, as if it belonged to someone else now, not me. The walls that once held my schedules and sticky notes were bare, the cork board stripped of photos and scraps of paper, leaving behind tiny pinholes like scars. Even the bed looked unrecognizable without the pile of blankets I usually kept heaped on top.

Natalie had barely started packing. I'm pretty sure she still had an exam next week and, true to form, she wasn't worried about packing or about saying goodbye. She slipped out earlier that day to study after overhearing me on the phone with my mom. I left a brief note on her desk, two sentences, nothing more than *thank you* and *good luck*, and even that felt like the most I could manage. We weren't close, but the silence of her absence still pressed in on me.

A familiar car horn sounded outside, sharp and eager. I grabbed my keys, my chest tightening with relief, and hurried out the door.

I practically flew into my parents' arms as they walked up the path to the dorm, their car in the loading zone with the trunk already open. For the first time in months I let myself lean fully into their hugs, inhaling the comfort of laundry soap and coffee and something that was simply home.

"Here we go," I said, trying to sound lighthearted. My voice cracked anyway.

They both sighed knowingly and followed me inside. They had helped me move enough times to understand I was no light packer. Even after a few weekend hauls, the room still looked somehow untouched, stuffed with more things than seemed possible.

We spent the morning shuttling box after box to the car, my dad muttering about how one girl could own so many pairs of shoes, my mom rearranging bags with the precision of an expert mover until they fit just right. The hallways filled with the sounds of other families doing the same. Doors slammed, tape ripped, someone laughed so loudly it echoed down the stairwell. Every so often a gust of warm air rushed in from the propped-open door and rattled the tiny name tags taped to each room.

At last, after the final box had been wedged into the trunk, we shut it with a loud, echoing thud.

I hesitated before leaving. I wandered back into the building one last time and stood in front of the heavy beige door of my dorm room, the same door I had opened and closed a thousand times this year. With one final push, it closed, this time with me on the outside. The click reverberated through me. That was it. The year was over.

I stood there for a breath and then another, remembering the girl who dragged her suitcase down this hallway last August, heart pounding, eyes stinging with homesickness. The girl who cried herself to sleep that first night, convinced she had made a mistake. The girl who stumbled through classes, through almost-friendships, through heartbreak, always searching for her place. And now, the girl who was leaving. Changed. Not perfect, not whole, but stronger.

Outside, I traced the map of my year through the courtyard. Past the bench where I nervously ate my first lunch alone. Past the tree where I called my mom almost every day, whispering that I couldn't do this, that I wanted to come home. Past the path where I bumped into the girls I thought would be my friends, and the spot I avoided afterward when I realized I wasn't. My steps slowed near the oak tree that had been Oliver's and my spot, the place of our first kiss, the place where too many nights had started or ended. For a heartbeat I felt the pull to linger, to let the memories wash over me. I shook my head and kept walking, eyes on my parents waiting by the car.

I knew some part of me should be sad, and maybe it was. Mostly I felt restless, itching to leave like any kid at the start of summer. Excited to go, to breathe again.

That summer I never unpacked my boxes. It wasn't laziness. It was because I knew I wasn't staying home for long. Tuition would be lower now that I was in-state, which meant the extra loan money could cover rent. I wasn't moving into another dorm, and I wasn't getting a roommate. This time it was going to be just me.

By July, I found the right place. The moment I walked into the small one-bedroom with my mom at my side, I felt it. The apartment wasn't new. The carpet was old. The floor-to-ceiling windows were square and a little cloudy at the edges. The kitchen opened into a modest living room with a tired, black, brick fireplace. But it felt like a beginning.

"The previous tenants just moved out, so it will be ready by the end of the week," the leasing agent said, leaning on the door frame. "Rent is lower than most in the area. End unit, balcony.

It probably won't last long."

I looked at my mom with wide eyes. We had planned for August but the apartment was waiting here for me.

By the following Wednesday, I was moving in.

I wasn't ready in the practical sense. I didn't have enough furniture, and I hadn't figured out how I would afford groceries. Emotionally, I was more than ready. Forty-five minutes from my parents, five minutes from my new campus, far enough from the past year to feel like a reset. Leaving everything in boxes had been the right call, but standing there surrounded by cardboard towers and plastic bins, I realized how much work I had ahead of me.

I closed the beige door and leaned back against it. The empty rooms held a hollow echo. It wasn't the silence of my dorm room, thick with unspoken words and missed chances. This silence carried the weight of possibility.

Still, an ache remained. For what I thought the year would be. For the people I lost. For the version of Oliver who promised to cheer and never showed. A part of me feared the ache would follow me forever, that I would keep searching for him in every crowd, hoping for the impossible. But as the cool paint pressed between my shoulder blades, I knew I could not live anchored to someone else's absence.

I walked the apartment slowly, running my hand along the kitchen counter, the chipped fireplace mantle, the rough balcony railing. The balcony looked over a parking lot and a strip of elm trees that held birdsong like it was treasure. Each surface I touched was a reminder that this was mine, flaws and all. My place. My reset.

Winston's little travel container sat nestled in a box by the window. I set the tank on the counter, rinsed the gravel until the water ran clear, and poured it in, a soft clatter like rain on tin. When the filter hummed to life and Winston flicked his fins in the current, the apartment felt less like a stage set and more like a home.

I made a list on a sticky note. *Shower curtain. A lamp. A thrifted table if I could find one. Groceries.* I texted my mom a photo of the empty living room and another of the view through the window. She sent back a string of hearts and a promise to bring dish towels tomorrow.

Before the afternoon got away from me, I drove to the nearest store and bought a set of cheap white plates, a pot, a spatula, and exactly four forks. A plant caught my eye on the way out, a pothos with long green vines. The tag read *hard to kill*, which felt like a blessing. Back at the apartment, I opened the balcony door and let warm air pour in. Somewhere in the distance, a child laughed. Someone's radio drifted the scale and faded.

I set my phone on the counter, pressed play on a playlist I had made months ago, and let the first notes echo against the bare walls. I opened a box. Then another. Sheets smoothed, books stacked, a favorite mug placed gently near the sink. I tucked the notebook that carried this year's hardest sentences into the top drawer of the nightstand. I slid a photo of my family onto the windowsill and watched the glass catch the light.

When the sun tipped low, I boiled pasta and ate it out of the pot at the counter, leaning on my elbows, letting the steam fog my cheeks. Winston circled the same loop again and again as if practicing for his own small performance. I laughed once, quietly, at the kindness of that thought.

Later, I unrolled my rug in the living room and laid on my back to smooth the corners. The ceiling had a faint swirl from a paint roller. The music drifted to an old song I loved. For a minute I let my eyes close and pictured the year ahead like a blank page. Registration for classes. The education building with tall windows. Children's books stacked on future desks. A calendar with boxes I could fill or leave empty on purpose. Maybe a friend's laugh next to mine. Maybe mornings that felt like mine from the start.

I stood and clicked off the kitchen light. The apartment fell into a softer brown. I didn't feel like I was drowning. I didn't feel like I was running. I felt like I was building. One plate, one plant, one small room at a time.

Chapter 38

I had been living in my new apartment for a week when I finally figured out what was missing. The nights were too quiet. Every creak in the walls, every hum of the fridge made the silence feel louder, and I caught myself leaving music on all the time just so I wouldn't feel so alone.

The dorm had always been noisy, doors slamming, footsteps racing down the hall, someone's playlist leaking through thin walls at all hours. Here I had peace, but it was an unfamiliar kind of peace. It felt hollow, like a stage before the audience arrives. I wanted something, someone, to share it with.

That is how I ended up pulling my blue KIA Soul into the parking lot of the local pet store and staring at the bright red and blue adoption banner that fluttered in the hot air. My heart was racing, but not from nerves. It was the quiet thrill of knowing I was about to make a choice that belonged only to me.

Inside, the store smelled like cedar chips and clean glass. I walked past the aisles of food and toys and straight to the cat adoption corner. A row of enclosures lined the wall, each with a card clipped to the front. Sleepy faces blinked back at me, whiskers twitching, ears angling toward my footsteps. Each pair of eyes seemed to tell a different story.

And then I saw her.

A tiny tabby pressed close to the glass. Brown and black swirled across her fur, and a white stripe ran down the center of her face like it had been painted there on purpose. Her small tail flicked once, then twice. She stood, stretched in a long curve, and padded closer until her nose almost touched the glass.

"Oh, this little one likes you," said the woman cleaning behind the enclosures. She wore a volunteer badge and a smile that reached all the way up to her eyes. "She has been shy all week. Let me know if you would like to meet her."

I laughed softly and crouched to meet the kitten's gaze. "I think I already do."

The volunteer unlocked the door and lifted the kitten out, careful hands and a practiced swing. She placed the ball of fur in my arms and the room changed shape. The kitten tucked herself under my chin and purred like a tiny engine. The sound vibrated into my bones. I felt my shoulders drop for the first time all week.

"What's her story?" I asked, rubbing a thumb along the white stripe.

"She and her litter were found under a porch. She is healthy and curious and becomes very attached once she decides you're hers." The woman's voice softened. "You look like a good match."

It didn't take long. I filled out the forms and answered questions about pet care. I showed a photo of my apartment and the carrier I had brought just in case I found the right one. There was a fee, a small bag of food and a list of local vets. The volunteer tucked an adoption certificate into the folder like a diploma.

By the time the sun shifted past noon, I was driving home

with a carrier strapped in beside me. The kitten pressed her paw through the door grate, and I rested my fingertips against it at every red light.

At home, the apartment felt new again. I set the carrier down in the living room and opened the door. She stepped out with careful paws, low to the ground, tail high and alert. She circled the sofa, sniffed the corners, and hopped onto the windowsill like it already belonged to her. She watched cars glide by and the tops of trees sway, her tail swishing, the white stripe bright in the light.

The litter box tucked neatly beside the washer. Food and water bowls found a home in the kitchen where the tile was cool. A cardboard scratcher went by the balcony door. I dangled a string and she pounced with the fierce seriousness of a hunter, then tumbled end over end and landed in a pile of her own paws. She climbed my leg and settled in my lap as if she had always known I was the softest place to land.

Naming her felt impossible until suddenly it was not.

Juniper.

Junie for short. Sweet and woodsy and steady. It fit the way the white stripe ran between her eyes. It fit the tiny trill she made when she meowed. It fit the way she went straight for the sun.

That evening I sent a picture to my mom of Junie asleep like a comma on my knee. My mom sent back ten heart emojis and the words *she is perfect*. Later I texted Cole and he replied with a joke about me turning into a cat lady and a request for more photos. I sent him five without pretending to be embarrassed.

The rest of the summer slowed into a different rhythm. I worked shifts at a little shop down the road, learning the regulars and which hours were best for reading at the counter.

But the real joy was coming home. Juniper met me at the door with a chirp, circling my ankles like a ribbon. She claimed the windowsill and the top of the couch and the one patch of afternoon sun that slid across the rug. I set a small basket with blankets beside my bed, but she preferred to curl right above my head, purring herself to sleep like a lullaby.

There were nights I danced across the living room barefoot, music low, Junie chasing my moving shadow on the wall like it was prey. There were mornings where I sipped coffee by the window and she batted at the steam curling out of my mug. There were afternoons when I read on the floor and she napped with one paw draped over my wrist as if she were pinning me in place.

It wasn't exciting. It wasn't loud. It was mine.

I learned small things the way you learn a new person. Junie liked the sound of running water and would sit on the tub edge to supervise my showers. She hated the vacuum like it was a villain from a storybook. She watched Winston's tank from a respectful distance and eventually lost interest when she realized the fish was untouchable. She stole the hair tie from my wrist every time I forgot to hide it and stashed them under the couch like treasure.

I bought a plant labeled *safe for cats* and set it on the bookshelf. She ignored it and instead fell in love with the crinkly paper bag I brought the plant home in. I learned to tuck the balcony door closed and to check the screen twice. I learned to sleep through the three in the morning zoomies that sounded like a miniature thunderstorm racing from room to room.

The apartment changed around her. A rug appeared and then a lamp that cast a warm pool of light in the evenings. A secondhand table found its way into the kitchen and made the space feel less like a temporary stop and more like a place where life was happening. I pinned a calendar on the wall and penciled in class registration dates and doctor appointments and a weekend to visit my parents. In the corner of the page I wrote Junie's first vet check and drew a tiny paw.

On the morning of that appointment she cried in the carrier for exactly two minutes and then went quiet, as if deciding trust would be easier. The vet called her perfect and brave. I bought her a green mouse in the shape of a bean as a reward and she carried it from room to room for the rest of the day like a prize.

Sometimes the ache still found me. It slipped in during the softest moments, when the apartment was golden and quiet. I would think about the version of the past year I had wanted and the way it had cracked in my hands. I would think about the note in the desk at school and the promise that had never been kept. The ache rose and then receded, not gone, not roaring, just a tide.

Juniper did not fix me. She didn't have to. She kept me company while I did the work of fixing myself. She sat next to me while I made a budget and a grocery list and a simple dinner without spiraling into the old thoughts. She watched me from the windowsill while I filled out forms for the fall, stacked a new pile of books for classes and set up a small clipboard where I could write lesson ideas for the elementary classrooms I wanted to be in one day.

The ordinary days stacked up. The quiet that had once rung in my ears softened. It had a heartbeat now. It had a cat shaped weight.

One evening, after a late shift, I came home to find the apartment washed in peach light. I opened the window and the warm air swept in. A bird called from the elm tree. Somewhere below a neighbor laughed. Junie hopped onto the back of the couch and turned her face to the wind like she was listening for something I could not hear. I sat with my palm on her back and let my shoulders loosen.

For the first time in a long time, I let myself be happy for no other reason than that I wanted to be. Not because someone else had chosen me. Not because I was trying to prove anything. Just because I had made a little space and filled it with a life that felt like mine.

In that small, ordinary summer, something shifted. The ache of the past didn't vanish, but with every slow moment it loosened its grip. Joy stopped feeling like a performance I had to audition for. It began to feel like morning light on a windowsill and a kitten snoring beside me and the simple relief of breathing.

Happiness didn't feel like a finish line anymore. It felt like Juniper curled against my ribs on a sunlit afternoon. It felt like breathing.

Chapter 39

The morning began quietly, the way I liked it. Rain drummed against the balcony, steady and heavy, the kind of downpour that blurred the world outside into nothing but gray. Juniper was curled into the crook of my arm as I stretched beneath the blanket, her purrs louder than the storm for just a moment. I had spent the morning reading in bed, the way I had most days this summer, soaking in the last of it before classes started at my new college.

I slid out of bed, my bare feet touching the cold floor, and padded into the kitchen. The scent of coffee filled the apartment, rich and grounding. I carried the mug to the windowsill where Junie had already leapt, her nose pressed to the glass as drops of rain raced one another down. I laughed softly and set the mug beside me.

This was what I had wanted: the slowness, the peace, the quiet. Not frantic rehearsals or the constant fear of letting people down. Not the ache of waiting for someone who never came. Just this. Me and Juniper.

I wanted a quiet, peaceful life, and was never quite sure how I ended up so far from it.

I thought about how I had started the year certain that love and success would save me, that being someone's person and being center stage would make me whole. Instead, I stumbled through loss, disappointment, and too many nights that felt unbearably lonely. Standing here now, watching June bat at the rain from the safety of my windowsill, I realized I was not lonely at all. I did not need to be anyone's person. I was my own.

The thought made me smile, not triumphant or loud, but small and steady, like a candle flame no storm could touch.

As the afternoon stretched on, I turned on music and let it fill the empty corners of the apartment. Junie tracked me from her perch as I twirled across the living room, arms wide. My laughter mingled with the song until I almost forgot the year that had come before, almost believed this joy had been waiting for me all along. Dance would not be my whole life anymore, but that didn't mean it was gone. Classes might be fewer, but dance would never fully leave me. I was in the middle of an improvised ballet that would never meet the light of day. I was spinning and jumping as if in the most prestigious performance.

That was when I heard a knock on the door.

I froze mid-step, the music still spilling its chorus. My breath caught in my chest. The knock came again, firmer this time, half-drowned by the downpour outside.

My heart hammered as I crossed the room. I told myself it was nothing, maybe a neighbor, a mistake, or maintenance. Still, my hand trembled when I reached for the handle.

I opened the door.

Rain pooled at the threshold, carried in on the storm. Standing in it, soaked through, hair plastered to his forehead, was Oliver.

His shoulders were tight, his chest rising and falling as if he had been running. His eyes, the ones I had sworn I would not look for again, locked onto mine like they had been searching all along.

For a long moment neither of us spoke. The rain filled the silence, steady and relentless.

And then, in spite of everything, I felt it, something warm, something undeniable.

Unbalanced hope.

About the Author

Hi, I'm Sydney Gommer. What started as a boredom breaker became a passion project that has threaded through my life over the past two years. I earned my undergraduate degree from the University of North Carolina at Charlotte and I'm now pursuing a master's in reading education while teaching fourth grade. My goal with this book is simple: to remind first-year college students that real life rarely looks like the movies, and that's okay.